PRAISE FC  E

"With clear, honest, and precise writing, Mario Busacca and Hoyt Byrum have created a work capturing our shared quest for purpose, belonging, and a higher union. *The Chase* embraces these central issues in a narrative that is simple enough to be accessible and layered enough to probe the deeper questions that define spirituality. This is a book to read more than once, and slowly, so that these questions might take proper root."

—Greg Fields, Author, *Through the Waters and the Wild*

"*The Chase* is an engaging and relatable book with valuable takeaways for us all. Told in story format, it will capture the reader's attention and expand their perspectives on what it means to be a Christian. The accompanying study guide will ensure that facilitators can easily lead small group discussions that are productive and meaningful. Kudos to Busacca and Byrum for making biblical concepts accessible and for introducing a model we can all follow in our complex modern world."

—Linda Cobb, President, The Coaching Company, Inc.

"I was drawn into the story of Tony, and even though I was brought up in a Christian home, I 'got' his position. And as the story unfolded, I was there like a fly on the wall, waiting to see what happened next. As a believer, I wasn't sure how this was going to relate to me . . . and then . . . there was an explanation of the parable of the Prodigal Son. Wow. Just wow. The insights. I do believe that this is a compelling story for non-believers to get an introduction—and even more so for Believers, whose beliefs may be strong, or not. There's something here for everyone to learn."

—Dr. Sony Jackson, President, Marketing Tools for Coaches

"If you ever feel like you're running all the time with no finish line in sight, pick up *The Chase* and receive hope for your journey. A warm and encouraging spiritual novel about how God has a plan for each of us and works through ordinary people, through the joys and sorrows of everyday life. A terrific book and study guide for small groups or church book clubs."

—Judy Christie, Author of Eighteen Books, Including the Gone to Green Series

"As a pastor who was always looking for creative ways to communicate the essence of the Christian life to those within my congregation, *The Chase* is a resource I welcome. *The Chase* is a unique book in that it is on the one hand a novel worthy of reading simply for pleasure. It is, however, much more than that. It is a book that takes the reader into the most important topics needing to be examined for those who want to embrace the Christian life to the fullest. It presents the good news of the Gospel and it leads the reader into deep discipleship. *The Study Guide* for small groups or book clubs is brilliant."

—Reverend Bill Anderson, Honorably Retired Presbyterian Church (USA) Pastor

"The story of *The Chase* has a marvelous way of pulling you in and allowing you to share the complex feelings of a man on a journey of discovery and a life-changing encounter with the Lord who loves him."

—E. Stanley Ott, Founder & President Vital Churches Institute

"I read tons of books each year and *The Chase* had me riveted to the story from the first chapter on. I loved how the key themes of God's grace and our resulting gratitude and generosity were illustrated by life examples and relationships. I was impressed by the quality of the unique study guide that accompanied this novel.

"*The Chase* book and study guide are tremendous resources for an existing or newly formed small group in a local church, in a neighborhood, or on a college campus. Spiritual seekers as well as growing disciples will benefit greatly from this book and will find themselves growing closer in their relationship with God."

—Bob Reusser, Veteran Navigator Staff, Founder and Former Director of the Navigators Encore Mission

"*The Chase* is a wonderful gift to Kingdom work! For seekers, it is a companionable walk; for believers, it is a thought-twisting serendipitous journey."

—Kathy Turner, librarian emerita

The Chase

by Mario Busacca and Hoyt A. Byrum

© Copyright 2021 Mario Busacca and Hoyt A. Byrum

ISBN 978-1-64663-374-6

Published by

◤ köehlerbooks™

3705 Shore Drive
Virginia Beach, VA 23455
800-435-4811
www.koehlerbooks.com

THE
CHASE

A NOVEL

MARIO BUSACCA &
HOYT A. BYRUM

VIRGINIA BEACH
CAPE CHARLES

CHAPTER 1

Tony was a runner. He could not tell you why he ran, but he knew he simply had to run. Sometimes it felt like he was running towards something, sometimes like he was being chased. But regardless, he had to run.

He wasn't really built for running. At 6'1" and 210 pounds, he was a bit heavy for the task. He didn't always enjoy the running itself. More often than not, he simply needed to burn off energy. And he usually felt better after he ran.

He had started running while in the Army. As an officer, he figured he had to set an example for the other men. So because they had to run, he ran. It also fulfilled some deep-seated need in him. It was something he could do on his own and measure his progress directly. The farther and faster he ran, the more he felt like he had accomplished something. He was in control. And being in control was all-important to Tony.

On this particular day, he was running to address his anger and frustration. He felt hurt and betrayed. He had been passed over for a promotion at work. A promotion he thought he deserved. So he ran, hard and fast. He hardly noticed the cars on the street or the people that he passed by, which was unusual for him, as he liked being around people. He got his energy from being around people.

But today, all he could see was the president of the company announcing giving the promotion to Charlie Prescott. Sure, Tony had to admit that Charlie had been with the company longer, but, dammit, Tony thought that he deserved it more! After all, he worked harder than anyone else, in his opinion. But here was another turn in the road to his advancement. And he was angry. So he ran.

He passed the shops and businesses in the downtown area without any thought of how they had been upgraded recently. He had lived in this town most of his life. He had met his wife here in high school. He was proud of how the town had grown and how it had become a center for several engineering firms, one of which employed him.

But today, none of that mattered to him. Today, it was all about how he had been glossed over. Finally, he ran out of energy. He stopped near one of the recently landscaped town squares and caught his breath. He looked at his watch and realized it would be dark soon. So he turned back and jogged home. He had to be more careful, as the night crowd was coming out. He worked his way through the crowds, being careful not to run into or upset any of them. Tony made it home before the streetlights turned themselves on. He stopped at the front door and tried to compose himself before he went in.

As he walked through the door, his wife, Beth, was sitting in the front room reading. Beth was a tall woman herself. At 5'10" with long red hair, she attracted glances wherever she went. And while she was normally soft-spoken, when she did speak, people tended to listen. She was a senior executive in a local accounting firm.

She and Tony had been married eight years. They were the perfect complement for each other. He was the emotional one who tended to react to both the good and the bad more viscerally. She was the more even-handed one. She took things more in stride and had a calming effect on Tony when he overreacted. She put her book down and looked up as he came in.

"Did you have a good run, honey?" she asked.

"I guess. I burned off some energy at least," he said somewhat sarcastically.

"Oh, did something happen at work today?" Tony had left for his run before she had gotten home. But Beth knew him very well, and seeing him with his attitude, she knew he must have had some issue on his mind.

"Yeah. Charlie Prescott got the promotion. The president announced it today at the all-hands meeting," he said.

"Oh. I'm sorry. I know you had your heart set on that."

"Yeah, well. Not happening."

Tony went into the kitchen to get a bottle of water. Beth called after him, "Aren't you going to ask me how my day went?"

Tony came back into the living room with his bottle. He took a long drink and said, "Oh, sure. How was your day? But before you answer, don't you think that I deserve that promotion? I mean, I work my butt off for that company!"

"Of course you do, honey." She set her book on the end table and waited for him to continue, as she knew he would.

"I mean, it doesn't seem fair. It's just like when I was in the service. You remember, I was up for that promotion to captain, and they passed me over?"

"Yes. I remember."

"Well, you know, if I had gotten that, I would likely have stayed in. But once you get passed over like that, it's a sign that it's time to go. I wonder if that's what's happening here?"

"Oh, I doubt that. This company has been pretty good to you."

"Yeah, that's true, though it doesn't seem that way at this moment." He drained his drink and started to walk back into the kitchen.

"You're not thinking about leaving the company, are you?" she called after him.

"I don't know. Maybe. I'll have to think on it. It just seems like I haven't been treated fairly, you know?" Tony walked back and stood in front of her almost pleading for some confirmation from her.

"I understand, Tony. You do work hard. You deserve to move up in the company. I'm sure you will, eventually. But they have treated you well. Haven't you been given some pretty big and important projects lately?"

He nodded reluctantly.

"You just have to have a little more faith, dear."

"I know you're right. But, you know, I'm tired of waiting for 'eventually.' And as for 'faith,' pffft." He made a raspberry sound. "I think maybe I need to look at my future plans and reevaluate."

"Yes, you may have to do that. But . . . " She paused and looked up at him.

Tony looked down at her. "What? But what?"

"But you'll have to think about it now."

"Now? What are you talking about?"

"I have some news that may affect your thinking."

Tony stared at her. "Does this have something to do with your day?"

"Yes. Yes, it does. I went to see Dr. Jamison today."

"Your gynecologist? Oh, yeah. You mentioned something about that. Is everything okay?"

She smiled a knowing smile. "Yes. You may want to sit down for this."

Tony just stood there. She continued, "Okay then. I spoke with Dr. Jamison about that fertility treatment."

Tony abruptly sat down on the nearest chair.

"What?"

"Well, we talked about it, remember? I said that we may have to do something if I'm going to get pregnant. I'm not getting any younger."

"So you have said. Repeatedly."

"Is this a problem?"

"Well, maybe. I mean, kids. They would change our whole life, uhm, lives."

"Of course they would. But I thought we agreed that we needed to start soon."

"You mean, YOU agreed." He moved forward on the edge of his seat. "Look, Beth, I know that you want kids. You've always been upfront about that. But I don't know. Isn't it good with just the two of us? And if I have to make a job change to move my career forward, well, kids might make that harder. And then there's your career. Wouldn't you have to put that on hold?"

"Tony, you are so stubborn sometimes. I thought that we agreed on all of this." She stopped and looked at him for a long time. Finally, she said, "I have made myself very clear. I think we should have children and the time is getting closer. So if you really don't want to have any, then . . ." she paused looking for the right words, "then I really need to know that soon."

She stood up and started to pace around the room. Then abruptly she stopped pacing and stood directly in front of Tony. Looking down at him, she spoke in very even tones.

"Tony, I have something to say, and you need to listen. Let me make this perfectly clear. I am going to have children and I desire to have them with you. And I desire to have them soon. I'm not waiting for some career advancement that may or may not come. I am not waiting until the finances get better. And if you don't get on board, well . . ." Her voice trailed off. "Do you get what I am saying?" She walked away from him and turned to look at him from across the room.

"Aw, Beth. Don't get like that. Of course, I get what you are saying. If you really, really want kids then, by all means, we should have them, eventually. I just don't know if now is the right time."

"On the contrary, now is exactly the right time. And we need to do something about it." She stood with her arms crossed, waiting for his response.

"You mean like right now?" He started to get up and looked towards the bedroom.

"No, that's not what I mean, silly." She walked over to him and put her hands on his shoulders. "I mean that we need to see if this treatment that the doctor talked to me about is the right one to use. That's all."

"Oh. Yeah. Sure."

"All right, then. It's settled. Now you go in and get cleaned up and I'll get dinner." She kissed him on the forehead and walked into the kitchen.

Oh, boy, thought Tony. *I guess we're moving forward now.*

CHAPTER 2

Several days later, Tony was running again. As usual, he was running toward something, or rather, someone. In this case, it was his longtime friend and confidant, Dave Worthington, who was waiting at the pub to have a drink with him. Dave and Tony went back all the way to grade school. They did everything together. Well, almost everything. But we'll get to that later.

Dave was 6'2", with deep blue eyes and blond hair. Tony was always envious of those eyes, as his were brown and, in his mind, not very interesting. He and Tony had gone through school together, including college. Then Tony had gone into the military service, and Dave had chosen the Peace Corps. When they finished their respective tours, they both moved back to their hometown and spent much of their time together.

The town was not too large. The downtown area had been revitalized over the last several years in a sort of 1890s look. It now had all sorts of shops and stores. The new look was rather quaint, Tony thought. And he was rather proud of it. As an engineer in one of the larger local firms in town, he had been asked to be on the review committee that oversaw the planning for the downtown revitalization. The streetlights resembled old-time gas lamps, which had been Tony's suggestion, and the color schemes of the buildings were very controlled. Tony rather liked that, being the control freak that he was. He always wanted to know what the next thing to do was, and he wanted to have a say in it. And he had enjoyed working with the local community leaders.

As he arrived at Charley's Brewpub, he opened the door to the sounds of laughter and clinking glasses. Dave and Tony had been going to Charley's since they were old enough to drink. It was a family sort of place, catering to the local crowd, decorated along the lines of an old English pub. The menu was a little more varied, but you could always get bangers and mash for lunch or dinner. They also made a great shepherd's pie, which was one of Tony's favorites, and they had a large number of different kinds of beers on draft. Tony knew all the waitstaff by their first names.

Tony walked in and immediately felt at home. He spied Dave over in their favorite booth, the one with a good view of the two big-screen TVs, and walked over to him.

"Well, it's about time!" said Dave.

"Oh, you haven't been waiting that long."

Tony slipped into the booth across from Dave and signaled to the waiter to come over.

"Hello, Mr. Hunter," said the waiter. "How are you today? Would you like your usual?"

"Just great, Jimmy. I hope you are well?" Jimmy nodded in agreement. "Good to hear. Could you please bring us a couple of shots of Scotch to go with the drafts?"

"Right away, Mr. Hunter," Jimmy said as he placed a coaster on the table in front of each of them then went to get the drinks.

Dave looked at Tony, "Scotch, huh? What's the issue?"

"What do you mean?"

"Well, usually when you drink Scotch, there's something you're working through."

"You know, my problem is that you know me way too well."

"True words," said Dave.

Jimmy returned with the drinks, set them on the table, and said, "There you go, Mr. Hunter. What's the issue today?"

Tony looked up at him then back at Dave. "Are my habits known to everyone in the bar?"

"Oops, sorry, Mr. Hunter. It's just that you don't usually drink Scotch . . ."

Tony cut him off, ". . . unless I have some issue on my mind. Yeah, Dave just reminded me."

"I didn't mean to offend," said Jimmy.

Tony smiled and waved his hand at Jimmy. "No offense taken, Jimmy. It's nice to know that I'm such an open book."

"Uh, okay. Uh, let me know if you need anything else." He turned and walked away.

"Good kid, that Jimmy," said Tony.

"Yes, he is." Dave paused and looked intently at Tony for a moment. "Soooooo, what *is* on your mind this evening?"

Tony downed his Scotch in one gulp.

"Beth is pushing for kids again."

"Ooooh. That issue."

"Yeah, she actually went to the doctor to get information on fertility treatments! I mean, she is getting really serious, Dave!"

Tony shifted around in his seat. He felt very uncomfortable. "I don't think I'm going to be able to put her off much longer. Actually, the whole kids and family idea is really Beth's. I would have been just as happy to have it just the two of us. But Beth and I get into bed at night, and she will say, 'Hey, do you hear that?' and I say, 'What? I don't hear anything.' Then she says, 'But it's so loud!' I say, 'What is it?' and she says, 'It's my biological clock ticking, you dummy. It's time to start working on children!'"

Dave was laughing so hard he couldn't drink his beer and spilled some on the table.

"Oh, you find that funny, do you?" said Tony.

"Yeah, it's hilarious, actually."

"Well, it would change my whole life. My whole life plan. Kids would, uh, *will* change everything, if we have them."

"Your life plan?"

"Sure. You know, career, moving up in the organization. If I have to spend time and money on kids, it will hurt my career. I mean I've already been passed over for promotion twice now."

"It doesn't have to, Tony. You can still have all of that. And your career isn't that far off track. You can't expect to be at the top until you get a little more experience. You just have to have a little faith."

"Oh, great, you are going to hit me with the 'faith' card, too? You and Beth. Don't go all religious on me right now, okay? I need some real advice here, so please keep your church philosophies to yourself. You and Sarah can do all that stuff all you want, but you know my history with that. I don't believe it. I don't need it. I don't want it. The church did nothing for me or my family when we most needed it. There is no God up there watching over us. So leave it alone, for today at least, okay?"

Dave smiled and put his hands up in submission. He had heard Tony's position many times before. "Okay, okay. No preaching today. But I will pray for you, of course." They were silent for a few minutes, each lost in their own thoughts. Finally, Dave broke the silence, "So what are you going to do?"

"To be honest, I'm not sure. This is really important to Beth. We are going to have to make some decisions. I'm just not sure how."

Dave said, "You know, you have said in the past you thought the idea of children wasn't terrible."

"I suppose. But man, it's a scary thing. Being totally responsible for another person like that. I'm not sure I'm up to the task."

"Tony, you can do anything you put your mind to. I've seen you do that more times than I can count."

"Yeah, but with kids, it's not the same." He looked at Dave, who was smiling at him. "Look, with you and Sarah, it's different. You both always wanted kids. And you are great parents to Katie. But with us, what if I don't do a good job?"

"Tony, all I can tell you is that it's always a work in progress. And I know that you would, uh, will be a great father."

"That's all you have for me? I was hoping for a little bit more."

"I'm afraid that's all there is, my friend." Dave finished his beer and smiled at Tony.

Tony finished his beer and got Jimmy's attention.

Jimmy came over to their booth and said jokingly, "Can I get you another round, or was one drink enough to resolve the problem?"

Dave spoke up, "No, Jimmy. Tony here is going to have to go home and work on it some more. So we probably need to have the check."

Jimmy looked down at Tony and said, "Aw, it's okay, Mr. Hunter. Please say hello to Mrs. Hunter for me. And I have faith that you will do whatever it is you need to do."

Tony looked at Jimmy, then at Dave, and threw up his hands. "I'm surrounded by 'Believers'!"

CHAPTER 3

The next day, Tony and Beth were getting ready for work. Their bathroom had separate sinks for each of them and they were across the room rather than right next to each other. This was by design, as Tony did not want to get in Beth's way when she was getting ready.

It also meant their backs were to each other most of the time. This also worked for Tony, as Beth had the annoying habit, at least Tony found it annoying, of wanting to talk about serious life things early in the morning. She, being a morning person, was ready for such discussions. Tony, not so much. It took him a while, maybe after a run and then some strong coffee. Even though he wasn't a morning person, the running helped him clear his head and get moving. But that usually didn't deter Beth. The fact that she had to turn around to get his attention was a good thing, as far as Tony was concerned. But this morning, she wanted to talk.

"So, what was it that Dave said last night that you didn't want to talk about?" she asked.

"I never said I didn't want to talk about it," as he picked up his toothbrush.

"Oh, so now we're going to do the tooth-brushing delay?"

"No, it's just time to brush my teeth, and I know how you hate it when I talk with my mouth full of toothpaste!" He immediately started to brush his teeth vigorously.

"Careful. You'll wear off the enamel. Okay, I can wait. You'll tell me when you are ready."

Beth started brushing her teeth as Tony finished. He turned and watched her and sighed heavily. He knew there was no getting out of this discussion.

"Okay, Dave said he would pray for me, uh for us," Tony blurted out.

"Oh, horrors! Not the 'I will pray for you' threat! Whatever shall we do?" She put her hands up against her cheeks in mock shock.

"Knock it off, will you? Look, I told him how I'm afraid that I won't be a good parent and that being a parent would affect my career. I had hoped he would give me some, well, more valuable advice."

"Oh, like what?"

"Heck, I don't know! If I did, I wouldn't need the advice." He turned around and started lathering his face with shave cream.

"So what else did he say, apart from the dreaded 'Prayer Threat?'" She made the quotes sign with her fingers.

"He basically said that you have to learn as you go along and that I would be a great parent. And that I 'should have faith.'"

"Does sound like he blew you off," she said sarcastically. She paused to look at him and realized he was really troubled. "Look," she walked over to him and put her hands on his shoulders from behind. "What else could he say? I'm sure he believes that you would, uh, will be a great dad, as do I. But we all have to work through all of this in our own way. And you won't be alone. Remember me? I'm along for the ride as well. And as for the praying thing, he truly believes that will help. Frankly, so do I. I've been doing my own praying as well."

"I know that. You believe that religious flap just like he does. Sorry that I take no stock in it. It gives me no comfort. You knew that when you married me." He started shaving.

"Yes, I did, but I think it may . . . someday. But until then, just trust in the two of us. We will be doing this together."

"Okay, just so long as you guys don't try to force this prayer stuff on me."

"Oh, I think we know better than that." She walked back to her sink. "All right then, as long as we all understand each other," she finished.

"Yeah, but what about my career? Or yours, for that matter?" Tony asked.

"Our respective careers will be just fine, dear. Have faith!"

"Right."

They both finished getting ready for work. They had a cup of coffee together, kissed each other goodbye, and went their separate ways.

Tony was an engineer in a large company. They had offices in several locations around the country. At his particular location, they occupied a fairly new building. It was only five years old. It was set up like many such offices, a set of cubicles in the center that were surrounded by offices for the management staff. The offices had windows, but the general area did not. Tony occupied one of the many cubicles, not having yet been promoted to management. Tony would have liked an office just because he would have been able to close his door when he really needed to concentrate, but he made do with what he had.

At about ten o'clock, Jerry Conway, Tony's supervisor, called Tony into his office. He told Tony to sit down and closed the door.

Tony started to become a little nervous. Jerry didn't often close his door. He watched Jerry go around his desk and sit down. Tony waited.

Jerry said, "Look, Tony, I know you are disappointed about not getting the promotion."

"Yeah. I am."

"Well, it's history now. But I wanted to make sure that you understood why."

"Okay," said Tony.

"You see, Charlie has somewhat of a history with the clients that he will have to be dealing with. They like him and will work well with him. Like it or not, that's how this business works. It's not always about skill or talent."

"Seems a bit unfair."

"Whoever said it was going to be fair?"

"No one, I guess," Tony replied.

"In any case, that's how things work, and that's how you move up. So to help you along those lines, I want to put you in charge of the Sievers' project."

Tony sat up in his chair. "You mean that big new office complex downtown?"

"Yep. That's the one. It's just getting underway, and while Charlie was on the proposal team, he won't have time for it as part of his new duties. And I think you are just the man to lead this one. It will be a big challenge and may require some travel and extra hours. But you will be out there in front of management. Do you think you are up for it?"

"You bet I am, Jerry! Thanks for the opportunity. I won't let you down!" He stood up and reached out to shake Jerry's hand.

"I know you won't, Tony," Jerry replied.

Tony walked back to his cubicle. His feet barely touched the ground. This was his big chance! He would put all his energy into this project. Then he sat down and thought about Beth. *This may put a damper on her plans for having kids,* he thought. But he loved Beth and did want her to be happy. Maybe he could do both? He wasn't sure if he could. Clearly, they were going to have to make some tough decisions. But Tony was very sure about one thing: he was going to give this opportunity his very best shot.

CHAPTER 4

For the next three months, Tony spent almost all of his time on the new project. He stayed late at work, often bringing work home as well. He ate and breathed the project. And it showed. Today, he had briefed top management on the progress, and they had all been very pleased. They had approved his proposed budget with no changes. That was highly unusual in his experience. He could hardly wait to get home to tell Beth the news.

"Tony, that's wonderful!" exclaimed Beth. "I am so glad the project is going well. I knew you would do great," she said as she sat across from him at dinner that night. "We should do something to celebrate."

"You know the project is getting to the point where soon there will be some more travel and probably some overtime," Tony said.

"Of course." Beth got up and went around the table to hug Tony from behind. "I am proud of you, honey." She squeezed him again and started to clean the dishes off the table. "Uh, we have something else to celebrate."

"Oh. What is that?" He got up to help with the dishes.

"Well, the fertility treatments are going well."

"Oh?" Tony turned back to the table to get the last of the dishes and stopped. He slowly turned around. "By 'going well,' you mean there are no bad side effects?"

"That, too."

"Too?"

"Yes."

"Beth, what are you trying to say?"

She turned around and leaned against the sink. She smiled and said, "They are working. I mean, they worked. Uh, I mean that we have procreated!"

"Procreated? Is that what we are calling it now?"

She laughed. "I know that sounds silly now that I've said it out loud. But yes, I'm pregnant!" She did a little jump for joy and waited for Tony's reaction.

"Uh, are you sure? You know sometimes those tests are not accurate. When exactly did you find out?"

"Oh, a few days ago. But I wanted to be sure, so I went to Dr. Jamison's office and they confirmed it. I didn't want to distract you from your project at work until I was certain. We are going to have a baby, Tony. Isn't that wonderful?" She ran over to him and threw her arms around his neck.

He hugged her back, sort of, then slowly disengaged himself from her and extended her out to arm's length. "So, there's no mistake. You're definitely pregnant."

"Yes. Yes." She paused and looked at him. He did not seem happy. Indeed, he was frowning. "What's the matter? It's what we have been wishing for. Isn't it?"

"I guess. But . . ."

"But what?"

"Well, I didn't think it would happen so fast. I mean, it's only been a couple of months."

"I know. I was surprised too, but Dr. Jamison said that it happens that way sometimes. I'm so excited. I need to call Sarah and let her know. But I wanted to tell you first." She started to go into the other room, but then turned and looked at Tony. He was clearly not happy. She sat down at the table and looked at him for a while. "Okay, spill it. What's on your mind."

He sat down across from her and said, "It's work. I mean, it will be hard by itself. Uh, having a child will be even harder."

"I don't see how."

"Oh, please, Beth. Kids take up so much time and energy. I won't have that with this project. You've seen how much of my time it takes."

Beth turned towards Tony and looked him directly in the eyes. "Tony Hunter, you cannot use this one project to make a case that we shouldn't have children. After you finish this one, there will be another, then another. Now is the time for us to have children. We can work through this. We can do it together. Didn't your father have a job that required him to work a lot?"

"Well, yeah."

"And didn't he do a good job of parenting with you? You're always saying what a great father he was. Is."

"True, but . . ."

"But what?" she asked as she folded her arms across her chest.

"Well, I'm not sure that I can do what he did. I'm not sure that I can be a good father," he said.

"Tony, you will be great at both your career and your parenting. You will be a great father. And I will be here to help you. Your dad had to do it mostly on his own after your mother died. If he could do this alone, think how great it will be with the two of us working together!" She reached out and held his hand and waited for a reply.

He finally sighed and said, "You always do get your way. Okay, we will work on it together. But if and when I screw it up, remember I told you so."

"Have I ever not done so? Now, I'm going to call Sarah." She giggled and kissed him and got up and went into the bedroom.

Tony sat there and sighed. "Boy, life is going to be different from now on," he said out loud.

CHAPTER 5

Tony slipped into the booth opposite Dave. He waved to Jimmy, who came to their booth.

"Two Scotches, Jimmy." Tony said. "And two beer chasers."

"Oh, do we have an 'issue' to deal with?" asked Jimmy.

"Sort of, I just came from the ultrasound."

"Well, that is exciting," said Jimmy. "I'll get your drinks right away."

Dave looked at Tony who simply smiled back at him. Finally, Dave could take it no longer.

"So how long are you going to keep me in suspense? Is it a boy or a girl?"

Tony raised his hand and shook his finger at Dave, "Now, that would be telling. We need to wait for the drinks."

"Oh, for Pete's sake, just tell me, will you? The suspense has been killing me all day!"

"Tut, Tut. Patience is a virtue, my friend."

At that point, Jimmy arrived with the drinks. "Here you go, gentlemen. Given the occasion, the boss says these are on the house. Congratulations, Mr. Hunter." He placed the drinks on the table.

Tony looked up and said, "Thank you, Jimmy, and thank the boss for me."

"Will do, Mr. Hunter." Jimmy walked away.

Tony raised his shot glass and Dave followed suit with his. "Here's to . . ." Tony paused for effect.

"WELL? . . ."

"Twins!" Tony downed his drink and slammed his glass on the table.

"Twins?" said Dave.

"Yep. Clear as day right there on the ultrasound." Tony pulled a piece of paper out of his pocket and unfolded it on the table in front of Dave who peered at it intently.

"Wow, you can really see the two of them clearly. Are they boys or girls?"

"Can't tell yet. Being twins, they're a little smaller than they would be if there was only one. Hopefully, we will know at the next test."

Dave pondered the picture for a moment. Then he looked up at Tony, handed the picture back to him, and said, "How is Beth taking the news?"

"She's still in a little bit of shell shock. To be truthful, so am I. I mean, *Twins*. We never planned for twins. We weren't even sure if we would have a second one after this. Well, I wasn't sure. I don't know how we are going to manage. I mean, there's double the expenses, more diapers, more food, then college, and, dang, what if they're both girls, two weddings to pay for!"

"That will be a lot, for sure," Dave said as he downed his drink.

"We're going to have to start saving! Just 'cause I'm an engineer and Beth is an accountant doesn't mean we're flush with money."

"Oh, you guys will be fine. Wow, what a blessing to have twins!"

Tony grimaced and said, "Okay, Dave, you don't have to start with the religious stuff right off of the bat, you know."

Dave raised his hands in surrender. "Oops, sorry. I'm just excited for you. I mean, God is good, you know."

"Dave, God had nothing to do with this."

"Oh, I beg to differ."

"Dave, you are a grown man, so I should not have to explain how this works." Tony went into a mode of speaking as if he were talking to a small child. "You see, Dave, when a man and a woman love each other, they get very close together and . . ."

Dave put his hand up to stop Tony from speaking, "Okay, okay, I get it. You don't want me to talk to you about God today. That's fine. I still think it's a blessing anyway."

The place was beginning to fill up and the background noise became a little louder.

Tony spoke first. "Actually, it is kind of a shock. I mean like I said, now we have to get two of everything. We had budgeted for only one. The money is going to be tight."

"I'm sure you guys will be able to manage," Dave replied.

"Yeah, yeah, I know what you are thinking . . . 'God will provide.' Well, I'm afraid I don't have your faith. But it's more than just that. I'm not sure how to deal with siblings. You know I'm an only child . . ."

"Which explains a lot!"

"Always a funny joke. But I'm serious. How do I address sibling rivalry and that sort of stuff?"

"Look," said Dave, "it's not like you're in this alone. Beth has two brothers and a sister. She knows all about sibling rivalry."

"True, I guess I can lean on her for that," Tony replied.

The two men sat silently for a few minutes, each drinking their beers and lost in their own thoughts. Tony finally broke the silence. "So, have you and Sarah ever thought about having more kids? I mean Katie is almost three now and you always said that having them close together is what you guys wanted to do."

"We have been trying, but nothing yet."

"Well, keep at it. You're such a great father."

"Thanks, I try."

Both men again were silent for a while. Then Tony said, "Man, I still can't get over it, twins. What if they're identical?"

"What if they are?"

"Well," Tony responded, "Aren't there like special issues with identical twins? I mean, you have to decide if you're going to dress them the same. And how would we tell them apart?"

"Oh, I'm sure you'll be able to tell who is who. But it doesn't matter, kids are a blessing no matter what."

"Really? You're going with the 'blessing' thing again? What if they have some rare disease or are missing a leg or something? How in the world could that be a *blessing?*"

"Hey, you're not usually the negative type. What gives?"

Tony took a deep breath before answering. "To tell you the truth, Dave, I'm just plain scared."

"Of what, may I ask?"

"To be honest, I'm not ready to be a father. Not sure I ever was."

"I don't think anybody ever is 'ready,' Tony. But you work through it."

"Easy for you to say. You always wanted to be a parent. Never been a part of my plan. If it wasn't for Beth wanting it so much, I never would have done it."

"I have confidence in you. You will be fine. In fact, I predict you will love being a father. But I will be happy to talk about the issues you will face as a parent, not that I am an expert. And, of course, I will pray for you as well."

"Oh, please, keep your prayers to yourself."

"As you wish. But here's to fatherhood." Dave raised his beer in a toast. "And to all the things that come with it, the good and the bad."

Tony raised his glass in response. "Well, I'll toast to the good things, and hope I can deal with the bad."

CHAPTER 6

Tony sat across the table from Dave and Sarah in his kitchen. Beth was in the living room, lying on the couch. Tony was grim.

"The doctor was very explicit," Tony said. "This preeclampsia thing can be serious. Beth has got to follow instructions, or she could get really sick." He spoke in low tones so that Beth wouldn't hear what he was saying.

Sarah reached across the table and grasped Tony's hand. "Thanks for calling us over. We will all get through this," she said. Sarah was a physical therapist. She had met Dave in Africa when they were both in the Peace Corps. They had actually gotten married during that tour. When Sarah met Beth, the two had fallen instantly in love with each other. They were closer than real sisters, which is how they sometimes thought of each other. They also shared the common bond of their faith.

Sarah noted that Tony's hands were sweating. "I know a little bit about this because two women at the church have gone through it. It's something that some women get when they are pregnant. Their blood pressure goes up, and they can have other symptoms like headaches; their feet can swell up, and their vision can be affected. But it all went away when the women gave birth. We were there for those women and helped them through it. And we will be there for Beth."

"Yeah," Dave chimed in. "We've got a whole community to help with this."

Tony looked at them in amazement. "I'm not a member of your 'community.' Why should they come to help me? And, anyway, I don't need them."

Sarah said, "First of all, Beth is a member of the church. But that doesn't matter. We are all members of God's community."

Tony glared at her.

"Oops," she said. She put her hands up in surrender. "Sorry, didn't mean to get all religious on you. But really, in terms of offering you some assistance, it doesn't matter to us that you don't come to church. You and Beth are our dearest friends. Of course we will help you. Beth is like a sister to me. Her problems are my problems."

"But what about your church mates? They don't know me from Adam, pardon the reference."

"Cute," Dave said. "Again, it doesn't matter to them either. They do it out of a sense of extending grace to anyone in need."

Tony looked at him quizzically. "Grace? Oh, yes, that all-encompassing feeling of 'good will?'" He rolled his eyes.

"Look, let's just say it's what we do and leave it at that for the time being. Okay?" said Dave.

Tony stood up and started pacing back and forth in front of them. He clearly had something else on his mind. So Sarah prompted him, "What's the problem?"

Tony sat down and leaned across the table and looked at them. "Here's the thing, I'm not one to ask for help."

"Tell me about it," said Dave. "Remember the time you wouldn't let me help you cut down that old tree in the backyard? How much did it cost you to get the roof fixed?" Dave started to laugh. He stopped when he realized Tony wasn't laughing with him.

"Sure, bring that up when I'm down!"

Dave started to speak, and Tony stopped him with a raise of his hand. "That wasn't fair. I know you're just trying to help, and, in this case, I am sure there will be days when Beth and I will need some help, as hard as that is for me to admit. I mean, I can't stay home with her all the time. I've got this big, important project at work that I can't neglect. It's too important for my career. But I can't leave Beth alone either."

"Good," Sarah exclaimed as she stood up. "It's all settled then; we will handle it for you. Now I'm going in to talk with Beth."

Tony got up and walked over to her and put his hands on her shoulders and looked into her eyes. "What she needs to understand is that she can't do all the things she always does. She has to . . ."

Sarah put up her hand to stop him. "I know the drill, Tony. She has to stay lying down on her left side. She can only get up to go to the bathroom. There ought to be someone here with her most if not all of the time in case something happens. We will have this covered. We will get a group of us to take shifts while you are at work." She gently pushed him back into his seat. "Trust me, Tony."

"So you're going to bring a bunch of strangers into my house?" He looked up at her with almost pleading eyes.

"Oh, please. Get over yourself." She gently slapped him lightly on the cheek. "You may not know some of them, but I'm sure Beth will. Unless you want to start an application process where you get to interview all of them," she said placing her hands on her hips. "Hmmmm?"

"No, no," Tony said as he raised his hands in submission. He was resigned to letting Sarah take charge. She had that effect on Tony. In fact, he would trust her and Dave with almost anything. "Now go and convince Beth," he said.

Sarah walked out and Tony looked at Dave who sat back with a smile on his face.

"This is going to be a long twelve weeks, Dave."

"Is that how long it is until her due date?"

"Yeah, that's on the short end. Could be as long as fourteen."

"Wow, that is a long time. But we'll get through it," Dave said.

"It's going to make Beth crazy! All that inactivity. Heck, she won't even be able to sit up and work on her computer! What in the world is she going to do all day?" Tony threw up his hands.

"Don't know. I guess she will have to figure that out. But at least she will have company pretty much all the time."

Tony leaned across the table. "Look, Dave, I didn't mean to say anything bad about your church friends."

Dave waved him off. "No offense taken, buddy. I know how you feel about your privacy. But if it makes you feel any better, you have probably met most of them at one time or another. So hopefully we're not bringing in a bunch of 'strangers' to your house."

"Thanks, Dave." Tony paused for a moment as if he had something to say. Finally, Dave asked, "Okay, spit it out, what's on your mind?"

"Well, I don't want to start an argument."

"Since when?"

"Funny. Look, seriously. You and Sarah have been supposedly 'praying' for us. Heck, even Beth talks about praying for the kids and a healthy birth and all that."

"Uh-huh, and?"

"Well, it doesn't seem like it's done any good!"

Dave paused a moment in thought. "So you think that because we have all been praying, everything should be going smoothly?"

"I'm not saying that. But if it doesn't help the situation, what's the point?"

"Oh, I see, you think that praying should fix everything and if you pray hard and long enough, you will have no troubles?"

"I'm just saying that if praying has no positive effects, why expend all the time and energy?"

Dave paused for a moment and collected his thoughts. Then he said, "Tony, it doesn't work like that."

"Okay, how does it work then?" Tony sat back and crossed his arms across his chest.

"Look this may not be an easy concept. Are you ready to listen?"

"Sure, I'm all ears," Tony said as he shrugged his shoulders.

"You may need to engage your heart as well."

"Sure. Whatever. Explain away." Tony rolled his eyes.

Dave took a heavy breath before he started. "Okay then. Prayer is not about getting results. It's about connection." Tony shrugged his shoulders. "It's about connecting with God," Dave continued. "We believe that God is always listening and striving to connect with us, always trying to move towards us. That He wants a relationship with each of us and that relationship is as different as there are people in the world. Just like the relationship that you and I have is different than the relationship you and Beth have. And prayer is the way to build that relationship. Think of it as an ongoing conversation."

"But it's kind of a one-way thing, isn't it?" Tony said. "I mean you talk, and no one answers."

"That's not exactly it either. We do get responses."

"Oh, you hear voices now, Dave?"

"I think some people do. I don't."

"Then what do you get?"

"It's hard to describe. And it comes in different ways. Sometimes, it's a feeling. Sometimes, things happen that I can't explain it any other way. It might be a dream. Sometimes, it's with an interaction with someone else. It varies."

"Sounds a little flakey to me. I like hard facts and solid reactions," Tony said emphatically.

"Like I said, it's different for everyone."

"Well, I still don't see it. I mean, what about this situation? You have been praying, Sarah has been praying, Beth has been praying, and then Beth gets sick. Sounds like a negative response to me! If God is so good and listens to you all, why this?" He raised his hand and swept it around.

"We were never promised a rose garden. There is no rule that says when you believe, life becomes a bowl of cherries. We still have trials.

Heck, the Apostles had lots of trials and Jesus told them to expect difficult times because they followed Him. The promise is, at its heart, about spiritual well-being rather than physical well-being. It's about connecting with God. I know that doesn't help you now, but it may in the future." Dave sat back as Tony was clearly finished listening.

"You haven't said anything to convince me, my friend. But I respect your right to believe it. So keep on praying your heart out, for all the good it will do. In the meantime, I guess I will have to accept the help from all you churchgoing folk." Tony started to get up to bring the coffee cups to the sink.

"All right then. Good talk. I will ask one thing of you, though," said Dave

Tony sat down again. "And what is that?" Tony asked cautiously.

Dave leaned across the table. "Just this. As you meet these people, don't be afraid to talk to them. You just may learn something."

"They're not going to try and convert me, are they?"

"No, I don't think so. They are pretty laid-back."

"Fine, whatever. I need a beer. Want one?"

"Sounds like a plan to me!"

CHAPTER 7

It had been a very difficult six weeks. Beth had had to stay lying on her left side pretty much the the entire time, which left her very frustrated, as she was an active person. She tried to not take that frustration out on Tony, but when he got home in the evenings, she was sometimes, well, testy.

It was not as if she was alone all day. There was a constant stream of folks from the church who came in and stayed with her. Tony had met some of them as well, but most were strangers to him. He had slowly gotten used to the idea of all these people being in his home. He had even spent a little time talking with some of them. And just as Dave had promised, they didn't try to lay a whole bunch of religious mumbo jumbo on him. They just seemed like regular folk.

On this particular day, he had come home to find Beth in a particularly foul mood. He thought that getting out of the house would be good for both of them. Well, it would be good for him, at least. He figured she could be left alone for half an hour without any grave consequences. So he gave her a bite to eat and went out for his run. When he got home, he walked into the living room and was immediately concerned. Her face was very red, and she did not look happy.

"What's wrong?" he said.

"I don't know. I just don't feel good. I feel kind of hot and maybe a little dizzy."

He went over to her and felt her forehead. She seemed a little warm to him but not overly so. "Maybe it's your blood pressure. Let me get the cuff."

"No, I'm fine." She tried to wave him off. "I just need some water, maybe."

"Look, let me just take your pressure, okay?"

She looked up at him and shrugged her shoulders. "Whatever," she said.

Tony went and got the blood pressure cuff and proceeded to take her pressure. When he was done, he whistled to himself.

"What's that?" she said.

"Well, it's 190 over 110," he responded. "That's a bit too high. The doctor said to call her if it got over 180."

"No, don't call Dr. Jamison, I'll be fine." She rolled over onto her side so that she wasn't looking at him.

"Look, I'm just going to see what she says."

She gave him a dirty look over her shoulder but said nothing. Tony went to the phone and dialed the doctor's number. When the doctor got on the phone and listened, she said, "Okay, get her to the hospital now. I will meet you there."

Tony hung up the phone and went to speak with Beth. She was still not looking at him. "The doc said we need to get you to the hospital. So I'm going to get your clothes," Tony said.

"Oh, I knew you shouldn't have called. Look, I will be fine. You are just overreacting!"

"Maybe, but she said she would meet us there, so let's get ready."

She turned over and stared at him as if to say, *I'm not going.*

He went and stood over her and said, "This is not optional. Let's go!"

She sighed and said, "Okay, whatever. Let's get it over with."

Tony helped her get dressed and she seemed to be resigned to having to go. They got into the car and drove to the hospital in silence. When they arrived at the emergency room, Dr. Jamison was already there. Even though the place was pretty busy, and the waiting room was full, they immediately moved her onto a bed and started to hook her up to a bunch of wires. They moved Tony into a waiting area where he fidgeted for about twenty minutes. Then the doctor came out. Tony thought she looked rather grim.

"Well," said Dr. Jamison. "It looks like you're having a baby, or should I say, babies."

"Yeah, tell me something I don't know, like how is Beth?"

"No, you don't understand, you're having your babies today! Like now!"

"What? Why? How?" He stood up and came face to face with the doctor.

"Now sit down and I will explain," she said.

Tony sat down as the doctor sat down next to him.

"So, here is the deal," she said. "Her blood pressure is spiking. It's now up to 270 over 180."

"What does that mean?" He was alarmed now.

"A couple of things. First, it is putting the babies under stress. They are not getting as much oxygen as they should. Second, it is putting Beth in a place where she could go toxic. You remember what we talked about if she experienced toxemia?"

"Yeah, you said it's really dangerous. Oh my God, is Beth in danger?" Tony stood up and started to go towards the door where Beth was. The doctor grabbed his arm and pulled him back down into the chair. Tony reluctantly sat back down but kept looking towards the other room.

"Easy, Tony. Beth is fine. But her condition has worsened and the only cure for this is birth."

"But she still has six weeks to go. And you said if something like this happens, you don't want to induce labor."

"We are not going to induce labor. We are going to do a C-section."

"A C-section? Isn't that extreme? Won't the babies be in danger?" Tony was very agitated now.

"Tony, calm down. We can control all of that."

"But the babies. They're not ready yet! Can't you do anything else?"

Dr. Jamison grabbed Tony by the shoulders and looked him squarely in the eyes. "Look, Tony, this is the best solution. We have to do this for both Beth and the babies."

Tony looked at the doctor and tried to think of a response. But he couldn't. He finally slumped back in the chair and said, "What do you need from me?"

"Nothing right now. We explained all this to Beth, and we are preparing her for surgery. We have her mildly sedated and are giving her fluids."

"Can I see her?"

"Yes, in fact, you can come into the operating room, if you would like."

"Yes, yes. Of course, I want to do that." He jumped up.

"Okay then, come with me and we will get you ready."

They got up and walked into the pre-surgical area. They fitted Tony with a gown and mask and brought him into where Beth was being prepped. There was a flurry of activity, but no one seemed to be in a panic. That reassured Tony a little. Then he saw Beth and gasped.

She looked flushed and completely out of it. It scared him.

He went to her and said, "How are you doing, honey?"

She fluttered her eyelids but did not speak.

Tony turned to the nurse. "Is she all right?"

"She is just sedated, that's all." The nurse continued to do her preparations. Tony grabbed Beth's hand and squeezed it. He didn't know what to do. He looked around at the people and watched them work.

He felt so helpless. *What should I do?* he thought. He wished Dave was here: he always seemed to have calming words in a crisis. Then he thought, *Dave would be praying, like that would do any good!* Tony looked up at the ceiling and found himself silently asking for help. *Please make this all go away,* he thought. Then he shook his head. *How ridiculous was that?* he thought to himself. *Nobody is listening up there or anywhere for that matter.*

Just then, the nurse gently touched his arm. "It's time to go," she said.

She led him into the operating room as they followed the gurney Beth was on. It was very bright in the OR. It seemed crowded as well. There was the doctor and a whole bunch of other folks. They were all busy doing their various tasks. Everyone seemed to know what they were doing. All the time, the nurse who had brought him in held onto his arm.

Finally, he said. "Look, you don't have to hold on to me, I'm not going to fall."

"I'm sure you're right, but Dr. Jamison wants it this way."

"Why?"

"Well, it seems that one time early in her career, she had a father faint during a birth and when he fell, he pulled all the tubes and wires out of the mother. So she always has a nurse be with the father during deliveries, just to be sure."

"Oh, I suppose that would do it."

She walked Tony over to the head of the operating table where the anesthesiologist was standing next to a panel of dials and flashing lights.

"Hello, I'm Dr. Vann," she said. "I'll be taking care of your wife during the procedure."

"Hello, Doctor," Tony said. Not knowing what else to do he said, "So how long have you been doing this?"

"Oh, this is my first case," she said with a straight face.

Tony looked at her in panic.

"Just kidding," she smiled. "I've been doing this for over fifteen years. Look, let me show you how it works."

Cheerfully, she proceeded to explain what the various instruments were and how they worked. While he listened, Tony glanced around the room. The various nurses and technicians seemed very relaxed. They were making jokes and acting fairly casual about the whole thing. Tony thought, *This must not be as bad as I thought. No one seems to be very worried.*

Had he known the truth, he would have not been so relaxed. When things are very serious in an operating room, the staff tend to try to keep it light to reduce their own tensions. But Tony was oblivious to that at the moment, which was for the best.

Being seated at the head of the operating table, Tony couldn't see all that was happening, but when the first baby came out of Beth's belly, he leaned around the screen to see. The nurse assigned to Tony watched him carefully.

What he saw reminded him of the movie *Alien.* There was this bloody head sticking up out of Beth's stomach. The doctor put something in its mouth and sucked some fluid out, then he pulled it up and out of Beth. The baby immediately started crying as he handed it to the nurse.

"You have a beautiful baby girl, Tony," the doctor said. The nurse brought the baby over to a table on the far side of the room and did something Tony could not discern. Then the second head popped out of Beth. The doctor pulled the baby out, but this one didn't cry. There was no sound. The baby was handed off to another nurse, who brought it over to another table.

"Is everything okay, Doc?" Tony asked.

The doctor ignored him as she kept working on Beth.

"Doc?"

"Be with you in a moment, Tony," she said.

There was silence in the room as each person did their job. The anesthesiologist was focused very intently on her machines. The nurses wrapped up the babies and carried them out of the room. Tony just sat there, not wanting to disturb anyone but at the same time wanting to scream out. Finally, after what seemed like an eternity to Tony, a nurse came over to him and gently tugged on his arm.

"Come with me, please," she said.

"Why? What's happening? How is Beth? Where are the babies?"

He looked over at Dr. Vann who looked at him.

"Go with the nurse, sir."

"What is going on?"

"Everything is all right. We are just stabilizing your wife," said Dr. Vann. She looked back at her machines and the nurse again gently tugged on his arm.

"Come on, let's go see your babies."

Tony was numb. He dutifully followed the nurse. Filled with so many questions, but unable to ask them. His last view of the room was of Beth lying there, blood all over her middle section, and the doctor with her hands inside Beth's stomach and a grim, determined look on her face. Then the door closed, and he was led away.

CHAPTER 8

They walked through several doors and then onto an elevator. As the doors closed, Tony looked at the nurse.

"Where are we going?" he asked.

"To the neonatal unit," she said.

"What?"

"Well, your babies are a little premature, so we have a special unit for taking care of them."

"Are they all right?"

"They are evaluating them right now."

"But I didn't hear the second one, it didn't cry when he came out! Is it a he or a she . . ."

"Yes, he is fine. They are both fine. You have a little boy and a little girl. The nurses are just evaluating them to see what they need."

The elevator doors opened. "Come, you can see them now," she said as she led him down the corridor.

They finally came to a place where there was a big glass window. On the other side was a room filled with what appeared to be clear plastic boxes. In each box was a baby. Some had tubes in them. Some had breathing masks over their faces. There were several nurses and technicians moving around the room, each checking dials and operating various machines.

"Are my babies in there?" Tony asked.

"Yes. Your two children are over there in the back, where the two nurses in red uniforms are tending to them."

"What are they doing?"

"They are evaluating them. To see what they need. Remember your children are six weeks early. They may need some special care. They will get that here."

"And what about Beth? My wife. How is she?"

"As soon as they are finished in the operating room the doctor will come and talk to you. Now, you can stay here as long as you like."

"Okay, I guess. But how will she know where I am?"

"Dr. Jamison has done this before. She will know to come here," she said. She gently squeezed his arm. "Not to worry, we have the best people here."

Having said that, she left Tony standing there by himself.

He stood there, not knowing what to do. No one acknowledged him from within the room, and there was no one else in the corridor. He didn't even know what time it was. He looked at his watch: it was almost midnight. They had been here for hours. He watched the nurses move about the room on the other side of the glass. He put his hand on the glass and pressed his face against it. His babies were in there, and he didn't know what was going on. He felt completely helpless, a feeling he was not accustomed to and did not like.

There was a light tap on his shoulder. He jumped around to see Dr. Jamison standing there.

"How is Beth?" he blurted out.

"She is out of danger."

"Out of danger? What does that *mean*?" Tony almost shouted.

"She had started to go toxic. We got her on the table in time, though. We were able to stabilize her. She is resting comfortably."

"So she's okay, then?"

"Yes, but I must warn you . . ."

Tony grabbed Dr. Jamison by the shoulders and squeezed hard. "Warn me of what?"

She gently disengaged Tony's hands and held them in hers. "Take a deep breath, Tony."

Tony backed off and breathed deeply. "Sorry, Doc. Okay, I'm calm. Tell me what's going on."

"Right. Let's go sit down." She led Tony to a bench across the hall. They sat down.

The doctor took a breath and began, "Beth had a close call. She went to the edge of toxemia. We have her stabilized. But we have to monitor her closely for a couple of days. And after that, she will have to take it easy for a couple of weeks."

"Okay, okay. What else? Are there any long-term effects?"

"We will have to see, but we hope not."

"Okay, I see." Tony looked down at his hands because he didn't know what else to do. Then he looked up. "What about the babies? One of them, the boy, didn't cry when he was pulled out, uh, when he was born. Is he okay?"

"Well, they are both six weeks premature."

"Right."

"That's why they are both in the neonatal ICU."

"ICU? The intensive care unit? Is it that serious?" Tony started to stand up. Dr. Jamison eased him back on to the bench.

"We are still doing some evaluations. Your daughter appears to be fine, just low in weight. You may remember when babies are subjected to preeclampsia, they tend to put their energy into developing their systems rather than putting on weight. Your daughter seems to have done that."

"And my son?"

"He also is low in weight. And he seems to have fully developed most of his systems, with the possible exception of his lungs."

"What does that mean? Is that why he didn't cry?"

"Perhaps. Ultimately what it means is that he will need some time to develop his lung capacity. He should be able to do that. We will ensure that he has that opportunity."

"He will be okay, right? I mean he won't have any long-term problems, right?" Tony almost pleaded.

"We will do everything we can to make that happen. In the meantime, they will both have to stay in the neonatal unit."

"For how long?"

"Until they put on enough weight. Probably for several weeks."

"Weeks! How long until Beth can come home?"

"Hopefully in a couple of days. We'll see how it goes."

"When can I see her?"

"Right now. Come on. I'll take you to her room."

They got up and walked to the elevator. Tony was none too steady on his feet. He was trying to process it all. He wanted to run but could barely walk in a straight line. They got out of the elevator and Dr. Jamison led Tony to a private room. When he saw Beth, he jumped a little. She looked terrible to him. She had all sorts of tubes and wires all around her. She was pale, very pale. And her face was slack. If he couldn't see the shallow breathing, he would have taken her for dead.

Dr. Jamison put her hand on Tony's shoulder. "She is stable, Tony," she said. "I know she doesn't look like it, but she is better. Now, you need to go home. She won't wake up for a while, and you will need your rest."

"No, I can't leave her or the kids. Kids, huh, that sounds so weird to say."

"I'm sure," Dr. Jamison said and smiled slightly. "But really, she won't wake up until morning, as we have her sedated. Go home and come back then. If anything happens between now and then I will call you."

Tony looked at her then back at Beth. Again, he had the feeling that he shouldn't have gone on his run. Had he caused this because he left her alone?

He turned to Dr. Jamison. "Doc, I left her alone for like an hour, maybe less. Maybe if I didn't leave . . ."

"Tony, you got her here in time. You did everything you needed to do. This is not your fault. And we will make sure she gets better. Now go home!"

Dr. Jamison turned Tony towards the door and gently pushed him out. Tony looked at Beth the entire way out of the room. He got in the elevator and pushed the button for the lobby. When it got there, the door opened and he walked into the lobby. He didn't know what to do. Then he thought of Dave and Sarah. That was where he needed to go.

CHAPTER 9

D ave opened the front door to see a tired and distraught Tony. Dave said, "Tony, what are you doing here. It's 1:00 AM!" He paused then grabbed Tony by the shoulders. "What's wrong? Is everything okay with Beth?" He proceeded to drag Tony into the house. Tony did not resist.

"I just came from the hospital," Tony blurted out.

"And?"

"I had to take her there. Her blood pressure spiked and . . ." Tony started feeling a bit woozy. "I need to sit down." At that point, Sarah came down from the bedroom adjusting her robe.

"What's going on," she asked. Then she saw Tony collapse onto the couch. "What's wrong? Where's Beth?"

Dave looked up at her, "Tony was just about to explain. Could you get Tony some water, please?"

"Of course," she said and went into the kitchen. She returned directly with a glass of water which she handed to Tony. He drank most of it in one gulp and handed the glass back to her.

Dave said, "Okay now, take a deep breath and tell us what's going on." Sarah and Dave sat down on either side of Tony on the couch and waited. Tony steadied himself and began speaking.

"It was like this; Beth wasn't feeling very good after I came home from a run."

"You left her alone?" Sarah blurted out.

"Yeah, I know I shouldn't have, but she seemed okay, and I needed some space . . ."

Dave gave Sarah a stern look. "It's okay, just keep going," he said.

"Anyway, when I got back, she said she was feeling kind of dizzy, so I took her blood pressure and it was high, so I called the doc. She told me to bring her to the hospital. I drove her there and when we saw the doctor, she said Beth needed an emergency C-section."

"When . . ." Sarah started.

Again, Dave raised his hand. "Keep going, Tony," he said.

"Well, right then! They rolled her into a room to prepare her."

"And . . ." said Sarah.

"They prepped her and me . . ."

"They let you into the surgery room?" Sarah was incredulous.

Dave said, "Sarah, please let Tony finish the story. Go on, Tony," he said after giving Sarah another stern look. Sarah folded her hands in her lap and sat back.

"Okay, so they delivered the babies and took them both out of the room. I guess they took them straight to their neonatal ICU 'cause that's where they took me. The girl was the first one out, and she seemed okay to me. But when the boy came out, he didn't cry, and they quickly took him away. It turns out his lungs aren't developed properly. Both of them are underweight and will have to stay in the hospital for some time, maybe weeks. They sewed Beth up, I guess, but they escorted me out of the room before they finished." Tony ran his hand through his hair. "When they brought me to her room, they let me see her. Man, she looked awful!"

Sarah seemed to soften her attitude and put her hand on Tony's shoulder. He continued.

"Then the doc told me to go home. I couldn't hold the kids or do anything for Beth. So when I didn't know where to go, I came here."

He put his head in his hands and started sobbing.

Sarah put her arms around Tony and held him close. "Of course, you came to the right place. You can stay here tonight."

"Thanks, I knew I could count on you guys." He lifted his head and wiped his eyes on his shirt sleeve.

Dave got up and said, "I'll go make up the spare room." He left the room as Sarah sat with Tony on the couch.

"Can I get you anything else?" she asked.

"I could use some more water?"

"Of course. You just sit there."

She got up and was back quickly. "Here you go," she said as she handed him the glass. He downed it in one gulp. Then she sat down on the coffee table directly across from him and waited for him to speak. Eventually, Dave came in and sat down.

Finally, Tony broke the silence. "I don't know what I would do without her!"

"It doesn't sound like you need to worry about that," Dave offered.

"I don't know. She looked so weak and, I don't know, just bad."

"It sounds like they have it under control, Tony," Sarah said. "Perhaps the best thing you can do is get some sleep."

"We can pray as well," Dave said.

"Really? That's where you're going to go now?" Tony spat out.

"Sorry."

"Aw. Look. I'm sorry. I'm just on edge. Of course, I know you two will pray, for all the good it will do."

"Okay, Tony. We get that you're angry. We are too," said Dave. He looked over at Sarah, who nodded in agreement. "Let's table this. Tony and I have had the discussion before. Come on, let's get you into bed, Tony." He helped Tony off of the couch. "Things hopefully will look better in the morning."

Tony allowed himself to be led into the bedroom, where he got into bed, fully clothed, and put his head on the pillow. "Thanks, guys." Dave closed the door and he and Sarah went into the kitchen.

"First thing tomorrow, I will make some calls," Sarah said. "They are going to need help when they all get home."

"Right," Dave said. "And I'll call Pastor Bob. I think they are going to need him as well." They turned off the light and went up to their bedroom, where they knelt next to the bed and prayed together before going to sleep.

CHAPTER 10

The next day, they all got up early. Dave got Katie ready for school, and Sarah made breakfast. Tony ate something, mostly to be polite, but he wanted to get to the hospital. The doctor had not called him during the night, and he took that as a good sign.

"Do you want me to go to the hospital with you?" Dave asked.

"No, I think I will be all right," Tony replied. He got up from the table and started to bring his plate to the sink when Sarah stopped him.

"I'm sure you want to get to the hospital, so don't worry about the dishes."

"Okay, I'll get going then. Look, I don't know how to thank you guys enough. I'll call you as soon as I know something."

"You just worry about what you need to do," she said. "Now get going! Oh, and please give Beth a big hug from both of us."

"I will," Tony replied.

Tony grabbed his jacket and went out the front door. All the way to the hospital, he imagined all sorts of bad things: Beth had died, the kids were sick, any number of awful scenarios. He pulled into the parking lot and found a spot. He turned off the engine and sat there, afraid to go in.

Then he did something unexpected.

He looked up and said out loud, "Look, I know nobody is listening up there. But just in case there is, please make sure that my family is safe."

He bowed his head and shook it back and forth. "Boy, I must really be desperate. Dave and Sarah have got me 'praying.' I must be out of my head."

He got out of the car and went into the hospital. The elevator ride was torture, and when he got out, he turned to the left, following the signs, and found her room number. But he hesitated at the door. What would he find?

He finally ventured in and there was Beth. She looked almost calm. He walked over to her side and looked down into her face. She seemed to be sleeping peacefully. Then her eyes fluttered, and she looked at him. She smiled slightly. She tried to speak but seemed to have trouble forming words.

"Hi, honey," he said. "How are you feeling?"

She tried to speak again, but all she could do was shake her head weakly.

"Would you like some water?" he asked.

She nodded yes. He picked up the Styrofoam cup next to her bed, the one with a straw in it, and put it to her lips. She took a couple of sips and then shook her head to indicate she was done. Then she spoke, weakly.

"How are the children?" she croaked out.

"I haven't seen them yet. They were okay last night."

"Last night? How long have I been here?"

"Just overnight. You had a pretty bad time of it. How do you feel?"

"Like hell."

"Oh. Can I get you anything?"

"No." She closed her eyes and appeared to be done with the conversation.

Tony was at a loss as to what to do next, as she didn't seem to want to talk any more. Finally, she dozed off.

Tony sat there. *What should I do?* Then he remembered the children. *Maybe I should go and see them?*

He got up and went to the elevator. He got off at the maternity ward floor and went to the glass wall at the neonatal ICU.

There were clear plastic boxes lined up in the room and eight or nine babies in there. Which ones were his? He couldn't read the names on the ends of the boxes.

Then he saw a call button next to a telephone to one side of the glass. He went over and pressed it. One of the nurses looked up and went over to the glass and picked up the receiver on her side.

"Yes?" she said.

"Hi, I'm Tony Hunter. My two children are in there somewhere?"

"Yes, of course. Would you like to see them?"

"Yes, please."

She put down the receiver and went to the far side of the room. She found two of the plastic boxes, all of which were on their own wheeled tables. She wheeled them over to the front of the glass.

Tony looked down at them. They looked so small! And one of them had what seemed to Tony like a hundred wires attached to him. He surmised that one was the boy because his blanket was blue, while the other was pink.

He picked up the receiver again. "How are they doing?" he asked.

"Oh, they are doing beautifully."

"But what's with all the wires on the boy?"

"Those are just for monitoring his vital signs."

"Why are you doing that? Is he sick?"

"He is doing fine. The doctor will give you all the details when she comes in to do her rounds."

"When will that be?" Tony was starting to panic a little.

"She usually comes in between 11:00 and noon. You can speak to her then. In the meantime, I will leave them here for you to look at." She hung up the phone and went back to the other children.

Tony stood there and stared at them. *How can we take care of anything so small?* he thought? *They are so helpless.*

Without thinking, he looked up and said, out loud, "This is what prayer has brought us? Thanks for nothing!"

After a while, the nurse came back and moved the boxes back to the other side of the room. Tony decided to go back to Beth's room. She was still sleeping or unconscious: he couldn't tell. He sat down and waited. It was 9:00 AM, so he settled in for a long wait.

Her nurse came and went, checking on Beth. She asked him if he wanted or needed anything. He told her no.

Finally, about 11:30, Dr. Jamison came into the room. "Good morning, Tony," she said.

"Hey, doc. What have you got for me?"

Dr. Jamison opened the clipboard she was carrying and read for a moment. "Well," she said, "looks like Beth is pretty much out of the woods."

"Pretty much?"

"Yes, her vitals are very close to normal. She should make a complete recovery."

"Should?"

"She had a very close call, Tony. And we will have to watch her for a while."

"Here in the hospital?"

"Just for a couple of days. Then she will be able to go home."

"And then?" Tony asked.

"She will have to take it easy for a while. You will have to take her blood pressure regularly and make sure she is not doing too much."

"That should be fun. She's been sitting at home for weeks with nothing to do. Now, with the kids . . ."

"Yes, you are going to have to pick up the slack for a while. But after that, things should get back to normal. Well, the new normal."

"New normal?"

"Yes, you have two children now!"

"Right! So how are they doing?"

"Your little girl is just fine. She just needs to gain some weight before she can go home."

"Okay. What about the boy, my son?"

"Ah, that is just a little more complicated."

"What?"

"You see, Tony, he has slightly underdeveloped lungs."

"How bad is it?"

"He is breathing pretty much on his own now, but he may need to stay in the hospital a little longer than your daughter."

"How much longer?"

"Not sure. We will have to see how things develop. He is under constant observation and excellent care."

"What are the long-term effects?"

"Assuming that he can put his energy into getting his lungs where they need to be, the effects should be minimal. But again, we will have to wait and see. He also will need to put on some weight."

Tony sat there for a while trying to process what he had heard. Dr. Jamison waited patiently for Tony to look up. When he did the doctor asked, "Do you have any other questions, Tony?"

"No, I guess not. It's just a lot to process, that's all."

"I know it is. We will be with you and Beth through all of this."

"Yeah, I know."

Dr. Jamison stood up and closed the clipboard. "I'm going on my other rounds. Call me if you need anything." She walked out.

Tony sat there, looking down at his hands. Then he looked up at Beth. She looked better. Almost peaceful. *How am I going to tell her all of this when she wakes up?* he wondered. Then he got up and went to see his children again.

CHAPTER 11

The next few months were a blur to Tony. Beth came home from the hospital three days after the births. She was still worn out and wasn't allowed to do too much. Again the house was "invaded" by church people, but this time, Tony was less perturbed by it all. They came and went on a fairly regular basis. But as Tony was staying at home some of the time, he got to meet them. They all seemed to be a fine lot. Never asking for anything, but always willing to help.

He also finally got to meet Pastor Bob. Bob Angler was a fairly small man, about 5'8". Also, he was rather quiet. This seemed odd to Tony, as he figured anyone who stood up in front of a church congregation would be loud and bombastic. And Sarah had described him as 'a mighty man of God,' so Tony had pictured him as a large man. Not so Bob.

Bob talked with Beth a lot. She seemed to find comfort in whatever he said to her because whenever he came by, she was less stressed after he left. She had not taken the condition of the twins, as they now called them, very well at first. She blamed herself. But gradually, she came to understand that it was not her fault.

Not having them come home right away was hard on both of them. Tony was less stressed about it, as he had to worry about Beth's health. But once he felt sure she was going to be all right, he was able to go back and spend more time at the office without feeling guilty. When they finally were both able to go together to the hospital and see how the twins were being cared for, they both relaxed a little.

Christina did very well and had gained enough weight in a month to come home. She was a happy and healthy baby. Not quite so with Joey. He was struggling to put on weight, and his breathing was difficult. Every day, either Beth or Tony went to see him. They had finally gotten to hold and feed him, and that helped their outlook. Tony was surprised how quickly he bonded with the children. He enjoyed being with them, something he had not expected.

The doctors and nurses were all very encouraging and finally the day came when Joey was doing well enough to be released. They brought him home to much fanfare from Pastor Bob and the congregational folks. There were presents and food and even a little party when they got home from the hospital that day. All put together by Dave and Sarah.

"Dave, what's all this?" asked Tony when he and Beth walked in with Joey in his arms.

"We thought you would like some help when you got home. Actually, the folks from the church wanted to see Joey. They have heard so much about him." He looked at the panic on Tony's face. "Don't worry, we won't stay very long."

Dave was true to his word. The people gathered around and oohed and aahed at Joey, then excused themselves. Some of the women made sure that Beth was okay, then, slowly, they all just left. Except for Dave and Sarah.

Sarah took Joey from Tony and brought him to the nursery, where Beth was checking on Christina. Dave went to the fridge, got out two drinks, and brought one to Tony. They went out onto the back porch and sat down. Tony took a long drink and sighed deeply.

"What's the matter, Tony?" Dave asked as he sat down across from him. "Things should get back to normal now."

"Normal now? What is that?"

"Oh, I guess that's true. Let's say the new normal then."

"I don't know what that is, Dave. I mean, we're not used to kids."

"You'll figure it out. That's kind of how it works."

"That may be true for Christina. She's fine. But Joey, he's got . . . issues."

"Yes, but you've got a great support system now. And he's got great medical help."

"That's true. They brought him through all of this."

"Yes, with God's help."

"Isn't that what you guys always say, 'with God's help'?"

"It's what we believe, Tony."

"I know you do. I've been thinking about that some."

"Oh, really? Do tell," Dave sat forward in his seat.

"Well, there were times when it seemed like the docs weren't so optimistic. In fact, one time the pediatrician at the hospital said something about 'praying for the best.' It struck me funny 'cause I had never heard a doctor talk like that."

"What do you think he meant?"

"I don't know, but I have to admit, I thought about praying that night. Actually, I told Beth about it and she said she would pray. I sat there while she prayed. I didn't feel any different when she was done."

"And?"

"And nothing. I didn't see any change in Joey's condition the next day. Or anytime soon afterward."

"And yet here he is."

"Yeah, here he is."

They both sat in silent thought for several minutes. Then Tony spoke.

"What is it with all your church friends, anyway?"

"I would say *your* church friends now, Tony. And what do you mean?"

"My church friends. That's funny. Before all of this, I didn't know these people. Beth knew many of them, but not all. And now they are suddenly a part of our lives. It's weird."

"What's weird about it?" Dave asked.

"Well, what do they get out of it?"

"Why do they have to get something out of it?" Dave asked.

"Because nobody does something for nothing. Everyone has self-interest and they do things so they can get something in return. It's just human nature."

"Maybe so, but the Christian philosophy teaches us otherwise."

"Yeah, yeah. I know what you're going to say: this is all about grace."

"Well, my, my, you *have* been listening all these years."

"I've listened. I just don't believe you."

"Not even when you experience it?"

"Is that what this has been all about? Getting me to 'experience' grace?"

"No, Tony. This has been all about us living by grace."

"Oh, please, do go on," Tony said sarcastically.

Dave grimaced at that. "Tony, I will be happy to explain it to you, but don't be flip."

"Fine, I'm listening," Tony said, though he was clearly annoyed by it all.

Dave continued, trying to keep his voice level as he was also annoyed with Tony's attitude. "What that means is, that grace is what we experience from God. He extends grace to us freely and there are no strings attached."

"No strings? Really? He just hands it out with no expectations in return."

"Yeah, that's pretty much it. And so we try to emulate that by extending grace to others. We live by the model that God provides for us. You see, Tony, when you understand grace, your heart is affected. And you want to be just like God."

He paused for a moment to let all he had said sink in. Then he continued, "I don't expect you to understand this, but my greatest hope for you is that in time you will not only grasp it, but you too will live it. Bottom line? Accepting God's freely given grace is very freeing. And that is what you have been witnessing! And I might be so bold to say that that is what you are missing."

"Fine," said Tony as he finished his drink. At that moment, Beth and Sarah walked onto the porch. Beth was excited.

"Come on, Tony. Christina and Joey are playing together," she said.

"What?"

"We put them together in one crib and they are, well, happy being together."

"You didn't put Joey in the oxygen tent?"

Beth put her hands on her hips and stared at Tony. "You are not going to worry constantly, are you? The doctor said we only needed to do that at night. Really, Tony, he has a condition, he's not going to break!"

"Yeah, I know you're right. I just . . ."

Beth went over to him and gently put her hands on his shoulders. "I know, honey. He is going to be all right. Now come into the nursery and see your children together." She gently helped him up and they went into the house.

Sarah went to Dave and put her arms around him. She looked up at him and sensing that there was something on his mind, she asked, "What's wrong?"

"He just really frustrates me sometimes. He has seen all these grace-filled people around him being generous to him and he doesn't get it! I'm not even sure he appreciates it."

"I know, honey. He's just really stressed. He's going to need help getting through this, Dave. We need to cut him some slack."

He sighed deeply. "I know, Sarah, I know."

CHAPTER 12

Tom Hunter was a rough man. His years in construction had hardened him. But he was likely that way before he went into the field. He had retired several years before, though he had probably wanted to keep working. But his back was giving him problems, and he couldn't quite keep up anymore.

He had never been a religious man. In fact, he pretty much rejected the church. Said it was a waste of time. That there was nobody out there or "up" there listening. You were born, you lived your life, then you died and there was no more. That was his philosophy. And, as Tony's father, he had tried to impress that view of the world on Tony.

Now, he sat across from Tony at their kitchen table sipping his coffee. Tony was uncomfortable under his gaze. Finally, Tony broke the silence.

"Look, Dad. It's what Beth wants to do. You know that I don't buy into all this, but what's the harm?"

"It sets a bad precedent, son."

"It's a simple ceremony. It's a baptism. It means nothing to me but means a whole lot to Beth."

Tom put his cup down more loudly than he needed to. "Aw, this is your mother all over again."

"Aha. See, you understand."

"What's that?"

"Mom made me go to church and Sunday school and all that. Even though you didn't want me to. And you didn't fight her on it."

"Oh, yes, I did! I just lost the battle."

"And why was that, pray tell?" asked Tony.

"I just didn't want to break up the marriage over it."

"Oh, you guys wouldn't have ever broken up. You always played the tough guy, but she could twist you around her little finger anytime she wanted!"

Tom stared at Tony for a long time. Finally, he shrugged his shoulders and sighed. "I guess you're right. That's why we moved to be near your Aunt Susan when she got sick after you went off to college. Damn, how I miss your mother."

"Me too, Dad. So let Beth have this, okay? No scenes, please. Look, it's not even a regular church service. We're doing it on a Saturday, so it will just be the family and a few close friends and no sermons."

"Sure. Fine. Whatever, but . . ."

"But what, Dad?"

"But . . . I hope this isn't the start of a trend!"

"Trend? What sort of trend?"

"A trend of, oh I even hate to say it, churchgoing!"

"Funny you should mention that," replied Tony.

"Funny, how?"

"Well, I've been thinking lately."

"Not a good sign, I expect," Tom picked up his coffee and drained it.

"Please let me finish, Pop," Tony said raising his hand.

"Okay, say on. I'll keep my peace until the end." Tom got up and went over to the coffee pot to refill his cup. Tony took a deep breath and began.

"See, here's the thing. I know you don't like the whole idea of church. Neither do I."

"True."

"But I went to church as a youngster."

"Because your mother insisted."

"Right. And when she died, you pulled me out of it all."

"Yes, because it didn't do any good. All that praying. Bible reading. Saying of the Mass. None of it did anything to save your mother! She still died. And she died in pain."

"I remember."

"Hey, you were only eleven! You didn't see the half of it!" Tom exclaimed.

"I saw enough, Dad. You tried to hide it from me. So did Mom. But I saw it. And yeah, I don't think that any of those 'church things' like praying did any good at all. So I was glad to leave the church after she passed."

"So why are you involved in that . . . that institution now?" Tom asked as he sat back down.

"Beth is a churchgoer. Just like Mom was. And she wants to be involved, so I'm not about to stop her. And, the thing is, these people have been there for us when we needed it most."

"That's how they start. They worm their way in and once they have you hooked, they start asking for money and time and whatever they can get."

"That hasn't been my experience with these people, Dad. It's been kind of surprising, really."

"Just wait. Mark my word. It will *be* your experience before too long." Tom shook his finger at Tony.

"Maybe. But here's what I've been thinking about. You always told me I have to make my own decisions."

"Of course."

"When Mom died, you asked me if I believed in God."

"Yeah. And you said you didn't."

"Yeah. I was mad. I was sad. And you were my role model. I didn't want to hurt you," Tony replied.

"What are you saying? Did you lie to me? You're a 'believer' now?"

"No, that's not what I'm saying. Far from it. But I had the background to call on to make that choice."

"What?"

"Because I had gone to church and learned the lessons and all that, I had a basis to make my decision. I had data. And I decided to not believe."

"So?" Tom asked cautiously.

"So if I want Joey and Christina to make their decision about their belief in God, they will need some basis as well."

"And?"

"And I think I need to give it to them."

"Go on," he said carefully.

"And I think the best way to do that is to join the church. Well, not join so much as to learn the details of the religion, so I can control the information that they get. Any religion would do, but since Beth is a part of this church, it seems the logical place to start."

"Let me get this straight, you want to join the church so you can teach them that *there is no God?*"

"Yeah. Well, no. What I mean is, I want them to have a solid basis for whatever decision they make. Mom's insistence that I go to church helped me because I knew how the church worked. Or didn't work in the case of Mom's illness."

Tom put his head in his hands and groaned. "You know if you get them into the system, they will be brainwashed. I don't like this. I don't like this at all!"

"I didn't think you would. But you see my point, right?"

"No, I don't. I think it is a really bad idea."

"I haven't fully made up my mind," Tony said.

"I assume you talked to Beth about this?"

"Actually, no. I wanted to float it by you first."

"Good. Then my answer is *no!*"

"Dad, I wasn't asking for your permission. I just wanted to talk about it."

"Well, you've got my input!" He got up and started pacing around the room. "I knew this was going to happen. Ever since you told me that Beth had started going back to church."

"Dad, Beth has always been a churchgoer. She just never made me go with her. I think that's one thing she misses in our relationship."

"I'll bet she does. Look, you know I love Beth. But I can't change her views. What I'm concerned with are the kids. I don't want them to be contaminated with all that religious crap."

"I thought of that," replied Tony. "But if I'm the one who will be controlling all of it, I can give them the other side. Give them an even perspective, if you will."

"Uh-huh."

"And at the end of the day, they are going to decide whatever they're going to decide. I have to let them make their own decisions about this. And it is a pretty big deal."

"Jeez, you think that bringing them to church is going to help them decide there is no God?"

"No. I think that this may help them to decide whether to believe in God or not. That is the goal."

"Fine. You do what you want to, but don't expect me to support it."

"I won't. But Mom would have."

"Hmff. Whatever."

Tom got up and went upstairs to his room. Tony usually loved having his dad come to visit, but he knew that Tom wouldn't let go of this easily. He just hoped his dad wouldn't make a scene at the baptism.

Tom came to the baptism and sat quietly. He didn't even roll his eyes during the ceremony, for which both Beth and Tony were grateful. Tony thought that Pastor Bob did a nice job. It was short and sweet without a lot of preaching. There was a reception held in the church's fellowship hall, which was a surprise to Tony. He had not expected that sort of thing, but apparently, all the folks that had helped them through the past several months wanted to be there to help them celebrate. It was nothing too fancy, but it gave Tom a chance to interact with the church members that attended. And there were a lot of them. Tom asked Tony who they all were.

"Actually, I haven't met all of them yet," he said.

"Then why are they here? If you don't know them, what is the deal?"

"That just seems to be the way they do things, Dad. I told you, they just sort of show up when you need them."

"I'm still suspicious," Tom said sipping his punch and eyeballing the crowd.

"I know, Dad. I was, too. Now, I've just come to accept it. Beth seems to know most of them, though."

"Figures."

"It was a nice ceremony though, don't you think?"

"It was short, I'll give you that." Tom looked at his watch and finished his punch. "My plane leaves in a few hours. I better get back and finish packing."

"Dad, won't you consider staying a little longer? I know Beth would love to have you."

"Just Beth?"

"Oh, you know what I mean. We both would."

"But?"

"Well, I just don't want to have any arguments about the whole church thing."

"No arguments," Tom said. "You are going to do what you are going to do. I just don't want to be here to see you ruin your children, my grandchildren."

"We are *not* going to ruin them!"

"We'll see. Just drive me back to the house so I can pack. I've already ordered a cab to get me to the airport."

Tony knew there was no arguing, so he let Tom say his goodbyes to Beth and the twins and then brought him home. Tom packed silently. When the cab came, they hugged, and Tony watched him as the cab drove away. He had a strange, uncomfortable feeling he couldn't shake. Finally, he shrugged his shoulders and drove back to the church.

CHAPTER 13

It didn't take long for life to fall into a more normal routine. Beth was back to her energetic self. She seemed to have no long-term ill effects from her ordeal. Christina was a happy, healthy baby. She was growing normally and had the most wonderful laugh, or so thought Tony.

Joey was also doing well, though he struggled a little more than his sister. He sometimes had to sleep in an oxygen tent at night to help him breathe. And they had to watch him carefully when he played with his sister too roughly. He could get out of breath easily.

Beth had convinced Tony to go to church with her more regularly. He agreed, as it seemed to work with his plan of learning more about the church. He didn't like leaving Joey in the nursery care, but they seemed to be able to do a good enough job with him. Tony was still trying to decide how to approach the whole religious training thing when Hurricane Selma hit.

It formed in the Gulf of Mexico almost overnight and strengthened to a Category 5 in just three days. Then it moved north rapidly and slammed into the Louisiana town of New Iberia. It was devastating! It left death and destruction over a relatively narrow path, but where it hit, the results were massive.

Two days after it passed, Tony got a call from Pastor Bob.

"Tony," he said. "I'm sure you've heard how the hurricane impacted Louisiana?"

"Yes, of course," Tony said. "Just terrible!"

"Yes, it is, I agree."

"What can I do for you, Reverend?" Tony asked, trying to get to the point.

"Do you remember Walter King?"

"Not really. Should I know him?"

"I guess not," Bob replied. "He is one of the elders of the church."

"I see . . . Oh, wait. I remember him now. Didn't he speak at service a couple of weeks back?"

Walter King was a retired businessman. He had for many years been the vice president of a Fortune 500 company. He was a short man, but when he entered a room, everyone knew he was there. Fiercely devout, he was one of the driving members of the church. At the service, Tony had been impressed with his directness. Walter spoke his mind and was glad to share his views with anyone who would listen. At the same time, he was very respectful in his dealings with others. To Tony, he had seemed sort of an enigma, but it had been a short encounter and he had forgotten all about it until now.

"That's him," replied Bob. "In any case, he has a friend that is the pastor of a small church in New Iberia."

"Wow."

"Walter, being who he is, has already gone down there to try and help them out."

"Okay," Tony replied slowly.

"We have decided, based on what Walter has told us, to get a group of us together and go there with supplies and spend some time helping them rebuild and do repairs."

"I see." Tony thought, *Here it comes: the begging for money.* But Bob surprised him.

"I was hoping you might be willing to be part of the crew. We will be leaving the day after tomorrow and stay there for about a week."

Tony was incredulous. "You want me to come with you?"

"Yes. Beth has told me you are a 'get things done' kind of guy and that you have some experience in construction. This sounded right up your alley."

Tony was a little panicked. This was not something he envisioned himself doing. Going with a group of holy rollers to help a bunch of total strangers? He thought quickly about how he could get out of it.

"Uhm, okay. I will have to talk to Beth. You know, to see if she can handle things without me. You know, handle the kids and all. And I will also have to check with my boss. We are in the middle of a really big project right now, and I don't know if he will let me off."

"Of course. I understand. There is no pressure. If you can't go, that will be fine. Just let me know as soon as you can," Bob replied.

"Will do. Bye."

Tony hung up the phone and stared at it for a minute. *What am I going to do?* he thought. There were so many things to consider. Beth and the kids, of course. Could they get along without him? Probably. And would his boss let him off of work? But more importantly, did he *want* to go with these people?

This was a chance to get to know some of them better. And he did sort of like the idea of helping the people affected. Of course, he had more envisioned writing a small check.

He went into the nursery where Beth was putting the kids down for the night. At nine months old, they were so beautiful to him. The oxygen tent made a low humming noise that he had finally gotten used to. They didn't use it every night, but today Joey had seemed to be having trouble breathing, so Beth put him in it. He walked over to Joey and made some minor adjustments to the tent, then turned to Beth.

"That Pastor Bob from the church just called," he said.

"Oh, what did he want?" she asked as she finished tucking Christina in. They walked out into the living room.

"Apparently, they are putting together a relief trip to Louisiana. You know, to help with the hurricane victims."

"Oh?"

"And they are going down there with a bunch of people to help."

"Uh-huh."

"And he wants me to go with them." He followed her as she went into the kitchen and started putting the dishes away.

"Okay," she said.

"That's it? Just okay?"

"What else would you have me say? I assume you are going to go."

"Why do you assume that?" He sat down at the table. She sat down across from him.

"Well, you do like to help people."

"Yeah."

"And this would be a chance for you to get to know some of the other folks in the church. You have hinted at wanting to do that."

"Yeah. That's true. Okay, but . . . can you manage without me?"

"Of course I can. And if I need help, the folks at church will be here, as always." She reached out across the table and held his hand. "What is the problem? Can you get off from work?"

"I don't know, maybe."

"But?"

"Well, I don't know most of those people."

"You know more of them than you think. And they don't bite. But you already knew that. So what is the problem, really?"

"It sounds like such a 'church thing' to me. Lots of praying and spiritual stuff. Don't know if I can take a whole week of that," he replied.

"Honey, you will probably be so busy that you won't have time to think of that. Besides, I'll bet Dave will be going. You can hang out with him."

"So you think I should go?"

"Yes, I think it will be good for you. And we will be fine here." She squeezed his hand.

"Okay, I guess I'll check with Jerry and see if I can get off."

The next day, Tony walked into Jerry's office and closed the door. Jerry looked up from his computer and said, "What's up, Tony?"

"Well, it seems that Beth's church, uh, the church we go to, is sending a crew down to Louisiana to help with hurricane relief."

"What do they want, a donation? You will have to go down to HR. I think they have a fund for that sort of thing."

"No, that's not it."

"Oh, then what?"

"Uh, they asked me to be part of it," said Tony.

Jerry turned away from his computer, "What does that mean, exactly?"

"It means that they are putting together a crew of folks to go down there and help. You know, clean up, do repairs, that sort of thing."

"Uh-huh. And they want you to go with them? I didn't think you went in for that sort of church stuff."

"I don't, normally. But I've been getting a little more involved there, 'cause of the kids, you know."

"I see," Jerry said carefully. "When are they going?"

"Day after tomorrow."

"Uh-huh."

"So I was wondering if I can get time off to go with them."

"Gee, I'm not sure, Tony. We are in the middle of the Sievers' project. And you're in charge. Can you afford to take that much time off?"

This is exactly what Tony had been concerned about. And he could hear his dad whispering in his ear, *See, I told you so.* But he had thought this through and had an answer ready.

"Phil can handle the work, Jerry. He is fully up to speed and frankly is ready, I think, to take on some more responsibility. And it would only be for a week."

"I suppose." He paused, then said. "Well, if you go, you will have to take vacation time."

"What?"

"I can't authorize administrative time for something like that, especially since it's not local. Sorry Tony, that's the deal."

Tony thought for a moment. Then he said, "Uh, okay, I guess that is what I will have to do. I'll get Phil and the rest of the team up to speed."

"Fine, and I hope you're right about Phil." Jerry went back to his computer and Tony walked back to his cubicle.

What was I thinking? They need me at work. This could really negatively affect my career. Is Phil up to the job? Does Jerry think I'm doing the wrong thing? Should I stay and not risk it?

But the more he thought about it, there seemed to be something inside him saying, *Go to Louisiana.* Something else said this experience was going to be very different than he thought it would be. And that's how it would turn out: not the way he anticipated it at all.

CHAPTER 14

There was a dozen of them. There was, of course, Pastor Bob, as well as Tony, Dave, and a fellow named George Stavros, the custodian at the church. George had been many things in his previous life: a drug addict, a car thief, and other nefarious occupations. He had found God through the prison ministry of Pastor Bob and when he was released, he gravitated to Bob's church. Bob hired him as the church part-time handyman, and eventually he was hired there full-time. He was a quiet man, very grateful for his second chance in life, as he demonstrated regularly. There wasn't anything you could ask George to do that he wouldn't get accomplished.

James Callahan, a young doctor, a pediatrician just three years into his practice, was also part of the team. Having met him through the church, Tony and Beth had begun taking the twins to his practice, and Tony had been impressed with his level of expertise and caring. He was glad that James was along because he viewed this as a chance to get to know his kids' doctor better.

Calvin Lowe, a crusty old fellow who was one of the founding members of the church, was also along. Tony didn't know much about Calvin's history, but he had experienced Calvin's views on more than one occasion. Calvin was not shy about sharing his thoughts with anyone who would listen. There were others, but these were the folks who would eventually become most influential in Tony's life.

The team met in the church parking lot the morning they were to leave. Bob had rented a twenty-six-foot truck, now filled to the brim with supplies: water, medical items such as bandages and over-the-counter medicines, nonperishable foods, blankets, diapers, and other items the storm victims would need. They had the two church vans packed with their own personal supplies: sleeping bags, clothes, and tools. They also had to bring all their own food for the week ahead. They would not be using the items brought for the victims.

So it was a pretty cramped group that loaded into the vans and truck for the start of the ten-hour trip. Tony was asked to drive the truck, which he was more than happy to do, as it got him out of the crowded vans. He had hoped that Dave would join him in the truck, but somehow, Calvin ended up riding with him. Calvin kind of reminded Tony of his father, so he decided perhaps it wouldn't be so bad. As they set off, however, he quickly realized that Calvin was going to give him an earful on the spirituality of what they were doing.

It wasn't long after leaving the church parking lot that the usual small talk had run its course. It was when Tony asked Calvin, "So Calvin, is this your first mission trip?" that the deluge began.

"Far from it," Calvin replied. "I think this is my seventh mission trip altogether, and my third trip sponsored by the church. How about you?"

"Oh, this is my first one," Tony indicated. "I guess you could call me a true rookie."

Calvin jumped at the chance to let Tony know his perspective on why these trips were so important to him. "Well, Tony, I hope this isn't your last trip. Doing for others is what it's all about."

"How's that?" asked Tony.

"Well, young man, do you want the 'Cliff's Notes' version or the full-blown answer as to why I go on as many trips as possible?"

Tony replied, "Well, Calvin, we do have a long ride ahead of us. How about you share all the gory details?"

"Okay," said Calvin, "Don't say you didn't ask for it." He took a deep breath and began, "You really don't know me, but I can guarantee you that you have a totally inaccurate impression of who I am. You probably see me as a crusty old man who has been a Christian his whole life—a true churchgoer who has taught Sunday school, been on the church leadership team, and devoted himself forever to being a good guy."

"Well, I don't have any preconceived notions about anyone at the church," Tony said.

"I'm sure I don't buy that, my friend. Anyone who isn't a churchgoer has preconceived notions about who we are."

"Well . . ."

"Well, nothing. Whatever you thought, you're wrong, at least about me being a goody-two-shoes. Nothing could be further from the truth. In my younger years, I was a real hellraiser. I grew up in a home with three children, myself being the youngest. My older sister and my older brother were extremely obedient to my autocratic, domineering father and my quiet, submissive mother.

"For whatever reason, I committed myself early on to be a real boat-rocker. I can't tell you how many times my father laid his thick, wide leather belt to where the sun don't shine."

He paused for a moment, apparently in deep thought, as if picturing something that was confusing to him. Finally, he continued.

"I truly don't know why I was so different than my siblings, but I couldn't wait to leave home and strike out on my own. I knew there was freedom and frolic out there, and I wasn't going to wait for my turn to experience it. And I can tell you for sure that God and church and mission trips were nowhere in sight."

Tony seemed surprised that Calvin was so open about his "wild hair" days. So he asked Calvin, "At what age did you leave home?"

"I was sixteen when I set out on my own."

"Sixteen! That was pretty darn young to leave the nest. Tell me," said Tony, "how did you fare on this 'rebellious adventure,' if I can use that term?"

Calvin looked over at Tony as if sizing him up. Could Tony take the whole story? He replied, "We don't have enough time for me to tell you all about the next thirty years, but if you really want to know, I'm okay with sharing some of the highlights."

Tony replied, "Please, whatever you are comfortable sharing with me, I'd love to know."

"Good. No problem," replied Calvin, "I have nothing to hide. I knew my father had a stash of cash he kept in the shed behind the house. He did not trust anyone with his money, especially not the banks. He'd lived through the Great Depression and saw how the banks had failed, leaving everyone without any cash and in real financial hurt. So Dad stashed his cash in a place he thought no one knew about." He chuckled to himself. "No one but me. I came upon it one day when I was looking for a place to hide a pin-up I had ripped out from the center of a magazine I found. Every once in a while, I would sneak out to the shed and count the money Dad had hidden to see if he was spending any of it or adding to it. I never counted less than the time before. So when I decided I was going to make my break from home, I grabbed about half of it and took off. I knew that Dad would discover the missing cash, and he would know it was me that took it, so I resolved myself to never returning home. He would have killed me, or so I thought."

"That was a huge price you were willing to pay just to sow your oats, wasn't it?" asked Tony.

Calvin paused again, looking off into the past. "Looking back on it now," said Calvin, "it was a stupid move and a huge price to pay. But I didn't see it that way at the time. All I could see was that I had a wad of money, freedom from the tyranny of my father's law, and a chance to see how the other half of the world lived. I'm not sure why this desire to escape rules and regulations was so strong in me, but it was as if it wasn't my choice. It was more like there was something inside of me saying I had to get out. This thought had me in its grip, and it deceived me into thinking it would be fun to go and now was the time."

Tony interrupted. "So you said there was a thirty-year window of time that you would describe as a 'rebellious adventure?'"

"Yes, Tony, I lived out of this paradigm for the next thirty years of my life. Maybe not in the same way as when I was a teenager, but basically the same pattern. I wanted to be my own boss and not live under anyone's thumb. I jumped from job to job, city to city, wife to wife—I've been married three times. Thank God I never had any children. I knew I would follow in my father's footsteps as a hard taskmaster and any kids I might have would probably want to be as far away from me as I wanted to be from my father."

He looked over at Tony to see his reaction. If Calvin expected Tony to be shocked, he was disappointed. Tony just seemed genuinely interested.

Calvin continued, "I told you that your impression of me as the 'good little church boy' was not even close. Anyway, there's no point in giving you any more of the gory details of that part of my life. Just suffice it to say, that if sin was in front of me, I couldn't wait to experience it."

Tony was curious. "Did you ever return home? Did you and your dad ever patch things up?"

"No," he replied. He paused again. "And it never really bothered me until recently. My father passed away before we could reconcile and up until then, I wasn't sorry for never making things right. I had just accepted the fact that we were not in the same world. But recently, I wish I had the opportunity to make amends."

"Why the change of heart?" asked Tony.

"Well, for the past fifteen years, I have turned a corner. I can't even explain it very well. But fifteen years ago, I started to think about my legacy. I started to think about how those in my life would remember me. I'm not sure why this began to matter to me, but maybe it was because of my age. You know, we are not going to live forever."

"That is so true."

"I guess I wanted in some way to have at least a few people who would think I had made a positive influence on them. One day, I saw in the paper where a pastor was starting a new church in our community and was looking for help. I said to myself, 'What could be better than helping a pastor?' I showed up at one of the initial organizational meetings. I liked the people, and they obviously needed some help, so I signed on. Before I knew it, I'd become one of the charter members. I didn't have much experience in the church, but we started classes and Bible studies and started learning about God. That's when I knew I had done the right thing."

Tony grinned to himself. "How did you know? Was it 'God's voice' who told you?"

"Not exactly. One of the first books of the Bible we studied was Matthew."

Okay," replied Tony. "I'm afraid you are going to have to help me with this. What does the Book of Matthew have to do with your knowledge that you had done the right thing by getting involved in the church?"

"Well, Matthew 20:19 and 20 states, *Do not store up for yourselves treasures on earth, where moth and rust consume and where thieves break in and steal; but store up for yourselves treasures in Heaven, where neither moth nor rust consumes and where thieves do not break in and steal.*"

"Uh, okay?" Tony was confused.

"Don't you see, Tony?" Calvin asked. "I saw that the point of doing good works is how I can store up treasures in Heaven. We have to do good for others down here so we can get in up there and have lots of good stuff when we get there."

Calvin waited to see the effect his proclamation had on Tony. Tony shrugged his shoulders as if to say, *Okay, I get it.*

Calvin continued. "So that was the first thing I did to start racking up brownie points with God so someday when I die, I will have something to point to on the good side of the ledger. I've only had fifteen years to start racking up those brownie points, but I have had thirty years of the bad stuff, so I have a lot of catching up to do. That's why when

I have a chance to go on a mission trip, man, I jump at it. Believe me, the bad stuff I've built up is still way more than the good stuff. I just hope and pray that God gives me enough time to at least get the scale balanced so when I meet St. Peter at the gate, and he looks over my life, I have a chance of sneaking into Heaven by the skin of my teeth.

"That is why you are so lucky, Tony. You are young. You don't have thirty years of debauchery behind you. Why, if you follow my example and start adding to your good stuff now, your scorecard will be on the positive side before not too long, and you will be able to breathe easier much sooner than me."

Tony began to feel a little more comfortable. Calvin had opened his life to him in ways he never expected. However, he wasn't prepared to bare his soul to Calvin and hoped that Calvin did not want a blow-by-blow of his "bad stuff" at this point in their adventure.

However, Calvin seemed satisfied to bare his own soul without interrogating Tony about his. In a way, if there was a God, this made a lot of sense to Tony. He did believe that no one did anything without expecting something in return. Calvin's story simply reconfirmed in Tony's mind that philosophy. People in the church were doing good things for other people so they could get into Heaven. Yeah, that made sense to Tony. If the people in Dave's church had done things for him and Beth, the reason they hadn't asked Tony for anything was because they were expecting something from God.

Tony sat back in his seat. He thought that this was vindicating his philosophy of life. *Yes*, he thought, *I've already learned a lot on this trip.*

Calvin shared more of his life during the long hours they were driving. And the more he talked, the more Tony realized he had been right all along. The good deeds church people did was in their own self-interest. Little did he know how that view would ultimately be changed.

CHAPTER 15

The church was a mess. Trees were down everywhere. Trash was strewn all around the grounds. But that was the condition pretty much everywhere in New Iberia. The members had managed to clean up the sanctuary enough for Bob's crew to lay out their sleeping bags and other stuff. Power was, of course, out all around the city, as were the phone lines. Cell towers had been knocked down by the dozens, so there were no communications across the area.

Except for the church itself. By some act of fate no one could explain, the church's land phone line continued to operate. Walter King, being the opportunistic fellow that he was, immediately saw the value in the situation.

By the time Bob's crew had arrived, Walter had essentially established the church as a logistics center. Trucks and cars moved in and out regularly, either bringing supplies in or sending them out based on the needs in the community. Walter was firmly in charge of the whole operation when they arrived. Even though it was evening, they were immediately put to work.

First, they unloaded their truck and piled all their supplies into the church's Fellowship Hall, which had been turned into a warehouse. While they were doing that, several small trucks arrived loaded with bags of ice. Tony and the guys loaded all the ice into their now-empty truck, and George asked Tony if he could ride with him and help to distribute it. "No problem, George. Hop in," said Tony.

As Tony drove through the streets, he marveled at the level of destruction. Trees and power lines all down. Roofs ripped off houses. Cars turned over. Some of this debris had been moved off the streets, but Tony still had to navigate around various obstacles. Along the way, people would run out of what was left of their homes, and Tony and George would stop and hand out ice bags to grateful people. It made Tony feel good that he was bringing them something they needed.

As they got closer to downtown, they passed a parking lot for a local shopping center. There, the police had set up a distribution center for blankets, food, and clothing. The amazing thing to Tony was that the people were very calm. In fact, they didn't crowd around the tables: they formed this long snake-like line in the parking lot and waited patiently to get whatever they could. "Only in America would you see that," he commented to George.

"What do you mean?" asked George.

"I mean, we are so trained here in this country that we just form a line whenever we want something."

"I suppose that is true. Never thought about it before."

They drove on to the local fire station where they parked the truck and handed out ice bags until the truck was empty. Then they drove back to the church. Tony again noted how everyone was working to clean up their yards and houses. And they all waved at Tony and George as they passed.

When they got back to the church, it was getting dark. The operations had slowed, and finally, Walter stopped issuing orders. The church members had made the workers dinner. The pastor said a blessing, they were all served a hot meal, and they all ate quietly, as they were all pretty beat. Tony helped with the cleanup and then crashed onto his sleeping bag. He had forgotten to bring his air mattress, so he did his best to use his clothes and such to make some padding. People were sitting in groups talking when Dave came over to his sleeping bag, which was set next to Tony's.

"Haven't seen you all day, Tony," he said as he plopped down. "How is it going?"

"Fine. Man, you should see the mess out there. These folks are going to be cleaning up for a long time!"

"I haven't left the church since we got here. Maybe I'll get to see it tomorrow."

"It's not pretty."

"I'm sure it's not." Dave paused for a moment then said, "I'm glad you're here Tony. I wasn't sure if you would come."

"Why not?"

"Well, I know you're not all that comfortable with everyone in the church yet. Besides, I figured you wouldn't want to leave Beth and the kids alone."

"I didn't, really. But Beth encouraged me to come. And your folks are not all that bad, most of the time," he chuckled. "I sure would like to call home, though. But there's no cell phone service and I don't think Mr. King will let anyone use the church's landline for anything but 'business.'"

Dave laughed. "You're probably right. If it makes you feel any better, Bob was able to get a message home to let everyone know we got here safely. All the families have been or will be notified."

"That's good to know." Tony paused and looked around the room and sighed.

"What?" asked Dave.

"I don't know. I guess I kind of expected there to be some sort of religious thing. You know, a service or something."

"We don't always do a worship service whenever we get together, Tony. Everyone is tired and we need to focus our energy."

"True. Speaking of tired, I'm beat."

"Me too, let's turn in. Again, glad you're here, Tony. Good night."

Dave turned over into his sleeping bag and was soon breathing softly. Tony watched the crowd for a few minutes, then rolled up in his bag and was soon fast asleep.

CHAPTER 16

Tony woke up before most of the others. He had always been a light sleeper, and even though he was tired, he put on his running shoes and went out for a short run. He liked to run in the morning, as it gave him a chance to clear his mind for the day.

The area around the church was covered in downed tree limbs and debris, so he had to be careful where he stepped. Even at this hour, there were people out cleaning up their yards and houses. How would he deal with this kind of disaster?

When he got back, breakfast was being served. He grabbed a plate and found Dave and sat down next to him.

"So, what's the plan for today?"

"No clue," said Dave.

"Fair enough."

They finished breakfast in silence, each with their own thoughts. Walter again took charge of the day. No one seemed to want to challenge his authority, even though there was not an obvious reason he should be in charge. Tony was assigned to sort inventory as it came in. And come in it did. From all over. Tony and his crew had quite a time keeping up with the inflow. No sooner did a shipment come in than a request came for some of it and it had to be sorted and loaded and sent off.

Around midday, several cars and SUVs drove onto the church grounds. The local pastor, Reverend Paul, went over to the caravan and spoke for a while with the apparent leader. He then rushed over to where Walter was talking on the church's land line telephone. Tony happened to be standing within earshot and heard the conversation.

"Walter, I need to speak with you for a moment."

Walter put his hand up to silence Paul.

"It's really important, Walter," Paul insisted.

Walter put his hand over the receiver and gave Paul a nasty look. "I'm busy right now," Walter said and went back to his conversation.

Paul shuffled nervously for a moment then tried to interrupt Walter again. "Please, Walter," he pleaded.

Walter again covered the phone with his hand and shot back, "What is it that is so blessed important?"

"The governor is here," said Paul.

"And?"

"Well, he's heard about what your team of guys are doing here and wants to thank and congratulate you, uh, us."

"Tell him I'm busy. You talk to him," said Walter and went back to his phone conversation.

Paul was flabbergasted. He stood there for another minute and finally went up to Walter, who had turned his back, and tapped him on the shoulder.

"Please, Walter. It's the governor of the state of Louisiana! He wants to talk to you!"

Walter turned on Paul and said in a very stern manner, "I'm doing God's work here! You tell the governor of the state of Louisiana he can wait!" And he turned back to the phone.

And wait the governor did. Until Walter was ready to see him. After about five minutes of Walter speaking with the governor, the phone rang again. At which point Walter said, "That's for me. Goodbye,

Governor. Send more ice." He turned away and the conversation was over. The governor stayed another fifteen minutes talking to various people, but Walter gave him no more heed after that.

Tony had witnessed the entire exchange and marveled at the audacity displayed by Walter. He was not sure he would have had the courage to act that way. Yet there was something about it that energized Tony. The rest of the day, somehow his load seemed lighter.

CHAPTER 17

T he rest of the week seemed to pass quickly for Tony. There was always something to do, somewhere to go. And everywhere he went, he found people working together and helping each other. He had half expected to be breaking up fights and settling disputes among neighbors. But he did not see that anywhere in his travels.

Around the middle of the week, the church members decided that feeding their neighbors was the next thing they needed to do. So they started providing breakfasts to anyone who wanted them. People could come in and pick up meals and go on their way. Or they could stay and eat at the church. As the week wore on, more and more people stayed to eat. They seemed to want or need the company of others.

Tony got to visit with many of them as he either served them or ate with them. And one thing stood out to Tony he had not expected. No one was complaining. You could see many were hurting deeply, and you could see the fear in their eyes, but no one complained. *Pretty remarkable*, thought Tony.

Tony was also impressed with one story after another story of heartfelt gratitude from pretty much everybody. One man told of how his employer had come to his house and helped cut up the tree that had fallen on his garage. Another man said his company had given everyone a week off, *with pay*, to allow them to clean up their homes. And they weren't going to have to use their vacation time either. The company was simply paying them to be home.

Then there was the woman who had lost her dog in the storm and a bunch of her neighbors set up a search party to find him, which they did two days after the storm. Tony had never seen anyone so glad to be reunited with her dog. She hugged everyone who was on the search party and didn't seem to want to let them go.

Tony was amazed. There was no bitterness or anger that he could discern in those who had lost so much. He mentioned it to Dave, one evening as they were getting ready for sleep.

"These people are amazing, Dave," he said. "They aren't mad about the storm."

"Oh, I wouldn't say that exactly," Dave replied.

"What do you mean? I haven't heard anyone bitch and moan about it."

"I didn't say they were bitching about it. But I think you can tell they are not happy."

"Well, of course they aren't happy. But they're not complaining. At least I haven't heard any."

"I think they are coping as best they can," Dave said.

"But they just keep saying how thankful they are for the way others were helping them. I have to admit this has been good for me to see all these people a little happier because of what we have done for them." He paused. "Still, two weeks from now, they won't remember me or anything I've done. It's all just so fleeting."

"Perhaps, but does that really matter?" shot back Dave.

"Kind of. I guess I like being appreciated."

"Is that the reason you are doing this? So people will appreciate you; be beholden to you?"

"No, I guess not. Still, it would be nice. I mean what about all your church friends who came over to our house while Beth was sick? Don't they want something from us? Now that we are past needing them, don't they still expect Beth and me to continue thanking them for what they did? I think that is pretty normal, don't you?"

Dave could feel himself getting angry. He took a deep breath and moved to sit face-to-face with Tony.

"Is that what you think, Tony? After all this time? Has anyone asked for anything from you?" he said through clenched teeth.

"Well, no, no one has asked. But it doesn't mean they're not going to or that they don't expect me to do something for them if they were the ones in need. I mean there must be some motive, right, and some expectation of a little praise for doing good?"

"Let me tell you about some of these folks," Dave said slowly. "Okay, I will tell you about one. Remember Mary Johnson who came to your house almost every day?"

"Uh, I guess?"

"Mary, she is the woman with the short red hair that you commented looked so nice."

"Oh, yeah. Sure. What about her?"

"She lost her husband to cancer two years ago."

"Oh. I'm sorry to hear that."

"Well, during Ted's illness, the church rallied around them. And while it was a difficult time for them, Mary saw God's hand in her life; in their lives."

"How was that?" asked Tony.

"The community came together and provided support. And in the end, Ted found a kind of peace. He told me before he died, he knew Mary would be all right, as she was surrounded by a caring family of friends. And through that experience of Christian community, they were able to get her finances in a place that would not leave her wanting. He was thankful for that. And he felt a closer experience with God. In the end, he passed very peacefully."

"Sounds wonderful," Tony said sarcastically.

"*Damn it*, Tony, do not make light of it," Dave said so forcefully that others around them looked up.

"Okay. Okay. Sorry," said Tony putting his hands up.

Dave took a deep breath to calm himself down. Then he continued, "Mary, having seen God's hand in Ted's passing, has developed what I call a 'sacrificial heart.' But she will not talk about it with anyone."

"Why not?"

"Because she wants it to be about God and not about her. If you ask her why she does things for others, she will tell you about how God provided her with the much-needed support she received during that awful time in her life. She doesn't want to draw attention to herself. And she doesn't want any reward for what she does for others. Her generosity with others is born out of her deep sense of gratitude to God for how He comforted her through the people at our church. That's how it works, Tony."

"I'm still not sure I see what you are getting at. The guy still died!"

"Tony, you're just not getting it! And I'm too tired to explain it to you again. Good night!" Dave turned over in his sleeping bag.

Tony looked at his friend and said, "Dave . . ."

"What, Tony?"

"Thanks for trying."

"Whatever!"

Tony turned over in his sleeping bag but could not go to sleep right away. Dave had given him a lot to think about. The whole concept of doing something for someone else, especially someone you didn't know or care about and not expecting something in return was strange to Tony. While he always liked helping people, he also kind of expected at least a thank you. Yet hadn't he been doing just that this whole week? No, he hadn't, he realized. He still expected them to thank him. To remember him. To want to do something for him in return. He had gone in with that expectation, and he hadn't even realized it.

The question was if he dropped that expectation, would he still enjoy helping as much? Was his happiness at helping these people predicated on the fact that he received something from them in return? He would have to ponder this more fully. He dozed off into a troubled sleep and dreamed of hurricanes.

CHAPTER 18

The last day of the trip was a hectic one. There were many things to wrap up. Everyone had a sense there was more to do.

Tony had not seen much of Dr. Callahan during the week. Dr. Callahan had spent most of his time out in the community, tending to those who needed medical attention. For a pediatrician, he seemed to do well with triage medicine. Turns out, he had been in the Peace Corps with Dave and that is what he had done while there, tending to the natives in and around the villages they worked in. As they were packing things up, Tony got to talk to him.

"So, Doc, how was your week?" Tony opened.

"Busy. Very busy."

"How so?"

"Oh, lots of minor things. Cuts and bruises, mostly from the cleanup efforts. People are so wanting to get things done quickly that they aren't as careful as they should be. The chainsaw is the most dangerous part of a hurricane, I think."

"Kind of different work than what you usually do though, right?"

"True, though this is what I did while was in the Peace Corps."

"Oh, that's right. You were in Africa with Dave."

"Yes, that's where we met, actually."

"So he's the one who got you into the church?"

"Yep. When we got back, he introduced me to the congregation because he knew I was looking for a church home. Been there ever since."

"Ah, don't you find it a dichotomy?"

"What's that?"

"You know, the church and the medical and scientific fields?"

"No, not particularly."

"Really? I mean, you deal in facts and the church deals in, well, not facts."

"I see. You think that a scientific view can't relate to a religious view?" Dr. Callahan asked.

"Yeah, something like that."

"It doesn't work that way for me," replied Dr. Callahan.

"It doesn't. What about something like, oh say, evolution? The 'church' doesn't believe in it, but scientists do. How do you reconcile that? Or don't you believe in evolution?" Tony asked warily.

"Oh, I don't believe in evolution."

"Oh?"

"No, I said I don't *believe* in evolution. However, I do accept it as scientific fact."

"Help me understand that." Tony was interested now.

"Okay, let me explain. Evolution and other scientific facts are simply that, *scientific facts*. That means they are provable through the scientific method. That means they are testable and reproducible. That's how the scientific method works. A theory or idea can be put through a rigorous testing process by multiple people and the results are the same. Scientific facts change as we continue to test theories. You know, it was once a scientific fact that the earth was flat."

"Okay, how about the 'facts' of religion?"

"Ah, there is where the difference lies. You see, the facts we have about our spiritual lives are based on beliefs."

"Uh-huh."

"The big difference is that 'beliefs' are not based on necessarily 'scientifically testable' facts."

"Not following you," said Tony.

"We believe things for various reasons. Those reasons typically are because of our experiences. They are not reproducible, at least not in a scientific sense. My experience with God is mine alone. I can tell you about it, but I can't expect your experience with God to be exactly the same as mine.

"An example?"

"Okay, when I pray, I hope for an answer to that prayer. Now, I believe that I always receive an answer, but I never know what form it will come in. Or when it will come. And, most importantly, if you offer the same prayer, I would expect your answer to possibly be completely different from the one I receive. They are not reproducible. If they were, then we could scientifically prove God, and that, my friend, is not possible."

At that point, George Stavros, who had been working close to them, loading the truck, walked over to them. "Sorry to interrupt, but I couldn't help but overhearing your conversation."

"Hi, George," Tony and Dr. Callahan said simultaneously.

"I just wanted to put my two cents in, if I may?"

"By all means," said Dr. Callahan.

"Sure," Tony offered.

"Dr. Callahan is right. It's different for everyone. When I first started praying, I didn't get any answers, or so I thought."

"When was that?" Tony asked.

"When I was in prison. Pastor Bob taught me how to pray. It was very discouraging at first. To spend all that energy and feel like no one was listening. I almost gave up."

"Sounds about right. Doesn't seem like anyone is there," Tony said pointing up to the sky.

"Yes, but then I started looking at it differently."

"How so?" Tony said.

"Well, I started looking at what was happening rather than what I wanted to happen."

"How did that help?"

"I saw the answers," replied George.

Tony looked dumbfounded.

George continued, "Let me give you an example. One day I was praying, wishing really, that I could have my own cell. My cellmate had been moved to another block and I kind of liked not having to share my cell."

"Sounds reasonable," replied Tony.

"The next day, I got a new cellmate."

"Now that sounds about exactly the opposite of what you wanted," said Tony.

"I thought so at first, too. But it turns out it was a young kid who was just incarcerated. He was scared stiff and cried the whole first night."

"Again, sounds like your worst nightmare," said Tony.

"No, it wasn't. You see, it turns out this kid needed help. He had no idea how to survive in there. He had been caught selling some drugs and had just been convicted. He needed someone to keep him on the straight and narrow. To stay away from the drugs that are everywhere in prison. He needed to just do his time and get out and straighten his life out. That, I realized, was my job, my opportunity to help him do all that."

"So you're saying that the answer to your prayer to be alone in your cell was to help someone else?" Tony replied.

"Exactly! I wanted peace and quiet. But God wanted me to help Jason find peace and quiet and that was a real blessing to me. I'm so glad God didn't answer my prayer the way I wanted."

"Wow, that is a wonderful story, my friend," Dr. Callahan interjected.

"Sounds backward to me," said Tony.

"At first it might," said Dr. Callahan, "but that is a great example of what I was saying. Answers to prayers are individual and unique. And not reproducible."

"Amen, brother," George piped in. "Just so you know, I have been in contact with Jason, that young man, since I got out. He has done his time and is back in school and doing very well. I thank God for that opportunity. Oops, looks like they need me in the kitchen. See you later." He walked off leaving Tony and Dr. Callahan to finish the packing of the truck.

They finished in silence. When they were done, Dr. Callahan said, "Well, that's a fine job. I think we deserve some lunch. What do you say?" He patted Tony on the shoulder and started towards the dining area.

Tony followed slowly.

Dr. Callahan turned around and asked, "What's wrong, Tony?"

Tony looked up. "Oh, nothing, Dr. Callahan, just pondering George's story and your explanation. Both are a little confusing to me."

"Oh, you will get it, I'm sure. And how 'bout you call me James from now on?"

"Okay, James," said Tony shaking his head. "Maybe I will get it one day."

James laughed and put his arm around Tony's shoulder. "Now that that's settled, let's go get lunch. I'm starved!"

CHAPTER 19

Tony was sitting in Charley's across from Dave and Bob. It had been two weeks since they returned from the mission trip. Charley's was not too noisy on this night, as it was a weeknight, but there was a pretty good crowd anyway.

Tony was more nervous than he thought he would be. He decided, based on his experience with the mission trip, that these "church folks" were not so bad after all. And he had been trying to figure out how he was going to learn about all that "church stuff" he had talked with his father about.

Now, here he was, sitting with two important people. His best friend, a Christian who had been trying, subtly, over the years to win him over to the faith. And this new guy, this pastor whom he had gotten to know a little bit on the trip. It seemed like the perfect storm of coincidences that had led him here. How better to learn all he needed to know than from his best friend and this pastor who didn't always seem like a pastor? At least not the vision of a "holier than thou" type of fellow that Tony projected upon all pastors. But now that the reality of it all was setting in, he wasn't so sure.

Bob finally broke the silence. "So, Tony, can I be so bold as to ask why you called us both here?"

Bob looked over at Dave questioningly. Dave shrugged his shoulders. He wasn't quite sure why either.

Tony cleared his throat and started nervously. He had been practicing this speech for several days and now it had all left his brain.

"Well, as you know, I've fairly recently become a father of twins. And given that, I've been thinking about their future."

"Of course," encouraged Bob.

"And the events of the past several months have got me to thinking. The church you have . . ."

"It's not really *my* church. I merely oversee the operations."

Dave jumped in, "Oh, that's not true. You do much more than that, Bob. You are the spiritual leader. You're the hub of it all."

Bob looked sideways at Dave, mildly bemused. "I suppose."

Tony jumped back in, "That's kind of why I asked you here. You see, I want to come to you, uh, and your church, to study the Bible. I want to better understand the doctrine and processes and all that stuff. And the reason for this is so I can give my children the same religious training I had when I was a kid. Why? So I can better help them understand why they shouldn't believe all this religious stuff. Does that make any sense to you?"

"I think so," said Bob. Then he leaned forward towards Tony. "Tony, I'm not sure I get how coming to church will help you convince your children that there is no God. That's kind of the opposite of what we do. However, if it will help *you* understand the faith, then of course, you can come to the church to study at any time. And you don't have to be a member to study with us. We have several study classes that would help you. We are open to learning from each other. Oh, and you can drop the 'Pastor' bit, it's just Bob."

"All right, uh, Bob. But you must understand that I don't believe in God and this is just a means to an end."

"Okay, I get that," said Bob. "Anything else driving you to do this now?"

"I guess, it may also be, in part, the mission trip."

"How so?" asked Bob.

"Don't tell me you heard God on the trip, Tony," jested Dave as he lifted his beer to his lips.

"No, nothing like that. But I did see and hear some interesting things."

"Oh? Like what?" Bob leaned in across the table.

"Well, Dr. Callahan had an interesting perspective I hadn't heard before. About the difference between scientific facts and religious beliefs."

"Yes. I've heard him speak of it before," said Bob. "He explains that pretty well, I would say."

"Me too," chimed in Dave. "Made sense to me."

"It kind of did to me, too," said Tony. "And the stories I heard from the people we were helping. They were inspirational. So much wreckage and yet so much hope. I didn't expect that."

"Yeah, it was very cool in that way," Dave said as he took another sip of beer.

"And then there were other things. Like this, for example." He pointed at Bob's beer.

Bob looked down, then up at Tony. "What about this?" He paused for a moment. "Oh, me having a beer?"

"Yeah. I didn't expect that either. I mean, you're a pastor and all."

"What a surprise," Bob said sarcastically.

"Yes, it is a surprise." Tony said seriously.

Bob paused for a moment, then said, "I know many pastors do not believe it is appropriate to drink alcohol. And I respect that. However, many pastors, including myself, believe that while the abuse of alcohol is wrong, it is okay to have an occasional drink. Whenever I am with someone in recovery, I show respect for their commitment to sobriety by not having any alcohol myself."

"Okay, I get it, but I guess I have certain expectations of a 'man of the cloth,' as it were. And while Dave here has spoken about you . . ."

"That I have," said Dave.

"I guess I didn't believe some of the things."

"You expected a holier-than-thou sort, I expect," Bob said.

"To be truthful, yes."

They were all quiet for a while. Then Bob spoke. "You know, Dave has spoken about you often."

Tony grimaced. "That doesn't sound good."

"No, no. It's all good." He turned and smiled at Dave. "But I think I have a small sense of what it has taken you, emotionally speaking, to come to me and ask to study the Bible."

"Uh, thanks."

They were again quiet for a while, each in his own thoughts. Finally, Bob spoke up. "So, as I know something about you from Dave here, you know very little about me, apart from what you saw on the trip." He paused for a moment then took a deep breath. "As you have put yourself out there, I would like to share something with you that I don't share with very many people." He turned to Dave and said, "I don't think I have shared this part of my life with you either, Dave, but I trust you to understand."

Tony and Dave looked at each other and Dave shrugged his shoulders. It was clear he didn't know what was coming any more than Tony did.

Bob took another deep breath and said, "Okay, then. Here goes. Let me share a few things with you about my life that are part of my 'private' side. These things are a bit difficult for me to share, but if you and I are going to experience the Christian life together, we might as well start right now. And in so doing, I hope you will understand more fully how the Christian life begins and ends with grace."

"Okay, Bob. Sounds fair," said Tony.

Dave looked at Tony, then Bob, and nodded in assent.

"So the part of my story I want to share with you has to do with my going through a divorce years ago."

Tony had no idea that Pastor Bob would jump right in about a divorce. He didn't even ease into it. He just put it on the table and there it was. Bob's divorced? Both Tony and Dave were surprised, and it showed on their faces.

"You see, I met my first wife, Susie, while a freshman at college. We fell in love, and after dating for over a year, we decided to get married right after graduation. From day one of our marriage, we recognized that we were experiencing a significant amount of stress in our relationship. It didn't take me long to start thinking about a divorce. But I did not want to pursue that option. I had made a vow that for better or worse, I would remain in the marriage.

"Fast forward a few years. We adopted two children as babies, in part because I believed that bringing children into the marriage might make us feel more like a 'completed family.'" He did air quotes with his fingers.

"I guess I hoped that it would have a positive effect on our marriage. Well, it did not. I won't go into all the gory details, but suffice it to say my home life was not satisfying. So I started putting more of myself into my professional life, first as a public-school teacher, then as a counselor, and then as a pastor. I worked long hours, and over the seventeen years we were married, I became an absentee father and a less than devoted husband. My work became everything, and by work, I mean the ministry. I even thought that I must be a really spiritual guy for having stayed in a marriage that lesser men would have walked away from much earlier. But after some futile efforts at counseling, I came to the place where I couldn't stay anymore. And I mean it seriously: I *couldn't* stay.

"So I filed for divorce. I immediately went from the good guy wearing the white hat to the villain wearing the black hat. I lost my family. I lost my calling. I lost everything."

Bob stopped there to take a drink. *Wow*, thought Tony, *I never expected this of a pastor.*

Both Dave and Tony were on the edge of their seats. Dave seemed particularly interested. He had never seen this side of his pastor before, and he was curious for more.

Finally, Dave said, "Bob, I can't imagine how difficult this must have been for you. I bet no one wanted to be around you."

"That's an understatement, Dave. A lot of people in the church shunned me after that. Anyway, for three years, I floundered. I worked various jobs, barely making enough money to keep Susie and my children living at the house while I lived in another city. For the first two years, I was thankful that I was out of the ministry. I needed to work on me. But in the third year, I grew stronger and desired to return.

"Then one day in late December, I received a call from an elder in a church close to where I lived. He asked if I could preach on the first two Sundays in January. I was surprised, but I welcomed the opportunity. I preached those Sundays, and then the church board asked if I would continue preaching every Sunday.

"I was elated. God had restored me to my calling, and it was in that little church where I met my wife, Carol. The only reason I am here now, pastoring a church, is because the board of that little church was willing to extend grace to me rather than judgment and condemnation. They did not hold my divorce against me but welcomed me into their fellowship as I was."

Bob sat back and downed the rest of his drink. Tony and Dave looked at each other, both at a loss for words. Bob set his glass down and looked at each of them in turn. Then he smiled. "Bet you didn't expect that little story, did you?"

They both shook their head "no."

Bob continued, "To be honest, neither did I. I told you this story about myself to assure you that you are not getting caught up with a 'holy roller.' I am just like you, full of faults and foibles. I hope sharing this with you doesn't discourage you from wanting to study with me."

Tony considered this for a few moments. Both Bob and Dave watched him intently, especially Dave.

Finally, Tony said, "You know, Bob, I think it does help. At least a little. And I suspect that was hard for you to talk about, which also helps."

"Good," said Bob. "I'm glad. And yes, it is hard to talk about. While it isn't any big secret, it's not something I share with everyone. So, please, let's keep this to ourselves?"

"Of course," said Dave. "Thank you for putting yourself out there like that."

Tony interjected, "Yes, I appreciate it as well. Especially as you don't know me very well. Yet."

Bob continued, "Well then, we will have to see how we get you involved in classes. There are a few options, and I will have to think about it some. Is there anything or any particular book of the Bible that you want to learn about?"

"No, not really. Just basic doctrine and theology. Like, this whole idea of doing good works here on earth so you can earn a place in Heaven."

Bob sat up straight in his chair. "What's this, then?" he asked.

"You know, the idea we have to do good things to deserve or pay for the treasures we supposedly will receive in Heaven," Tony replied.

"And where did you get that idea, Tony?" asked Bob.

"Well, Dave here has sort of alluded to it, right, Dave?"

Dave was taken aback. "I don't know if I've said exactly that."

"But it was Calvin who really delineated it for me," Tony said.

"Calvin? Calvin Lowe?" Bob said.

"Yeah. He rode with me on the way to New Iberia. Gave me an earful, I can tell you."

"He is one to do that, for sure. Anyone else?"

"Yeah, several of the folks from the church who went with us all seemed to agree on that. A 'you've got to work to get into Heaven' sort of philosophy. Calvin was pretty straightforward about it. Said that the mission trip was one of those 'God-given' opportunities to rack up the brownie points he needed to get into Heaven. Said it made the trip all that more worthwhile."

Tony looked back and forth at Bob and Dave. Dave seemed to be noncommittal about it. As if he was buying into it. But Bob had a very concerned look on his face. He sat for a moment in silence. Finally, he spoke. "Would you say that most of the folks who went with us had the same idea?"

"I guess so. I didn't talk to everyone about it. But I did hear some of them say stuff like, 'God is happy we are here,' and 'we're furnishing our heavenly homes,' you know, stuff like that."

Bob turned to Dave. "Are you of the same thinking, Dave?" he asked.

"Well, we do talk about receiving treasures in Heaven, don't we?" he said hesitatingly.

"Yes, but that's not quite what it means." Bob sat silently for a time. Neither Tony nor Dave wanted to break the silence, as he seemed to be deep in thought.

Finally, he started speaking, but as if he was speaking to himself. "Have I not been clear? Is that the message I have been promoting? Man-oh-man, I have got to correct this."

He looked at the other two men. "Gentlemen, it appears that I must correct some misconceptions. That is not the message of the cross, nor the message I thought I have been sharing. If everyone on the trip is thinking this way, I must find a way to help them understand the truth."

"I'm afraid you have me at a loss, Bob. It's the one message I have always thought I heard. And Calvin was adamant about it," said Tony.

"Yes, I see that," Bob replied. "But it's a lot more complex than what you have heard." He was silent for a few more minutes. Then he stood up. "Well, the only solution is to get everyone together and discuss it. We shall have a retreat. Yes, that's it. A retreat for all of the folks who went on the mission trip. A de-brief, if you will."

He seemed to have established the idea in his mind. He turned to Tony. "Thank you for bringing this to my attention, Tony. You may not realize it yet, but you are already doing your part in God's plan."

"My part? I'm afraid I don't believe in all of that." He waved his hand as if to push it away.

"I know. But you are anyway. Good night, gentlemen. I have some work to do. And Tony," he placed some money on the table to pay for his drink and reached out his hand to shake Tony's, "welcome to the community."

He walked out, leaving Dave and Tony to watch him in wonder.

"What was all that about?" Tony asked Dave.

"I'm not sure. But when he gets like that, something very interesting is coming!"

CHAPTER 20

Beth sat across from Tony, sipping her coffee. Tony had just come in from his morning run and was rehydrating with a tall glass of orange juice. He clearly had something to say, which Beth had discovered was often the case after one of Tony's long runs. So she waited patiently for him to tell her what was on his mind. Finally, he finished his juice and placed the glass carefully on the table. Then he spoke.

"I think I know how I want to proceed," he began.

"Proceed with what?"

"With the whole 'religious training' thing." He did finger quotes.

"Can you be a little more explicit, please?"

"Sure. I've told you how I want to get smart about the whole 'Christian thing.'" Again he did air quotes. "But now I know how I want to do it."

"Okay, I'll bite. What is your . . . 'proposed method?'" She did air quotes too.

He made a face and continued. "Very funny, but I'm being very serious here!"

"I know you are, honey. I'm sorry. Go ahead."

"Okay. I spoke with Bob, the pastor at your, uh, the church. And he said I could study with him. Maybe go to some classes at the church. So that will help in learning about the doctrine and all that. But I don't think it's going to be enough for me to just study the Bible. I think I have to immerse myself in the culture."

"Oh, how do you mean?"

"I mean, I think I should go through all the motions."

She made a face at him.

"Whoa, that sounds bad," he admitted.

"Yes, it kind of does."

"Let me rephrase. I plan to not only study the Bible but go to church regularly with you. And try to do all the activities that you Christians do."

"Like what?" She was intrigued.

"Like. I don't know, say praying. I'll try to learn to pray. And volunteer for whatever mission sort of things the church does. You know, try to live the life so I can fully understand it. Only then will I be able to teach it to the kids." He sat back and waited for Beth's reaction.

She looked at him for a long moment. Finally, she said, "Well, Tony, I guess I have two thoughts that pop into my head. My first thought is, I think that is just wonderful. I would so like to share the church with you. The second thought is this. I know how important it is to you to be real, to be who you are. With what you are suggesting, won't you feel hypocritical just *going through the motions* while still not believing?"

Tony paused before replying to that second question.

"You raise a good point. Being true to myself matters to me. But I see it like this. Doing the Christian things for the reasons I am doing them is the real me. I'm trying to find out what doing Christian things is like so I can answer any questions the kids have about it, uh, religion, that is. So I don't think I will feel hypocritical doing them." She got up and walked around the table and hugged him from behind.

He looked up at her and said, "Now, understand I still don't buy this mumbo jumbo, but I need to understand it better if I'm going to discuss it intelligently with the kids."

"Oh, I understand. That's fine. As long as you are trying." She paused then said to him. "Does that mean you're also going to start tithing?"

"Tithing? Oh, you mean giving money to the church?"

"That's right. It's one of the *things we do.*"

"Oh! I don't know about that." He looked at her for a moment. "Look, I know I agreed that we would 'tithe' from your salary. I mean, that's sort of your money and while I never thought it was a good idea, I couldn't very well tell you not to. You did earn that money and it seemed only fair that you should make that decision. But as for the money that I earn, I'm not comfortable giving it away for no good reason."

Beth shrugged her shoulders. "Okay, that's fair, I suppose. I was just wondering, that's all."

"Don't hold your breath on that one. I don't think I will need to do that *Christian activity.* It just seems like a waste."

"I won't bring it up again, honey."

"Okay then. Now, there is something else."

"Oh?" She sat back down across from him. "And what is that?"

"It's my understanding that one of the things that is done is to go on retreats."

"Sometimes."

"Well, Pastor Bob called last night after you went to bed."

"Uh-huh?"

"It seems as if he wants to get all of the folks together who went on the mission trip to New Iberia and do some sort of de-brief."

"I see. When will this happen?"

"He wasn't sure, but sometime in the next couple of weeks. I guess it depends on when he can get everyone together. And the thing is, he wants it to be a multi-day thing. Like Friday night through

Sunday afternoon. And he wants to do it at some cabin up in the woods. Apparently, Walter King, you know, the guy from the church who got us all to go down to New Iberia in the first place, has a cabin somewhere and has offered it up for the retreat."

"And?"

"And I want to make sure you are okay with me going. I mean, I just got back from the mission trip not that long ago. Can you handle the kids all by yourself again?"

"Of course, I can. If you are committed to this mission of yours, I will support it."

"Okay then," he said.

They were silent for a moment. Finally, Beth spoke.

"What's the matter, Tony? You seem like there is a problem."

"It's just, now that I have said it out loud, it's sort of real."

"What is?"

"Getting involved in the church and all. It's kind of scary. I'm not sure I know what I have let myself in for."

"Oh. Well, I will be here with you the whole time. I think you will find this *Christianity thing* is not as scary as you may think. We are actually pretty nice people, in case you haven't noticed, hmmm? You have found that to be true, haven't you? I mean you like all the people you have met so far haven't you, including me?"

"Yeah, I guess. Of course!"

"All right then. Now, let's get the twins up. They need to be fed." She got up and went over and kissed him on the forehead and walked out of the room towards the nursery. Tony looked after her and took a deep breath then followed her out thinking to himself, *Well, I guess I'm jumping in with both feet now.*

CHAPTER 21

Pastor Bob scheduled the retreat for the members of the mission trip for two weeks after Tony and Beth's discussion. Tony and Dave drove together to the retreat. On the trip, which only took about an hour, Tony told Dave about his plan. Dave was overjoyed. It was all he could do to stop himself from letting go of the wheel and hugging Tony, but he managed to restrain himself.

Tony tried to set Dave's expectations low, but Dave would not be deterred. When they got to the cabin, most of the others were already there. Walter had a grand dinner ready for everyone—steak, potatoes, and all the fixings. After dinner was over and everyone helped to clean up, Bob assembled everyone in the big living area.

"Good evening, gentlemen," he began. "I want to thank you all for being willing to take the time to come together and talk about your mission trip experience. I know from past experiences that a retreat like this can have very significant benefits in the way one understands the faith. Jesus frequently went off to a lonely place and spent quality time with God the Father, and from those isolated places, He drew His strength for all the demands that were placed upon Him. And so I hope you have come to this retreat with an openness to experiencing God in a new and deeper way. That is my expectation for me as well."

He paused for a moment then said, "I also wanted to address some things I heard were discussed on the mission trip."

"Oh, what's that all about, Bob?" Calvin chimed in.

"Just some things regarding our purpose," replied Bob.

"I thought our purpose was clear," said Calvin. "Did someone from down there complain about our work?"

"No, nothing like that. But I would like to address some theological issues before we actually discuss the trip itself. Would that be okay with everyone?"

"No problem, you're in charge, Pastor," Calvin said. He sat back in his chair and folded his arms in sort of a defiant posture.

Oh, boy, thought Tony, *this hasn't started very well.* But no one else around the room seemed to be perturbed.

Bob continued, "I would like to delve into the parable of the Prodigal Son. And I hope that by the end of the retreat you will benefit from this discussion of the parable. So let's dive into our text. I hope everyone has brought their Bible?" Bob looked around the room.

Tony became a little panicked. He had not considered bringing a Bible. He didn't even own one. He felt suddenly very stupid for not asking Beth for hers. But Dave was prepared. He reached into his bag and brought out a well-worn bible and handed it to Tony.

"I got you covered, brother," he said softly.

Tony looked at him and mouthed a "thank you" to Dave. Once everyone had their Bibles out, Bob continued. "Let's go to Luke, Chapter 15."

Tony was floundering to find this in his Bible. He didn't know where to look. Dave again came to his rescue: he gently took the Bible from Tony's hands and opened it to the proper page and handed it back to Tony.

Bob continued, "To understand what we are about to read, it is important to understand that Jesus had a tendency to tick off the local religious leaders of His day. Jesus clearly was not one of those preachers who said whatever pleased the people so they would like Him—a temptation I fight all the time."

"That's not all that obvious to everyone," piped up Calvin jokingly. "You don't have any problem telling us things we may not like to hear!" That drew a chuckle from everyone.

"You guys aren't going to not like me when we end our retreat, are you?"

"That remains to be seen," Walter said. Everyone laughed again at that.

Tony was relieved. He wasn't sure if they were serious or not until they laughed. He relaxed a little.

Smiling, Bob continued, "Here is what the text says, *'Now the tax collectors and sinners were all gathering around to hear him. But the Pharisees and the teachers of the law muttered, 'This man welcomes sinners and eats with them.'* Let's stop there. In that day it was questionable whether a true man of God should be mingling with tax collectors and sinners. Tax collectors were the pawns of the Roman empire, extracting unfair taxes from the Jews. And the 'sinners' mentioned here were persons whom the whole community knew were the dregs of society—the kind of people no righteous person would fellowship with. To eat meals with them was absolutely forbidden. A meal was to be shared only with fellow righteous persons, not with the enemies of the Jewish community and lowlifes.

"Okay, let's jump into the Prodigal Son story. Jesus said, *'There was a man who had two sons. The younger one said to his father, "Father, give me my share of the estate." So he divided his property between them.'* In Jewish tradition, a respectable son would never ask for his inheritance until after his father had died. This younger son was essentially saying to his father, 'I wish you were dead.' At this time the Pharisees would expect the father to slap his younger son across his face and say to him, 'Listen, you little twit, if you don't want to live here under the rules of my house then, take your little rear end and leave. Go get a job and do as you please.'

"But that is not what the father said or did," he continued. "The text says the father divided his property between them. Now, it is important to understand the implication of this. The father did not have a large sum of money stashed away in his home where he could simply count out a large number of bills, give them to his son, and wish him well. The text says he divided his 'property' among his two sons. What the father likely did was turn over to the younger son the deeds to one-third of his property and probably designated a certain amount of farm animals that he could sell. Jewish tradition said the older son was to receive two-thirds of the estate upon his father's death and the younger son was to receive one-third.

"The younger son simply wanted cash so he most likely started calling on his father's friends and others in the community to see if anyone would purchase the property and livestock and give him cash. The loyal friends of his father would have given him a kick in the butt, told him to get off their property, and never come back. But as is always true when economics are involved, the son would have found some persons in the village who would give him pennies on the dollar for the property and be pleased to do so. However, now the whole town knew what the little snip had done and this would have brought shame to the father."

Calvin spoke up, "Why would the father do such a thing?"

"Great question. We will get to that, Calvin."

"Ungrateful little piece of . . . ," muttered Calvin, but he caught himself.

Bob smiled and continued, "The younger son did not have much time to turn the property into cash. This is because the whole town was now aware of what he was doing to the father and they were ready to throw him out of the city gates. So he had to get as much cash together as quickly as he could.

"Now, when the text says he set off for the 'far country' this is a euphuism for a 'Gentile' town. It becomes clear later in the text that that is exactly where he went—to the Gentiles—because he ends up working for a pig farmer, and no Hebrew would have pigs on his farm.

"The text also says he 'squandered his wealth in wild living.' Some translations say 'loose living,' some say 'reckless living,' but the true meaning of the word 'prodigal' means 'extravagant.' So he was living high on the hog—no pun intended.

"We cannot say," he continued, "that the younger son lost his inheritance with immoral living, even though the older son accuses him of this later in the text. We can be sure that when he left home, he wanted a taste of the 'good life,' the place where the 'grass was greener on the other side.' After all, the Gentiles didn't have to live under the weight of all the laws the Jews had to abide by.

"Now, the younger son is separated from his family. He has squandered the money he once had. He is in a foreign country, and no one cares about him, nor will they help him in any way. And he is hungry."

Walter spoke up at this point. "I'm afraid I would have agreed with the Pharisees, Pastor. He got everything he deserved."

"That may be true. And we are going to unpack that. However," Bob looked at his watch, "it's getting late, and we have all had a busy day. What say we leave the story at this point and head for bed?"

There were nods of agreement around the room. Everyone closed their Bibles and picked up their glasses to bring them into the kitchen.

Walter stood up and said, "We will need someone to cook breakfast in the morning. I've done my cooking for the weekend."

Tony immediately raised his hand, as did Dr. Callahan.

"Good," said Walter. "Let's plan to eat around eight. Does that sound all right with everyone?"

There were no dissensions. Tony and Dr. Callahan spoke briefly to coordinate when they would meet in the morning. When they had settled that, Tony found his room. He was sharing a room with Dave, for which he was grateful. This "cabin," more of a lodge really, was huge. Tony asked Dave about it.

"Yeah, apparently Walter built it when he was still with his company. Used to use this place for retreats and meetings. I think he said it can accommodate up to thirty people, a few more if people want to get real cozy."

"Wow, I guess he was really in the money, then," said Tony.

"Guess so. But you couldn't tell it from watching him. He never flaunts it nor talks about his money, really."

They prepared for bed in silence. Finally, Dave asked Tony, "Are you happy you came, and are you getting anything out of Bob's teaching?"

"Yeah, I guess. I do like the way Bob teaches and is open to questions. I mean these guys aren't afraid to push back on Bob, at least a little bit.

"I suspect there are several things that will surprise you about *us Christians*," Dave said with a smile. "See you in the morning."

"Good night, Dave," Tony replied.

However, he stayed awake for a long time, thinking about all he had heard and seen so far. *What have I gotten myself into?* he thought just before he nodded off.

CHAPTER 22

The next morning, Tony was up early. Dave was still sleeping, so he quietly got dressed and went down into the kitchen. There he found James already working on breakfast.

"Wow, you're up really early," Tony said to him.

"Yeah, it's a holdover from my days as a resident. I got used to not getting much sleep and I could wake up very early and quickly. Drives my wife a little crazy sometimes."

"Okay, then. What are we making for breakfast?"

"Actually, Walter has laid out a menu for each meal for the entire weekend." He held up a pad of paper with instructions printed out. "Very efficient, that man."

Tony and James split the work, and when they had breakfast ready, they called everyone in. They had laid out the food as a large buffet, and everyone dug in. There was lots of jovial conversation. Tony mostly listened to the others. Everyone seemed to be enjoying themselves along with the food. It made Tony feel good to have cooked some of it. He did fancy himself a fairly good cook, so here was something he could do to contribute to the weekend.

After breakfast, Bob brought everyone together again.

"I hope you all had a restful night. I sure did. Let's pick up the story from where we left off last night."

"At this point, the story takes a turn for the better, or at least it appears that way to the Pharisees. The text says, *'When he came to his senses, he said, "How many of my father's hired men have food to spare, and here I am starving to death! I will set out and go back to my father and say to him: Father, I have sinned against Heaven and you. I am no longer worthy to be called your son; make me like one of your hired men."'* This is the first time that we can assume that the Pharisees like the parable. The boy has 'seen the light' and he is willing to go home and work his way back into the good graces of his father. But there is a problem, and the Pharisees are fully aware of it.

"In the culture and tradition of a Jewish village at the time of Jesus, there was a ceremony that would prohibit the younger son from reentering the village. The tradition was called the Kizazah ceremony. It went like this. If a Jewish man either married a woman who was immoral—meaning a prostitute—or lost his family's inheritance to a Gentile, the whole village would gather in the middle of the town, with the man in the middle of them. One of the elders of the village would take a large earthen pot, and break it into a thousand pieces while declaring, 'As this earthen pot has been shattered, so has the relationship with this man and his family and the people of this village been shattered. As this pot cannot be restored neither can the relationship between him and his family, nor with those in this village.' The people would then throw him out of the village. He would never be allowed to live in the community again.

"So even though it appears that the younger son was repentant, in reality, he knew he could never return to live with his family in the village. He asked to be a hired hand because a hired hand was a tradesman who usually lived outside the village but could work for a village family. So if the father in the parable said 'yes' to the request of his son, the son could enter the village and earn a living but couldn't live there. What do you all think of his plan?"

Bob stopped and looked around the room. There was silence for a while. Finally, Walter spoke up. "It kind of sounds a little sneaky to me. Like he is trying to beat the system."

"Yes, I agree," said Calvin. "He wants to have his cake and eat it too, no pun intended."

George spoke up, "I don't know. I think the kid was genuinely repentant. And I would like to think that if he did become a hired hand for his father, that he would repay his father for the lost inheritance."

To that comment, a number of the men groaned, as if to say, *George, you are a dreamer.*

"Either of those positions could be true. We don't know for sure. However," Bob continued, "Jesus completely turns the story upside down. And this is what grace does. Grace turns everything upside down, giving us blessings we don't deserve.

"The actions that we now read about in the text are the most extravagant expressions of grace possible. The actions of the father are completely inappropriate in the mind of every Pharisee listening to Jesus and possibly to some of you. The text says, *'And he arose and came to his father. But while he was still a long way off, his father saw him and was filled with compassion for him; he ran to his son, threw his arms around him and kissed him.'* It's as if the father is chasing after his son as opposed to the other way around."

Calvin blurted out, "The father does what? Was he out of his skull?"

James jumped in, "What I don't get about all this is how anyone can be hurt so deeply by someone he or she loves and be able to forgive them unconditionally as it seems like the father did in this story. I know it would take me a very long time, if ever, to welcome back someone who wished that I were dead and did that to me."

Calvin said, almost to himself, "Like my father might have done if I had gone back. There are days that I wish that I had given my father that chance."

Tony looked at Calvin and said, "I'm sorry, Calvin." He turned to James and said, "Yeah, I'm not sure what I would do either, James."

Bob waited to see if there were any other comments, then said, "It *is* hard to understand, isn't it? I mean this would be considered outrageous even today! No Jewish father would do any of this. No respectful Jewish man would run in public, for it would expose the lower part of his legs and this would bring shame upon himself. And the father, after being shamed in the community by the younger son asking for his inheritance while his father was still living, was expected to remain distant emotionally and physically from the scallywag son.

"The father in this parable, however, paid no attention to these expectations. The father is portrayed as standing daily on his porch, looking through the gate to the city, to spot his son should he ever return. Why? For many reasons, but the main reason is so the people in the village didn't seize him first and perform the Kizazah ceremony. Once the villagers performed the ceremony, all hope for the restoration of the family would be lost. So on that day, when the son did return, the father ran immediately to the son before the son entered the village. He had to get to him before the villagers nabbed him."

"I'm not sure what I think about this guy," Calvin said.

"What do you mean?" asked Bob.

"Well, first he gives up so easily when the son asks for his money, uh, his inheritance. The father should be completely done with this rotten kid. Yet he keeps giving in to the son. What is it that the son has over his father?"

"So you think the father was somehow forced into giving the son his inheritance and welcoming him home?" Bob asked.

"Well, why else would he do it? And what about the other son?"

"Great observations, Calvin. Hold those questions. I hope we can answer all of them by the time we are done. But let me again point out the key element of this parable. It is ultimately all about God being outrageously grace-centered and extravagantly full of love for people who are so undeserving."

"Okay, your ballgame, your rules." Calvin went back to sipping his coffee. Bob continued.

"Next, the text says that the younger son says to his father, *'Father, I have sinned against Heaven and before you. I am no longer worthy to be called your son.'* At that, the father interrupts the son and instructs his servants to go and put his best robe around the son, put a ring on his hand, and sandals on the son's feet. Then he orders a feast to celebrate the return of his son. He says, ' *. . . this son of mine was dead and is alive again; he was lost and is found.'*"

Bob looked over at Calvin. "Still think the son had something over the father, Calvin?"

"Yep. Why else would he keep embarrassing himself in front of the whole village, for crying out loud?"

"It is perplexing, isn't it? Did you notice that because the father interrupts the son, the son does not get the opportunity to ask if he could become a hired hand? This third part of his planned speech was his 'works-righteousness plan.' But the father will have nothing to do with his son's works-righteousness plan.

"Instead, the father places his best robe on the son. The robe is significant." Bob continued, "because when the father places his own best robe upon his son, the son now has his father's identity covering him. His father can now gracefully and slowly walk back through the town to his home with his son on his arm and his son is now to be seen by the villagers in the same light as his father, whose robe he is wearing."

"Wait a minute," Walter interjected. "Are you telling us that the act of simply putting a robe on the son absolves him of all his sins? That's just too easy, Bob."

"Good point, Walter. But that's not exactly what I'm saying. You see, there is specific imagery here. And the Pharisees would have been fully aware of it. It's the imagery the prophet Isaiah used. He used the idea of God placing His robe of righteousness around the nation of Israel—a nation that continually sinned against him and committed adultery against him. We see this in Isaiah 61:10 where God was saying to all of Israel, that they have no righteousness on their own. The only righteousness they have is the righteousness God imputed to them. The Pharisees standing before Jesus listening to the parable would have been fully aware of this Scripture and would have had no rebuttal."

Bob sat forward in his seat and spoke very deliberately. "Now, listen carefully, guys. God is the One who runs to us and He will have nothing to do with us earning our way into His family. We become members of His family through His offer of grace, not our efforts, called works. And that is what is happening here in the Prodigal Son story. It was a radical teaching for the Pharisees, and from some of your comments, it seems radical to us today, as well.

"But it is not only radical," he went on, "it is the only plan God has for including us in His family. He chases after us and extends to us grace. We need to let go of trying to earn our way into His family. We humbly receive God's grace and ultimately, we get to join a great party in Heaven and celebrate this good news from God."

Walter pondered this for a moment, then said, "So what you're saying is that the father in the story is like God giving forgiveness to us? Even though we sinned?"

"You're getting the idea, Walter." He turned to the rest of the group. "Does everyone else see this?"

There was a nodding of some heads. Others were trying to take it all in. Tony watched the others. He was surprised at how many folks didn't just simply agree. *Was this all news to them?* he thought.

Calvin spoke up, "But the son didn't deserve it!"

"Ah, that is the whole point, Calvin." Bob replied. "The son didn't deserve such extravagant grace. You don't deserve such extravagant grace. And neither do I.

"The second action I want to comment on is the party. The father is going to throw a party. The party is not in honor of the son. The son who sinned does not deserve a party. The party is in celebration of a resurrection and a restoration. The son was dead. He was dead to the town. Most importantly, he was dead to the father. The son was very much alive physically, but his sin had separated him from his father and the community. And dead people cannot do anything for themselves. The son could not do anything to restore the broken relationship with his father except to turn toward his father. The party is to honor the father and his willingness to cover the son's sin with his own robe of righteousness and invite the whole village to celebrate with him. It is a celebration of the father's raising his son to life and restoring him to family and community."

The room remained quiet for a long time. Bob looked around the room at each person and allowed them to process. Finally, he said, "That is a lot to process. It's almost lunchtime, so why don't we break for lunch. Who is up for preparing lunch?"

Two of the men that Tony didn't know well stood up and went into the kitchen. Everyone else got up and either went to their rooms or out onto the deck. Tony watched them go and was confused. They all seemed to be startled at what they had heard. *Some of these guys have been in church all their lives, and they are just now getting the meaning of this well-known story? Didn't they know this stuff already?* he thought. *Maybe I'm not the only one who is clueless here.*

Finally, he got up and went out onto the porch for some fresh air. It was brisk outside, and he took some deep breaths. Dave came up to him and handed him a cup of hot coffee.

"How is it going for you, Tony?" he asked.

"Dave, I'm not sure what to think. But I will tell you one thing."

"What's that?"

"It's not boring!"

CHAPTER 23

After lunch was finished and the dishes were all cleaned and put away, Bob gathered everyone together. "Are we all ready to keep going?" he asked. There were general nods around the room, so Bob continued with his story.

"Although the parable told by Jesus is best known as the Parable of the Prodigal Son, the prodigal had an older brother, as you pointed out, Calvin. As I mentioned earlier, the friends of the father have gathered at his home and they are participating in this joyful occasion only out of respect and love for their friend, not the wayward son.

"Because the relationship between their friend and his son has been restored, the father is 'in his glory,' and the friends simply could not reject the father's invitation to celebrate, even if they disagreed with the father's actions, as that would have been in poor taste. The older son is clearly not pleased with his father and is in no mood to celebrate his brother's return. The text says, *'But he was angry and refused to go in.'*

"Now, this refusal to go into the house and join the party may seem justified to most of us, but to the father, his older son's refusal to go inside was heaping shame upon him. It was the custom in Jesus' time that the meal would not be served to the guests until the oldest son offered a blessing. So the people who had gathered inside were likely getting tired of waiting for the food to be distributed. It is like some weddings: when the marriage ceremony is over, all the guests have left the church and traveled to the site of the reception, and they have been waiting for an inordinate amount of time for the wedding photographer to do her thing. Remember, the younger son has shamed his father by asking for his inheritance. The older son has now shamed his father by making the guests wait for their food because he refuses to join the party and say the blessing. With great embarrassment, the father has to excuse himself from his guests and go outside to confront the older son."

Bob went on. "We would expect that the father has every right to be upset with the older son and maybe grab him by the ear and drag him into the house, put him on the spot, and make him say the blessing. But the father does not do that. When the father approaches the older son, the son confronts his father. He says, *'Look, these many years I have served you, and I never disobeyed your command, yet you never gave me a young goat, that I might celebrate with my friends. But when this son of yours came, who has devoured your property with prostitutes, you killed the fattened calf for him!'"*

Calvin again spoke up. "Seems like the older son has a legitimate point here. The father treated him very badly."

"It would seem that way, wouldn't it?" Bob looked around the room to get confirmation. "But remember, Jesus is telling a parable. Everything and everyone in it represents something. Now, if the younger son represents the sinners in our world, who does the older son represent?"

James spoke up, "The Pharisees?"

"Bingo!" exclaimed Bob. "Clearly, the Pharisees would have identified with the older son, and you can bet they are squirming at this point, not knowing what the father in the parable is going to do. The doctrine of 'fairness' is probably at the forefront of their minds. They are thinking, *The older son is right! He should be ticked since he has been*

so faithful. It is too bad the townspeople hadn't enacted the Kizzazah
ceremony before now. If they had, none of this would be taking place."

"That's what I'm saying," said Calvin. He stopped for a moment and whistled to himself. "Wow, I'm agreeing with the Pharisees?"

Bob chuckled. "It's okay, Calvin. It's a logical response. Which is why the father's response is so radical. The parable seems to be getting out of hand.

"And what does Jesus do with the parable? Well, in the face of the older son's attack, the father remains calm. He does not address the embarrassment he is feeling due to his older son's actions. He does not 'pull rank' and insist his older son fulfill his responsibilities. What he does do is explain the profound gratitude he has that his fractured family has been restored. The text says, *'And he said to him, 'Son, you are always with me, and all that is mine is yours. It was fitting to celebrate and be glad, for this your brother was dead, and is alive; he was lost and is found.'*

"And then Jesus does the most amazing thing. He says nothing else. He does nothing else. The parable abruptly ends.

"So, what happened? How did the story end? Did the older son ever enter into the house and give the blessing—since he was 'so obedient' to his father, or so he said? Or did his self-righteousness never allow him to embrace the pardon his father extended to his sinful brother? Did the Pharisees listening to Jesus ever connect the dots and choose to respect Jesus for the grace he extended to the tax collectors and sinners with whom he often shared meals?"

Bob paused for a long moment, letting what he had said sink in. No one spoke up, as they all seemed to be processing. Bob waited patiently.

Finally, George spoke up, "So what is the answer? I mean the whole parable thing is sometimes really confusing. What is the answer, Pastor?"

Bob looked around. "Does anyone have 'the answer?'" He did air quotes.

Calvin said, "I'll bet the older son stomped off and didn't come to the party."

"That is certainly possible. Why do you think Jesus stops the parable here and doesn't tell us what happens next?"

After a long silence, Tony tentatively raised his hand. Bob looked and him with a small smile on his face. "Yes, Tony?"

"Well, it sounds like the story is not about the older son."

"Okay, who is it about, then?"

"The father?" Tony said questioningly.

"*Yes*! I think you are onto something. So how does the story end? Jesus leaves us exactly where he left the Pharisees; allowing us to make our own ending. And that is important because it forces us to think about what the true meaning of the story is."

James spoke up, "So he gave us a homework assignment?"

Everyone in the room chuckled at that.

"A good way to put it, James. Yes, I think much of what Jesus said was a series of homework assignments. We are called to read the Scripture and understand what it means, not only for those who were present when Jesus told the parable, but maybe more importantly, for us. For each of us. But here is what I want to leave you with right now. In this story, both sons shamed and embarrassed their father. Both sons believed they could earn their way into the good graces of the family. But, and this is the really important part, the father extended grace to *both* sons, and *both* sons were supposed to join the party in celebration of the extravagant love extended to them by their father. The parable is all about extravagant grace—lavish grace—grace that goes beyond anything we might expect from God. Grace we don't deserve."

Bob paused, then said, "That's a lot to think about. Let's hold on to those thoughts. Why don't we break till after dinner? You all can have the rest of the afternoon to ponder what we have talked about. As for me, I am going to take a nap. Then, when we get together later, we can also delve into the next topic: gratitude."

Bob got up, and it was clear the discussion was over. Small groups started to form, but Tony went outside by himself. This was more interesting than he had imagined. And the fact that he had come up with an answer to a theological type of question had surprised him. He was not sure what was happening to him, but he was more engaged than he expected to be.

CHAPTER 24

Dinner was a little quieter than the previous meals. Everyone seemed to be in thought. It was clear that Bob's teaching had gotten people to thinking.

Tony spent most of his time watching and listening to the others. He hadn't expected this. He figured this would all be one big *amen* weekend where they all just accepted everything that Bob would say. The fact that they had to think about this and that they all clearly were learning something new was, well, surprising to him. He had been forced to think about things that he had never considered before. It was, at the same time, both stimulating and frightening. He wondered what the evening session would bring.

After the dinner dishes were all cleaned up, they gathered again. Bob began, "So, how were you feeling at the close of our afternoon session? I suspect you were feeling a little disappointed that you were left hanging about the meaning of the story. Tonight, I want to wrap up my comments about why I think the parable of the Prodigal Son is all about grace. Then I want to briefly introduce to you two consequences that will automatically occur in your life *if* you have truly grasped the significance of God's grace. Let's begin, then.

"Anything I might say from this point has to be understood in light of Isaiah 55:8–9, *'For My thoughts are not your thoughts, neither are your ways My ways, declares the LORD. For as the heavens are higher than the earth, so are My ways higher than your ways, and My thoughts than your thoughts.'*

"One of the very first things anyone who wants to know and follow God has to deal with is that God does not think or act the way we do. I suspect that as we were going through this parable, many of you thought something like, 'Man, this father is a fool' or 'This father is unfair' or 'This father is one card short of a full deck.'"

There were several tentative nods around the room.

"Having those thoughts is not sacrilegious," Bob continued. "It simply gives evidence to what Isaiah said in Chapter 55. To be honest, every time I preach a sermon, I realize that if I have done a really good job of *accurately* sharing with you God's perspective on an issue, your first reaction should probably be, *I think Pastor Bob has lost his mind.* That is what I pray for—that I will lose *my* mind and embrace *God's mind,* knowing that it is different from mine and yours. Most importantly, God's mind is far better than ours, for it contains a plan for our lives that is far better than our plans. Remember, it takes faith to believe that."

Now that startled Tony. *Wait a minute,* he thought. *What the heck does that mean? God has a plan for my life?* Tony wanted to interrupt Bob but chose to keep quiet.

Bob continued, "Having said that, let me return to the story so we might see the Prodigal God that is embedded in it. Keep in mind that even though I will be speaking about the father in the story, the story is really about Jesus. Jesus is using this parable to reveal who He is to a group of Pharisees, and because they are so deeply embedded in works righteousness, He has to reveal Himself to them as a father who is off the charts with extravagant grace. A grace that allows Jesus to eat meals with the dregs of society, tax collectors, and sinners.

"Let me summarize the father's expressions of grace. First, he lets his younger son leave home, requiring him to reduce his estate by one third. Second, he welcomes him back. Third, he throws a party. Finally, he reaffirms his love for the older son. Every single thing the father does in this story rubs against our sense of wisdom and fairness. But every single thing the father does is to reveal to us how extravagant is his grace and how much we don't deserve it and can't earn it. That is why I say that you can summarize the Christian life with I call the 3 G's."

As he continued, he marked them off with what his fingers. "First, it is all about Grace. Second, it is all about Gratitude for the extravagant grace extended to us by a profoundly loving God. And finally, it is all about Generosity—first God's generosity towards us and then our generosity towards others.

"Now, let me ask you this," he went on. "Why would you want to give your life to a God who appears to be unwise and unfair from our human perspective?"

He paused to look around the room. There was a sense of discomfort. Tony could feel it and he had the same question but was afraid to voice it.

Then Bob continued, "There can be only one reason: God is a God of grace and love. To the Pharisees, the father was unwise and unfair. To the oldest son, his father was unwise and unfair. But to the one who was broken, the one who was fully aware of his unworthiness to be part of the family, to this son, his father was not unwise or unfair. His father was gracious, loving, and generous.

"The text doesn't address this, but I think we can assume the younger son was grateful for his father's generosity. The younger son could only hope to become a hired hand, but he received so much more. His father restored him to the family. Because of this lavish grace, I like to think that he found as many ways as he could to thank his father after all of this. But the important point here is when one receives unexpected grace, one becomes grateful. I know I am personally grateful for God's grace and I suspect most of you are as well. But we often don't think about it that way because we think we have earned all the blessings we have received, and we don't associate them with God's free grace.

"As a Christian, I believe that all of my blessings come from God's grace and I did nothing to earn them. And that fills me with gratitude, which becomes the basis for how I respond to God and why I give my life to others."

Bob paused to let the group absorb this point. He took a sip of water, then continued.

"Of course, all of this begs the question: What set of eyes do you bring to this story? The eyes of the Pharisees and the older son? Or the eyes of the younger son? As long as you believe you do not need extravagant grace because you haven't been all that bad, and you have earned everything you have, then the power of this parable will be lost to you. It will just be a story told by Jesus that portrays a father and his two sons in a way that is unsettling more than comforting."

Bob let that sink in. The silence was deafening. Finally, Tony spoke up. "So you're saying that we're supposed to get comfort out of this story because God gives grace to us regardless of how good or bad we are?"

"Yes, that's it."

"And there are no levels of grace?"

"How do you mean?" asked Bob.

"Well, if I'm a person who has murdered someone, don't I need more grace than the guy who goes to church and follows all the rules?"

"Oh, I see. Let me be very clear: it is not a matter of degrees of sin. Sin is absolute. All sin separates us from God. And the only way to have a relationship with God is to receive His forgiveness and His extravagant grace, period. It makes no difference the amount of sin you have committed."

Bob waited for a response. When no one said anything, he said, "To be truthful, I don't know why we see people turn down God's grace, which is what we are talking about here. Believe it or not, some persons are prisoners to their anguish. They just can't get past the belief that nothing is free in this world and if anything good is going to happen in their life it will be because they worked for it and earned it."

Tony sat stunned. That was exactly his position. He looked around the room to see what everyone else's reactions were, but he couldn't read them. He decided not to say anything but caught Dave looking at him sideways. Tony looked back and shrugged his shoulders at him. Dave nodded knowingly and turned his attention back to Bob.

Bob continued, "Earlier, I said that when, and only when, a person embraces this radical grace will certain things happen. In the time remaining tonight, I simply want to alert you to two things that will be the evidence that you have grasped the depth of God's grace.

"The first thing to happen is a deep sense of gratitude. The second thing is that you will have a heartfelt desire to be generous with others the way God has been generous with you. And I mean 'generous' in the broadest sense of the word. You will desire to give your time, talent, and treasure to others, and this will bring you a great sense of joy. Giving won't be rooted in obligation. No longer do you perform acts of generosity to accrue brownie points with God or with others.

"Let's talk a little about being a generous giver. Generosity is not so much something you do as it is who you become. I believe many of our church members give financially to the church so they can rack up points so they will get into Heaven. That may even be true for some of you here tonight. And many of them give begrudgingly and minimally. Don't get me wrong, I am grateful for every gift, as it helps us do the work we are called to do as a church. But many also give very generously with a thankful heart. They are not paying God back for the grace they have received. They give generously because God has turned them into generous people and giving is a great source of joy for them. And one word of caution. When I say generous, I am not referring to the amount of a gift. For some people giving a thousand dollars to a favorite cause is not generous at all. For others, giving fifty dollars to the same cause may be extremely generous.

Tony snuck a look at Calvin. Calvin was deep in thought. *Bob is describing Calvin perfectly,* Tony thought. *That is exactly what Calvin thinks. I wonder how he is feeling right now.*

Calvin spoke up, "But aren't we mandated to give?"

"We are *called* to give. But to give through a generous heart. And it is not to buy our way into God's graces," replied Bob. "It is, however, a choice we make in which God rejoices."

Calvin remained quiet, as did everyone else. Finally, Bob broke the silence.

"Hey, guys, let's stop here for the night. I know too well that the mind can only absorb what the derriere can endure. You guys have been fantastic all day, and I don't know about all of you, but I am getting tired. So unless someone has some thoughts that you can't help expressing, let's sleep on all of this. Tomorrow morning we'll conclude with a few more ideas on the topic of generosity. We will start with breakfast at 8:00 AM sharp. See you in the morning."

He got up, and everyone else followed suit. Tony and Dave went up to their room. Dave looked at Tony and said, "I see something is on your mind. What is it?"

Tony looked at Dave for a long moment then said, "What's going to happen tomorrow?"

"What do you mean?"

"It seems like we are being set up for something."

"Like what?"

"Well, I have my suspicions, but don't want to say. Anyway, good night."

Dave didn't press him. They both got ready for bed. It took Tony longer to fall asleep than usual. He was concerned a little about the morning. Finally, he shrugged his shoulders, turned over, and fell asleep.

CHAPTER 25

Tony got up early Sunday morning. He put on his running shoes and slipped out before anyone else was awake. He had seen a trail the day before and thought this would be a good way to clear his head. There were just too many new ideas floating around in his brain. It was light enough that he didn't need a flashlight, but he kept a close watch on his feet lest he trip and fall. The woods were beautiful in the morning light. The birds had not yet awoken, so there was mostly silence. It was very peaceful.

After about twenty minutes, the trail emptied onto a beautiful open meadow. The sun was just coming up over the horizon and he stopped to watch it rise. The orange orb of the sun seemed so big that he could reach out and touch it. In fact, he did reach out his hand until he realized what he was doing. He lowered his hand and marveled at the beauty of nature.

"Wow, God does paint a beautiful picture," he murmured to himself.

Then he caught himself short. "What am I saying?" he said out loud. "All this talk of God has gotten me a little flakey. Dad may be right; they are trying to brainwash me!"

Then he chuckled to himself. "Get hold of yourself, Tony. You know what the deal is. Just go back and go through the motions. You'll sort this out later."

He shook his head and chuckled again. He looked at his watch and decided he better get back. He took one more look at the meadow and the sun, which was now too bright to look at directly, and smiled. It was beautiful, regardless of how it got here, he thought. He turned around and started the run back.

When he got to the cabin, breakfast was already being prepared. He jumped into the shower adjacent to his room and turned the water up to as hot as he could take it. When he got out, Dave had already gone downstairs, so he got dressed and went down for breakfast. Almost everyone was up, and the morning prayer had been said. The men were eating. Tony grabbed some coffee, bacon, and eggs and found a seat next to Bob.

"Did you enjoy your run this morning, Tony?" Bob asked.

"Yes, but how did you know I went for a run?"

"Dave said that was likely where you went. He said that you were an avid runner."

"Yes. I find it helps me clear my head, especially in the morning."

"Oh? Did you need to have your head cleared?" Bob said with a bit of a grin.

"Not exactly. It's just that, well, there has been a lot of information to process this weekend."

"I see," replied Bob. "Did you process it all, then?"

"No. But I will."

"Good," said Bob. "That's what all this is about."

Bob excused himself and went to bring his dishes to the kitchen. Tony finished his meal in silence. Bob called the folks to order about fifteen minutes later.

"Good morning, everyone," he started. "It being Sunday morning, I thought we might have a short worship service. There is a lovely stream out in the back of the cabin. I thought we could have it there. How does that sound to everybody?"

Everyone seemed to nod in agreement. They all grabbed their Bibles and marched down to the stream.

It was a lovely venue. Turned out that George had brought his guitar and was quite good. Tony wasn't sure if Bob had planned this all along and had asked George to be prepared, but he supposed it didn't matter much anyway.

The service was relatively short. They sang a few songs, none of which Tony was familiar with. Bob gave a short sermon. It was simply about how God created such a beautiful picture in nature, using the scriptures of the creation as part of it.

Bob continued, "As we are out here in this beautiful setting and have talked about creation and renewal and we have this wonderful stream, I thought we should celebrate communion."

Everyone seemed to be fine with that idea, so Bob brought out the elements and blessed them. Then, one by one, the men stood up to receive the elements. George was the first one to step up and then helped Bob administer them to everyone else. Clearly, he had done this before. Dave started to get up, then leaned over to Tony and said, "Didn't you say that you wanted to experience all the Christian rituals? Well, here's your chance." He offered to help Tony up.

"Uh, I don't think so, Dave."

Dave paused to look at him.

Tony explained, "Look, I know that this is a very serious ritual and that you put a lot of stock in it. But because I don't believe in it, I won't take it lightly. I won't be doing communion."

"Right you are, Tony. No pressure."

Dave smiled and went down to the stream. Tony breathed a sigh of relief. He certainly was not ready to do anything like that, and he was glad that Dave hadn't pressed the issue. In fact, no one pressed him. When everyone was done, they all picked up their things and walked back to the cabin where Bob gathered everyone for the last session.

"First, let me thank Walter for providing the food and this wonderful place. On some of my previous retreats, we woke up to only coffee and doughnuts, but not this retreat. You guys are shining examples of serving us with a gracious spirit and with an abundance of hot food—a great gesture of generosity. Like me, I believe all the men are here with a spirit of genuine gratitude. As I said last night, that's how it works."

All nodded their heads in acknowledgment.

"Let's dig a little deeper into this concept of generosity. To be honest, I believe the spirit of generosity is the greatest litmus test for knowing if God's grace has truly penetrated a person's heart or if a person is still suffering in a works-righteous paradigm.

"Let me put it this way. If a person is stingy, with either money or time, and what they give, they give reluctantly or even begrudgingly, then that tells me the person has not developed a heart of gratitude for all God has given them. I often become very discouraged when I include thoughts about giving in my sermons, only to find people who know me say things like, 'All he wants to talk about is money.' Or they don't come to church at all because they believe that 'all the church wants is my money.'"

Tony nodded his head without thinking about it. *Here it comes,* he thought. *Dad was right all along: they just want my money.*

Bob continued, "Let me tell you straight out, that couldn't be further from the truth. All I want is for everyone to be open to what God says about giving and how they can be—and it will take an act of God to do this—transformed into persons who find their greatest joy in giving their lives away to others. Note I said *lives,* not *money.* Jesus was absolutely right when He said, '*It is more blessed to give than to receive.*' And if a person is stingy and lacks a true sense of gratitude in his heart for all that God has given to him, that is an indication they have not fully grasped the concept of grace.

"Let's look a little deeper at this lifestyle of generosity," he continued. "And please don't sit there with a smug countenance whispering under your breath, *I don't care what he says, he's after my money.* That's just not true. Instead, I am asking you to open yourself up to what the Bible says about generosity. Fair?" He waited for them to take it all in. There were a few nods, but no one said anything.

He continued, "Generosity is first and foremost a characteristic of God. Our God is a generous God. If you were ever taught to memorize Scripture you probably started with what might be called the most famous Bible verse in all of Scripture, John 3:16. If you memorized this verse as a child, you can say it with me. *'For God so loved the world that He gave His only begotten Son, that whoever believes in Him should not perish but have eternal life.'* God could have left humankind in their dilemma and established some 'works righteous curve' where those who did a significant amount of good works would rise to the top of the curve and be saved. While the rest of us whose works did not reach the appropriate height in the curve would be turned away, only to experience death and eternal suffering."

Calvin spoke up rather tentatively, "That would seem fair, Pastor."

"I suppose it would. But it wouldn't be very generous, would it?"

"How do you mean?"

"Well, if only some get the reward, that means that there is only so much to go around, right? That's the doctrine of scarcity. Only so much grace to go around. But that's not the case with God. Would you agree, Calvin?"

"Yeah, I guess," replied Calvin.

"With a truly generous God, there is enough and more for everyone. That's the very definition of true generosity."

Calvin pondered that for a moment. "Yeah, I guess I see your point."

Bob continued, "Well then, let's look at this verse a little closer. First, God loves. Loves who? He loves the whole world. God is not stingy with His love. He can't love more generously. He loves *every single person who has ever lived* and that includes you and me. Now, as evidence of His love, the text says, 'He gave.' Do you see that? Loving and giving are linked together. Show me a man who loves his wife, and I will show you a man who delights in giving to his wife. On the other hand, show me a man who has stopped giving anything, including himself to his wife, and I will show you a man who has stopped loving her. Because God loves you, He gives good gifts to you, not the least of which is the gift of salvation. And it is a gift that is given freely. No strings attached."

Right, Tony said to himself.

"Ephesians 2: 8–9 says that we have been saved by faith, and that this is a gift of God's grace, not a result of works. There it is, that word 'grace' again. And close by is the word 'gave.' It couldn't be stated more clearly. Salvation is a gift of God. God is a giver at His core. And while His gifts came at a price, *we did not have to pay for it*. God gave His all—He gave His only Son. God didn't give a tenth of His Son. God gave 100% of His Son. There is no greater gift than salvation and it is offered to all for free! So make no mistake about it, God is a lover and God is a giver and He is profoundly generous to all. Not because He has to but because being loving and being generous are at the center of who He is."

Calvin jumped in and said, "So can I expect Him to provide me with a new riding lawnmower this Christmas?"

Everyone chuckled at that. Walter jumped in and said, "That's all you wish for? I think I would ask for more than that."

Calvin responded, "What can I say? I'm just a simple man, Walter."

Bob smiled and said, "Well, I suppose that's one way to look at it. But here's my point. Our goal in the Christian life is to become like Jesus. And that means we become loving and we become givers and our gifts are not the minimum to get by. We become generous givers. At the root of our generosity is *gratitude* for all God has done for us and a deep-seated desire to be as much like Jesus as we can."

He took a moment to let that sink in. Tony was thinking this was going to end in a "passing of the plate" kind of thing. He was sure Bob was going to be asking him for money before the day was out, despite what he said.

But to Tony's surprise, Bob looked at his watch and then looked up at the men gathered in the room. "Quite a lot to take in, isn't it? I suspect I have introduced you to some new concepts and ideas. I don't expect you to process it all at once. I am processing this stuff all the time.

"But our time is coming to a close. I hope you all have gotten something out of this weekend. You may remember when I invited each of you here, I wanted to debrief the mission trip. You may be asking yourself, when are we going to do that? What I will suggest to you is that that is exactly what we have been doing all weekend."

"Huh?" exclaimed Calvin. "What do you mean?"

"What I mean is I had heard that some folks went on the trip to 'build up treasures in Heaven.' Others came on the mission trip to earn brownie points that will help them get into Heaven. And I hope if you had either of these perspectives before this weekend, then what we have discussed these last couple of days will give you something to think about. Specifically, giving yourselves to others, as you all did on the mission trip, should be about having a generous heart. Not about duty, obeying the law, getting brownie points, or any of that. When you give to others, the basis of your giving is gratitude for all you have received. Then, and only then, are you doing it for the right reasons. It's what I earlier called the 3 G's of the Christian life: Grace, Gratitude, and Generosity. It's the lifestyle of the person who is becoming like Jesus. And that is the message I want to leave you with today. Amen."

Everyone was silent for a long time. Tony watched Calvin, who was clearly trying to understand the concept and perhaps was failing. Some of the others were nodding their heads in acknowledgment.

Dave was smiling broadly. Tony leaned over to him and whispered, "What are you so happy about?"

Dave looked at him and said, "I just love it when God reveals to me something significant that challenges me to become more like Jesus."

Tony shook his head. It was clear that Bob was done. They all got up and started tidying up the place. They left in small groups. As Dave and Tony drove home together, they were mostly quiet. But Dave had that silly Cheshire Cat smile on his face the whole time.

CHAPTER 26

I t had been several weeks since the retreat. Tony had been
engrossed in the Sievers' project, but he was finding that the
kids were taking up more and more of his time. Even though he
was taking his work home, he couldn't seem to get everything done
and still have enough time for Beth and the twins. Joey especially
required more time, and Tony was always concerned he would have
some sort of relapse. Beth tried to assure him Joey was fine, but Tony
still worried. That was the case this particular weekend, and while
nothing bad happened when they all went to the park, Tony still did
not sleep well on Sunday night.

So on Monday morning, Tony decided he wanted something
different. The coffee at work was fine, but he enjoyed the occasional
flavored coffee, and 7-11 had the best. Besides, he thought he might
need something stronger than what they had at work.

So he stopped by on his way to work. And lo and behold, they
had his favorite, blueberry. He got the extra-large cup and filled it.
He went to the counter to pay and opened his wallet and pulled out
a five-dollar bill and placed it on the counter.

But just before the clerk picked it up, Tony noticed it had some
writing on it. He looked and it was a Scripture verse. Ordinarily, he

would not have given it a second thought, but with his newfound interest in reading the Bible, he read what was on the bill. It said *ACTS 9:10.* Tony had no idea what that Scripture said, but he thought maybe he should look it up. So he took the bill back and put it back in his wallet in a separate compartment and paid with another bill. He promptly forgot about it.

When he got to work, his boss, Jerry called him into the office. This was not unusual, as he and Tony often started their morning together to plan the day. But today, Jerry seemed a little different. Perhaps nervous was a better description. That wasn't like Jerry.

Tony sat down at the little conference table in Jerry's office and waited for Jerry to join him. Jerry sat down and placed a folder in front of him.

"Jerry, you look so serious. What's up?"

"It's nothing bad. Well, not bad for you, anyway."

"What are you talking about?"

Jerry pushed the folder across the desk to Tony. "In that folder, you will find an offer."

"An offer? What sort of offer?"

"It's an offer for a promotion. To assistant director of the planning department."

"The planning department. But that's Tim Holden's job. Is Tim leaving?"

"No, Tim's not leaving. You are."

"Huh?"

"The job is in St. Louis. They are opening a new office there and they are offering you the position."

Tony sat back in his chair. His dream of moving up in management was here, but this was a surprise. He had no idea the top brass even knew he was alive. He opened the file in front of him and started looking through it. "But how did this happen?" he asked. "I wasn't up for any kind of promotion. I just got passed over, remember?"

"I remember. But your work on the Sievers' project has garnered you notice with management. Plus, I recommended you," Jerry said. "I know you can do the job, and I know you want to move into management. It was the right call. I will miss you, though. I have really come to rely on you."

It was true. He and Jerry had developed a very good working relationship. Jerry asked Tony to do lots of things he didn't trust to others in the organization. But St. Louis? It was so far away, and he knew nothing about the city. This was Beth's home and his as well. They had lived here all of their lives. She might not like the idea. And there was the . . .

Jerry started talking again. "As you can see, it comes with a substantial increase in pay, you get a company car, and all your moving expenses will be covered. A really good deal, actually."

Tony thumbed through the folder. "Yeah, it is. Uh, is this a mandatory thing?"

"What do you mean?"

"I mean I have to talk this over with Beth and she may not want to go. So if I don't take it, will it hurt my career here?"

"Oh, I don't know. I don't think so. I guess I just assumed it would be a no-brainer. I personally would love it if you stayed, but that should not play into this. It's about you and what you want to do."

"Yeah, sure. How long do I have to decide?"

"They want an answer by the end of the week. So look it over and go home and discuss it with Beth." He got up and reached out to shake Tony's hand. "Congratulations. I can't think of a better person for the job."

Tony took his hand and said, "Thanks, Jerry, I appreciate your confidence in me."

He walked out and went to his cubicle. *Wow*, he thought, *This is a very nice package. And my chance to move on up. So why am I hesitating?*

Tony had a hard time concentrating that day. He kept going back to the folder and looking through the details of the offer. It really was a generous package. But . . . He thought about calling Beth to tell her but decided he wanted to do it face to face. He finally put the folder in his briefcase and concentrated on his work as best he could. That night he got home and after dinner and the kids had been put down, he sat down with Beth at the kitchen table.

"Something happened at work today that I need to tell you about," he started.

"What? Was it something bad?"

"No, actually it is something good. But we need to discuss it."

"Okay," she sat back and waited. Tony put the folder Jerry had given him on the table.

He pointed at it. "This is a promotion package. They want me to be the assistant director of the planning department."

"Oh, Tony, that's wonderful!"

"In St. Louis."

"What?" She reached for the folder and opened it up and looked through the file. "St. Louis?"

"Yeah. They would move us there, help us sell the house here. The whole enchilada."

"Wow, and a big pay raise as well." She looked up at him with a questioning look. "And?"

"And this is not just about me. It's about us. We need to make this decision together."

"Tony, this is something you have been wanting for a long time. But it would require me to find another job there. I would probably take a pay cut. That would be a challenge for both of us, even though your raise might cover it."

"Yeah, that's true. Anything else?"

"Well, we would also be giving up our small-town lifestyle for life in the big city. I'm not sure how I feel about that, actually."

"Right. Maybe it's not such a good idea, after all."

She paused and looked at him for a moment. Then she said, "You know, this is what you have been waiting for—for so long. And all we have said about moving is true, but there's something else bothering you. What is it, honey? What's really on your mind?"

Tony took a deep breath. "It's just this. Wow, I can't believe I'm even saying this."

"Yes, go on." She gently grabbed his hand from across the table. "It's the Bible study thing." He let out a deep breath.

"The Bible study thing?"

"Yeah. I've started on this path to the whole Bible study thing. You know, I went on the retreat. I made some new friends. I met with the pastor, Bob. He seems like a pretty upright fellow."

"You want to stay because of Bob?"

"No, no. That's not it. Man, this is hard to put into words." He sat back and looked off into space then down at his hands.

"Okay," said Beth. "Take your time. I'm here all night." She sat back in her chair.

He paused for a long time. Finally, he looked up at her and said, "I can't put my finger on it. Something is niggling in the back of my head. It says, 'Stay, you're not done here yet.' It's crazy, I know. And there's something else."

"Oh, what's that?"

"Bob, the pastor . . ."

"I know who he is, dear," Beth said gently.

"Yeah. Well. He called me this afternoon."

"Yes?"

"He asked me to be in something called a Life Group. He said he was getting some of the folks from the retreat to form this thing and it would be the perfect place for me to pursue the, you know, Bible study thing."

"I see," she said cautiously.

"So that's another factor. I hadn't envisioned doing the study with a bunch of people. I just thought that it would be me reading and asking him questions."

"Oh. Well, that is the way we do it, you know. It works best if there is more than one opinion."

"That's kind of what Bob said. It's just so weird that he would call me today. You know, on the same day as the promotion offer."

Beth was quiet for a long time. "Do you think you're getting a message that you can't find a study group in St. Louis?"

He looked up. "A message?"

"Yes. A message from God?"

Tony stared at her. Could that be it? He shook his head. He didn't believe in any of that, did he? Maybe he *was* getting brainwashed, as his dad had said. There was no God and even if there was, He certainly didn't have the time to talk to Tony Hunter. Yet, there was something . . .

"Come on, Beth, you know I don't believe in any of that."

"I know, but you have committed to studying the Bible and learn about the church. And I know once you commit to something, you don't let it go. Yet this is a really big thing. This promotion is what you have been longing for for such a long time." She paused then leaned forward and put her hands out and held Tony's hands in hers and asked, "Would you like to pray about it?"

"What?"

"It's one of those 'Christian things,'" she said with a smile. You have been trying to do all the 'Christian things.' And this is one of those things. We tend to pray for guidance when we need to make a major decision."

Without realizing why, Tony responded, "Okay, I guess. Uh, you pray and I'll listen."

"Good," she said. She began, "Gracious Father, Tony has been given an opportunity. A very promising one. It looks like a wonderful promotion for him, but we are unsure. We ask that You give us guidance as to what *You* want us to do. We wish to do Your will in this. And we will abide by Your loving direction. We pray this in Jesus' name. Amen."

To Beth's surprise, and Tony's as well, he also said, "Amen."

"What now?" she asked. "When do you have to tell them?"

"By Friday."

"Then you have some time. Let's go to bed. You can sleep on it."

She took his hand and led him to the bedroom.

They got ready for bed in silence. When they got into bed, she kissed him gently and turned over.

But he couldn't sleep very well. He tossed and turned all night. At one point, he got up and went into the babies' room. They were both sound asleep in their cribs. He stood over them and just watched them for the longest time. *Every decision I make from now on affects you guys,* he thought. *How will this affect you?* He decided he needed another opinion.

The next morning, he called Dave and asked Dave to meet him at Charley's, their usual meeting place after work. As was his usual practice, Tony ran there: it was only a mile and a half from his house. And it gave him time to think.

Dave was already there when Tony walked in. He had ordered for both of them, so there was an ice-cold beer waiting when Tony sat down. He took a long drink and wiped his mouth on a napkin.

Dave started, "So, what's the big deal you wanted to talk about?"

"I need some advice."

"Okay, shoot."

Tony proceeded to tell him about the promotion offer. He also told him about all of his concerns and about his discussion with Beth.

Then Dave said, "Wow, it sounds like a really good opportunity. I will miss you and Beth."

"Whoa, I didn't say I was taking it."

"No? What is stopping you?"

"I'm not sure. There is something, something bothering me."

Dave waited patiently. Tony was struggling.

Finally, Tony said, "It's about the church."

"Church? What about the church?" asked Dave.

"Well, I've started on this thing to understand the Bible and it's important that I'm able to teach the kids. Well, you know what I'm trying to do."

"And you can't do that in St. Louis?"

Tony took a long sip of beer. He placed the glass slowly on the table and looked up at Dave.

"That's what Beth asked. It's not that I can't, it's just that I have this feeling that I shouldn't."

"That you shouldn't continue Bible study?"

"No, that I shouldn't do it somewhere else. That I need to stay here to do it."

"Wow, that is intense. Do you know why you feel that way?"

"That's the thing, I don't know. It's just this, oh, I don't know, a feeling. It's like I know something, but I don't have any facts to back it up."

Dave looked at Tony for a long moment. He hesitatingly said, "You know, it sounds a little like James' description of, dare I say it, faith?"

"*I know.* I thought that too. And it's making me a little crazy," Tony exclaimed.

"*Aah*, I see. Still worried about the whole brainwashing theory?"

"Yes!" barked Tony.

Dave sat back and put his hands up, "Easy, big fella. You know my position on the matter."

"Of course I do." Tony sat quietly for a while. Then he said, "And there's this other thing."

"Uh-huh?"

"Bob, uh, the pastor, asked me to be in a Life Group."

"Yeah, I know."

"You know, how?"

"Well, he called me and asked me about it first. He kind of wanted to know what you might say. He doesn't want to appear to be pushy."

"I see. And what did you tell him, if I may be so bold as to ask?"

"I told him that he would have to ask you," replied Dave.

"Not helpful, my friend."

"I didn't want to assume anything. Besides, I had an ulterior motive. He asked me to be in the same group, so I wanted you to join."

"Oh."

They were both quiet for a long time. Finally, Dave said, "So, do you still want my advice?"

"Sure. I trust you, David, you know that."

"Oh, it's *David*, is it? This must be serious."

Tony grimaced at him.

"Okay, seriously, it seems to me that God may be speaking to you. I know that you have not accepted that possibility, but that's what it sounds and feels like to me. But my advice is: when you make the decision, look at how you feel. If it *feels* right, you have made the right choice. If not, reconsider. But if it is God whispering in your ear, I suspect that you will feel good about it even if your head is fighting it."

Tony looked at Dave. He nodded and drained his glass. "Thanks, Dave. You are always a good friend." He stood up to go and reached in his pocket to pay.

Dave waved him off. "My treat."

"Thanks. I'll let you know what Beth and I decide." They both stood up, and Dave put some money on the table. They walked out, and Dave went to his car while Tony ran home.

When he got there, Beth was playing with the kids. He sat down and started to play with Joey. After a while, Tony said, "Beth?"

"Yes, dear?"

"I can't believe I'm saying this, but I think we need to stay."

"You mean not take the job?"

"Yeah, and before you ask, I can't tell you why. Every logical bone in my body says I need to take the promotion. But every time I make that decision, my stomach winds up in knots."

"What did Dave say?"

"Oh, the usual, you know, God's speaking to me. But what resonated was this. He said I would feel good if I made the right decision and bad if I made the wrong one. And that's what I'm basing this on."

"Seems like sound advice," she offered.

"What do you think, Beth?"

"I think I'm in the same place that you are. The right thing to do is stay here." She put her hands on his shoulders. "I would like to think that God is speaking to you, to both of us."

"Well, okay then, we agree."

Beth nodded to him and smiled.

"I'll tell Jerry in the morning."

Jerry was surprised at Tony's decision to not accept the promotion and stay where he was. Jerry promised that he would look for other opportunities for Tony locally. However, Tony had an inkling that things were going to be different.

CHAPTER 27

Bob was looking forward to this day. He had hoped that at least some of the men on the retreat would want to form a Life Group, but he had been surprised that all of them wanted to participate. As he wanted meaningful discussions, he needed smaller groups, so he organized the guys who went on the retreat into two groups.

One group consisted of Tony, Dave, Calvin, George, James, and Walter. Bob was particularly excited that Tony had agreed to be part of the Life Group. He honestly didn't think Tony would be willing to be involved. He knew he would have to be particularly careful with Tony and not scare him away. Bob also believed, based on what he had seen on the retreat, that God was doing something special in each of these men's lives. They all agreed that Saturday mornings fit best for everyone's schedule.

At the first meeting of the Life Group, Tony arrived first. He seemed a little ill at ease to be the first one, but Bob welcomed him warmly and offered him coffee and a donut. It wasn't long before the others showed up as well. They all fell into casual conversations, and Tony relaxed a little, especially when Dave came in.

Promptly at 8:00, Bob called the meeting to order.

"So," said Bob, "let me just say you're an amazing group of men arriving here for our first Life Group meeting right on time. Something my mother told me ages ago was, 'Bob, a word to the wise. Be gracious with people and ruthless with time.' And I have followed that faithfully. What that means is that we will start on time out of respect for those of you who were able to get here promptly. But that also means we will *end* on time. Some of my clergy friends do not buy into this practice because they think that the Holy Spirit should be the one who determines when the meeting should end. 'What if something really exciting is happening and you end the meeting and quench the Spirit?' they would say to me. Well, I respond to that question by saying that if the Holy Spirit knows we leave at 7:45 AM, then it is up to the Holy Spirit to get His rear in gear and do His thing early enough to honor our time limits."

Several of the men chuckled at that.

"So, having said that, if you are ever running late and the thought occurs to you that maybe you shouldn't come at all, please come anyway. I guarantee you that you will be welcomed with open arms, and you hopefully will still benefit from the remaining discussion. That also means that if you plan something after our meeting is supposed to end, you will not be held over and have trouble getting to your next commitment. We will end on time." He looked around the table and there were nods of agreement from everyone.

James spoke up and said, "Bob, thanks for running things with that perspective. Nothing bugs me more than getting to a meeting on time only to have the leader start ten minutes late and then keep us ten or fifteen minutes after we were supposed to end. I consider that abusive, so thanks for running a tight ship."

Bob smiled and simply replied, "Thank you, James, for that affirmation."

After saying an opening prayer, Bob continued, "Let me summarize the purpose of our gathering this morning and for however many meetings we may choose to have. At the retreat, I shared with you the idea that the heart of the Christian life is what I call the 3G Lifestyle, consisting of Grace, Gratitude, and Generosity. However, there's more to it than that.

"I believe there are a number of decisions we have to make to have peace with God. This morning, I want to look at one or two of those decisions and share with you how I made them years ago and how they contribute to having peace with God. Then, in the weeks to come, I would like to discuss with you several additional decisions a Christian benefits from making. Does that agenda seem acceptable to you?" No one raised any objections, so Bob continued.

"Before I delve into the first two of these decisions this morning, let me just say that all of them require faith. Why? Because our natural instincts cause us to resist them, and this leads to many struggles with God. So rather than just teach about these decisions in the abstract, I prefer to share with you how I overcame my natural resistance to these decisions. Is sharing my personal journey okay with you guys, or would you rather have me just teach you what the Bible says about these issues?"

Walter was the first one to jump in. "Bob, I like the idea of learning not only what these decisions are but how you wrestled with them. It lets me get to know you a little better, and it sounds like it will be far more interesting."

James affirmed Walter's point of view. "I agree with Walter. Stories of how people struggle with the key teachings of Jesus is always more meaningful to me than just some academic lecture on what the Bible teaches." Most of the guys nodded in affirmation.

"Okay, then," said Bob. "Thanks for affirming what I thought would be best. Here is where we are going this morning. I want to begin with the first major decision a person needs to make to experience peace with God, and that is the decision to receive God's grace by asking Jesus to be his personal savior. And if there is time, I want to look at a second major decision, and that is to accept God's Word as authoritative. What I mean by that is, making what God says about how to live life the blueprint for every aspect of one's life: marriage, parenting, time, money, and so on. As I said before, faith is central to all these decisions."

Bob picked up his Bible and said, "I'm glad to see that you all brought your Bibles with you."

Tony still had the Bible that Dave had lent him at the retreat, and Beth had reminded him to bring it.

"Okay, please turn to the book of Hebrews, Chapter 11, and verse 1." Bob paused for a moment or two, and when he perceived everyone was at that place, he read it from his Bible. *'Now faith is being sure of what we hope for and certain of what we do not see.'* This is the best and the simplest definition I know of for the word faith. Faith is being sure of what we hope for; being certain of what we can't see."

Tony surprised himself when he blurted out, "That doesn't make much sense to me, Bob. How can you be sure of what you don't have or can't see but only hope for? I'm not sure I get that."

"Okay, let me take a stab at what seems confusing to you." Bob offered. "Initially, faith is scary. Faith is choosing to believe something that still may seem difficult to believe. And let me explain what the Bible means when the word 'believe' is used. I think I am safe when I say that whenever you see the word 'believe' in the Bible it really means 'trust,' based on the Greek. It means to put your trust in what you choose to believe even though there are questions and doubts.

"Do you remember in the third *Raiders of the Lost Ark* movie when Indiana Jones read the directions that said he should step out into a chasm? His father, who was back in the cavern dying from a wound said, 'It's a leap of faith.' So Jones took a step out into the chasm and a bridge appeared under his foot and he did not fall into the chasm. The bridge was there all along, it was merely hidden from his view and he could not see it until he took that first step.

"That is a visual of what faith is about. Based on the Bible, you take a step and only after you take that step do you find yourself to be on solid footing. Faith starts with a step, or leap of trust."

"So you're saying we have to take risks to follow God?" asked George.

"Yes. That's why it is called faith. Every step of faith I have taken started by trusting God and His Word. That is why Proverbs 3:5–7 is so precious to me. Don't turn there, let me just quote it, '*Trust in the Lord with all your heart and lean not on your own understanding; in all your ways acknowledge Him and He will make your paths straight. Do not be wise in your own eyes.*' Did you hear that? Trust in the Lord. Do not be wise in your own eyes. What I am asking you to do is open yourself up to the idea that God is challenging you to do exactly what He is instructing you to do, even when it flies in the face of reason or human wisdom. Why? Because Hebrews 11:6 says, '*. . . without faith, it is impossible to please God.*' I only hope that you have a desire to please God. If you don't at this moment, I hope it happens within you over time. So if it is okay with you, let's get started on those critical decisions which lead to peace with God."

"Wait a minute," said Calvin. "Are you trying to say that every time we do something that we think God is asking us to do, it's going to be risky and make us uncomfortable? That doesn't sound like the promise of peace and joy we are supposed to feel when we accept Christ into our lives!"

"No, I'm not saying that. What I am saying is that when you *first* start listening to God and following His directions, it may be that way. It was for me. But it does get easier. And more comfortable. But you never know. He does tend to throw unexpected things at us from time to time that may seem pretty scary."

He continued, "I know that may not make sense right now, but hopefully, it will later. Let me begin right where some of you may be this morning by sharing with you how I made the first of many significant decisions, the decision to receive Christ as my Savior.

"When I was a freshman at college," Bob said, "I was in my dorm room on one fall Friday evening. I was not doing much of anything when a knock on my door startled me. When I opened the door, I encountered a large gentleman whom I had never seen before. When I say large, I mean *large*—probably 6'5." And in his hand was a Bible that must have weighed 20 pounds. Okay, maybe I exaggerated on the Bible.

"He said something like, 'Hi, I'm John. Tonight, I am seeing if anyone in the dorm would like to visit about spiritual matters and I wonder if I could come in for a few minutes and we could chat?'

"Trust me, that was the farthest thing from my mind. But back then, I was a total people-pleaser and I never said 'no' to anyone if I thought that might displease them. So, hesitantly, I invited John into my room.

"'Have you spent much time reading the Bible?' John asked.

"I said no. I had been given a Bible at my confirmation by my parents, but I hadn't opened it. I didn't consider it important to bring to college so I couldn't show him my Bible. Then he asked me if he could share with me a few verses of Scripture that meant a lot to him. What John shared with me was a very simple Gospel message involving four letters: PPPD.

"Here is what the letters stand for. They stand for Plan, Problem, Provision, and Decision. In essence, John shared with me that back in the Garden of Eden, God had a plan for Adam and Eve. It was a plan that placed them in a perfect environment, provided them with everything they needed, created them with perfect health and a perfect relationship with God.

"But then there was a problem," he went on. "The second P. That problem was called sin. Adam and Eve disregarded God's Word. God told them they could enjoy everything in the garden, but they could not eat the fruit on the tree of good and evil or they would surely die. They were tempted by the serpent to eat the fruit and they ate. Now, this caused a separation between God and Adam and Eve. There was a distance between them, and that distance was passed down to their descendants. Because of this, every person created since then has a sinful nature that separates them from God. And the penalty for sin, yours, mine, and every person since Adam and Eve, is death.

"Then comes the word Provision, the third P. Since man could not resolve this problem on his own, God chose to step in and solve it Himself. He sent Jesus to pay the penalty for the sin of the world—and that includes your sin and mine. Jesus was not born with a sinful nature like you and me. Unlike Adam and Eve, he resisted the temptations of Satan and never sinned. He became the unblemished lamb of God who died on the cross to pay the penalty for the sin of the world. He was God's provision for our sin.

"But it is not enough for Jesus to be the provision for the sin of the world. We do not benefit from God's provision until we make the decision, the D, to receive the gift of salvation that Jesus offers us. We can decide to receive the gift of salvation or decide to reject it. After John explained this to me, he asked me if I wanted to make the decision to receive Jesus into my heart and become a Christian."

Bob paused and looked around the table for a moment. Then he asked, "What do you think happened next?"

"You jumped at the chance to be saved and prayed to receive Christ?" Walter said tentatively.

"Ah, you'd like to think so, wouldn't you?"

There were several nods around the table.

"Well, what happened is this. I did not hesitate. I said 'no,' I didn't want to do that. He asked why I wouldn't want to receive such a gift. And I remember saying clearly that I did not believe that the Bible was relevant and there was 'no free lunch.'

"So I thanked him for his time, but I needed to return to my studies. That was a lie—I had no intentions of studying that night. He was very gracious and left without badgering me anymore. *Wow, what a religious kook,* I thought. *Out sharing Bible verses on a Friday night.* I was so glad to get him out of my room. And I didn't think any more about it that night, or the next day either."

"I hope this story gets better," Calvin said under his breath.

"Oh, but it does, Calvin," Bob continued. "Now, for some odd reason, which I didn't understand at the time, I kept bumping into John at various places on campus. When the conditions were right, he would ask to sit with me and share more Bible verses about what God had to say about a variety of topics. Again, being the people-pleaser that I was, I couldn't say 'no,' even though I wanted to. What ultimately became clear to me was John was basing his life on the Bible. He was the very first person I ever ran into who found Scripture passages relevant to current circumstances. For John, the Bible was not some antiquated book that didn't speak to today's world. Quite the contrary, it was a very up-to-date book that a person could use for real present-day living.

"Slowly my opinion of John turned a corner. I no longer thought of him as some religious nut. I slowly began to look forward to our sessions. I would ask him questions about God and life. I discovered that the Bible dealt with issues unique to the times in which it was written but also contained timeless principles that described the situations that people have been getting themselves into from the very beginning of time. And it offered sound counsel for those living today." Bob paused for a moment and took a long sip of coffee.

Tony looked around. He saw everyone was fully engaged and waiting for the next thing Bob was going to say. Then he realized he was doing the same. He was very engaged in the story.

"What was becoming attractive to me was John was living his life based on the Bible. And there was one Scripture that stuck with me, and I believe it was instrumental in me deciding to start reading it, trusting it, and applying it. Hebrews 4:12 says, *'The Word of God is living and active. Sharper than any double-edged sword, it penetrates even to dividing soul and spirit, joints and marrow; it judges the thoughts and attitudes of the heart.'*

"What that came to mean to me was that the Bible, according to the Bible itself, is alive and active. It isn't a book of dead literature. It reveals the condition of the human spirit. *Wow,* I thought. *The Bible knows me and speaks to me and assists me.*

"Now, I didn't come to believe this based on that one verse. After all, I still didn't believe all this stuff. But it was watching John believe in this verse that ultimately led me to believe it myself. And that, my friends, is the reason I wanted to have these meetings.

"What I want to do is share my life with you guys so you can see what it means to me to put my faith in the Bible. So the second decision we have to make if we are going to have any peace with God is the decision to accept the Bible as God's Word and to embrace it as an authority in our lives. These two decisions, to believe that the Bible is authoritative and the decision to receive God's offer of salvation, are closely related. The decision to receive Christ is how we *become* a Christian. The decision to make the Bible authoritative in our lives is how we *live* the Christian life. Does this sound confusing or does it make sense?" Bob asked.

George spoke up. "I think it makes sense to me. I can see that if you don't believe the Bible, then what it says about receiving Christ wouldn't mean anything to you. But if you believe the Bible, then what it says about how you become a Christian would make perfect sense to you. So I can see how you put these two things together."

"Thanks, George. I just wasn't sure if I had explained that very well."

There was a long silence.

Then Bob said, "Okay then, let's bring this to a close. "

James interrupted Bob. "Hold on a minute, Bob. Are you going to leave us hanging? You said you didn't pray to receive Christ in your dorm room that night, but you didn't finish letting us know when that happened."

Bob responded with, "James, that's part of what I want to share with you next week when we cover another important decision, which is living with the confidence of your salvation. Is that okay with you?"

James said, "Sure. I guess."

Bob continued, "Let's close with a prayer." Bob closed with a short prayer and got up to start cleaning up.

Then Walter spoke up. "Say before we all leave, I have an idea."

Everyone sat back down.

"What's that, Walter?" Bob asked.

"Well, while coming to the church for these meetings is okay, wouldn't it be nicer if we were in a more casual setting?"

"What are you suggesting?" Bob asked.

"Simply that we take turns hosting these at our homes."

"Oh, that does sound nice. What do you all think?" Bob looked around the table. There was a general nodding of heads. Even though Tony nodded his head, he thought to himself, *I can't agree to that. I need to talk with Beth first. And how will I be able to host this group while keeping the twins quiet the whole time? Beth will be burdened with that responsibility, and I'm not sure she will agree to that.* But he kept his concerns to himself.

"I will even offer to host next week at my house," Walter said. "Only seems fair, as it was my idea. And I will provide breakfast."

Bob again looked around the room. Everyone seemed to agree. "Well, that sounds wonderful, Walter. Thank you for suggesting it. If you don't mind, as I know where you live, I will forward directions to everyone this week."

"Sounds like a plan."

As they were walking out, Dave grabbed Tony by the arm. "So, what did you think?"

"I'm not sure," he replied. "A lot to think about. A lot I simply don't buy into. But at least I'm learning some things."

"Yeah? Like what?

"For one thing, you guys have a lot of faith in stuff that I don't. And for another, Bob is a pretty complicated guy."

CHAPTER 28

"**D**ad, it's good to have you here," said Tony as he flipped the burgers on the grill.

"Well, I wouldn't miss the first birthday of my two favorite grandchildren, son," Tom replied as he raised his beer in a toast.

"They're your only grandchildren, but let's not quibble. It's important to us that you stay involved in their lives. I know that's hard from a distance, but you can come and stay with us any time you like."

"I appreciate that, Tony. I'll take you up on that."

Tony decided the burgers were ready and started placing them on the platter. He checked the hot dogs and thought they needed a little longer.

"I'll take those inside," Tom said. He picked up the platter and walked into the kitchen. Tony continued to cook the hot dogs. Beth came out and walked over to Tony.

"How is it going with your dad?" she asked.

"Uh, fine."

"You know what I mean," she prodded him in the ribs with her finger. "Have you told him yet?"

"Uh, no. Not yet."

"What are you waiting for? You're not scared, are you?" She giggled.

"It's not funny, Beth!"

She composed herself then said, "I know. But there's nothing to be afraid of. He's not going to bite you or anything. He loves you!"

"Sure he does, he just won't love what I'm doing."

"Just talk to him. He'll come around."

Tony turned and looked at her. "How long have you known my father? He will *not* come around. He will be very upset, and I don't want him to do anything to make you or us unhappy."

"I think we can weather that storm, Tony."

"Well, I'm not going to talk to him till after the party. I don't want to ruin it for everyone else."

"Fine. I'll give you that. Now, if these things are done, can we get inside and eat?" She picked up the platter with the now fully cooked hot dogs and went into the house. Tony cleaned up the grill, turned off the gas, and followed her in.

The party was going full blast. As it was a first birthday party, the kids were not that involved. It was more for the adults. Tony looked around and realized there were more friends from the church than not. Somehow that surprised him. How had he gotten to this point? All of the members of his newly formed Life Group were there with their significant others. Except for George, of course. He did not have anyone. Tony went to the cooler in the corner and got another beer. He then went over to talk with Dave.

"How are the burgers?" he asked.

Dave looked over his burger and nodded. He couldn't answer, as his mouth was full. Tony took that as an acknowledgment he had done his job. So he went to get himself some food, making sure everyone else had gotten their first plates. As the host of the party, Tony was not going to eat before everyone else had. The thought came to him that that was just like Bob.

He sat down next to his dad and started to eat. They ate in silence for a while. Finally, Tom finished his burger and took a long drink from his beer. Then Tom said as he wiped his mouth with his napkin, "I see a lot of new friends here. From your wife's church, I presume?"

"Actually, yes. But I might say from 'our' church. I'm sort of attending now."

"Right! Learning the doctrine, I gather."

"Yes, that's the plan. But it's to give the kids some perspective."

"Well, they all seem nice enough," said Tom.

"Actually, they are very nice. I'm making some good friendships here."

"Of course, you are. That's how they do it."

"Dad . . ."

Tom raised his hand to stop Tony from speaking. "Look, I know the drill. Your mother and your Aunt Susan tried to hook me in too. Your aunt is still trying it on me."

"Aunt Susan is still trying to get you to go to church? Those must lead to some interesting conversations."

"Not really. She asks me to come, and I say no. Usually, that's the end of it. But since *you* have started to go, she seems to be asking more often. Did you tell her what you are doing?" He looked at Tony with a look that could kill.

"Yeah, I talked to her about it. She was very encouraging."

"Of course she was! She has always been, what do they call themselves, a 'believer.'" He did air quotes. "A lot of good it did for your mother!"

"Yeah, I remember."

"You probably don't remember it all. They would pray together. They would get together with that women's group of theirs and read the Bible and pray together. They even visited when she was in the hospital and prayed together. Your mother still suffered, and she still died. It did no good!"

"Right. But don't you think that maybe all that stuff gave Mom at least a little comfort?" asked Tony.

"Don't care." He looked at Tony, who seemed shocked. "Oh, I don't mean that giving her some comfort was a bad thing. I just found it to be futile and annoying."

"Yeah, I suppose so. But getting back to Aunt Susan, what did she say to you?"

Tom said, "Nothing new really, just asking me to come to church. I figured you talked to her though. You two always did have a good relationship. Huh, probably better than the one she and I have."

"Aw, she loves you, Dad. She only wants the best for us."

"Wait a minute." Tom put down his drink and looked Tony in the eye. "Did she push you into this church thing?"

"No. I did talk to her about it and of course, she was happy about it. She didn't like it after Mom died and you pulled me out of the church."

"Yeah, we did have quite an argument about it at the time. But she finally backed off."

They were both silent for a while.

"Soooo, how do you like my new friends?" Tony finally ventured.

"Like I said, they seem nice enough. Why do you ask?"

"As it turns out, I'm getting to know some of them well. Including Pastor Bob over there," he pointed across the room to where Bob was sitting.

"Oh, you mean the little guy over in the corner?"

"Yep. That's him." Tony paused to choose his next words. "Uhm, he invited me to join this discussion group." Tony waited for the explosion that he knew was coming. But it never did. Tom sat there and took another long sip from his drink.

Finally, Tom put his beer down and said, "I figured as much."

"What?"

"That's how they hook you. You get involved first in one thing and then another. Pretty soon you're signing over the deed to your house. I assume Beth is all over this. Is she a part of your group?"

"No. It's all men. Some of the men whom I went with on the trip to New Iberia."

"Un-huh."

"All pretty regular guys, really."

"Right."

"And we just sit and talk about stuff. You know, Bible stuff."

"Yep. Are they shoving Bible verses down your throat?"

"It's not like that."

"Oh, really?" Tom took another sip of his beer with a knowing smile on his face.

"Yeah. We've only had one meeting but, it's an open sort of discussion. Of course, Bob brings in a lot of Bible verses, but that's sort of the reason I'm there. So I can understand what their doctrine is and then give the kids the other side of the story. Then they can make an informed decision about God. It's just like me."

Tom looked sideways at Tony. "Really? How so?"

"Yeah. You see Mom and Aunt Susan gave me the religious side and you gave me the real-world side. That gave me the basis for my decisions about God."

Tom said nothing but finished his drink.

"Look, Dad, I'm with you on this. I mean Bob and the others have said a lot of things that I don't believe. Things that are in direct conflict with what you taught me. Quite frankly, I'm not sure I understand most of it. But the thing is . . ."

"Oh, no, here it comes. What is *the thing?*"

"Well, it's more them."

"Them?"

"Yeah. They haven't tried to convince me of anything. I mean they have some very strong opinions, but the approach is not what I expected."

"Yeah?"

"Yeah. I'm allowed to push back on anything they say. They are willing to discuss anything and listen to my opinions. And when all is said and done, we agree to disagree. It's much different than I thought it would be."

Tom pondered this for a moment. Then he turned and looked at Tony directly in the eye. "Don't you see what's happening here?" Tony shook his head. "They are being very devious. They are pretending to *understand you* while they slowly brainwash you. Be very careful here, son. Very careful."

Tony was taken aback. He considered it for a moment then responded. "I hear what you are saying, Dad, but that's a little harsh. It just doesn't feel like that at all. And besides, Dave is in the group. He is my best friend and I trust him implicitly. I don't think he would do that."

Tom looked around the room and finally found Dave. He waved at Dave who waved back. "Son, I know that Dave is a good man and your friend. But being around these believer types for too long can affect anyone. I'm just saying be careful or you might get sucked in too."

"All right, I will, Dad. Don't worry."

"But, son," he put both of his hands on Tony's shoulders. "I am worried. I am. And now I need another beer."

Tom got up from the table and Tony watched him walk away. He thought that hadn't gone as badly as he had anticipated. He looked around the room at the guests, especially the men in his group. Were they trying to brainwash him? He didn't want to believe they were, but as his dad said, he would keep his guard up.

CHAPTER 29

The second meeting of the Life Group was a little nerve-wracking for Tony because of the discussion he had with his father. *Was Dad right? Are these folks just feeding me some doctrine, leading me down a wrong path?* Tony had thought about it long and hard. *Should I continue attending or just back out?*

But the longer he considered it, the more he wanted to come. He couldn't put his finger on it, but somehow, he felt good when he was with the Life Group guys. They were not judgmental, as his father insisted they would be. They seemed to accept him for who he was. And they never seemed to press their ideas on him. In short, their agendas did not seem to jibe with what his dad was saying. Besides, Beth seemed very happy he was doing this, and that counted for a lot with Tony.

And after all, he had chosen to decline a significant promotion at work in large part so he could continue learning about the faith. To back out now would defeat that purpose. He hadn't mentioned that aspect to his father, and he wondered to himself why he hadn't. He finally decided it would have just made his father angry and served no real purpose. Somehow, it still seemed a little dishonest, but there it was. In any case, he decided he would keep going to the meetings but be wary of what they were saying.

When Tony arrived at Walter's house, he was surprised. He had expected some sort of mansion. However, while it was very nice, it wasn't gigantic. Nor was it ostentatious.

He was not the first to arrive this time. That was on purpose. He did not want to seem too eager.

When the last man arrived and everyone had their coffee, Walter spoke up, causing the flutter of chatter to come to a close. "Welcome to my home," he started. "I am so pleased you are here. While this is not the first gathering of exclusively church people I have ever had in this home, I hope the neighbors haven't noticed what a motley crew this is. When you leave could you please go out the back door, one at a time? I don't want the neighbors to be concerned about their houses going down in value."

Everyone laughed at Walter's joke. Tony liked the fact that the atmosphere was light and fun, and the unanimous laughter seemed to lift any tension he was feeling. Walter continued, "To be honest, I got dressed at the last minute. I thought it would be fun to come to the meeting in my jammies, but Donna insisted that that was overstepping my prerogative. As you probably noticed, I have made lots of coffee and a little breakfast food. The omelet is kind of my specialty, so please try some. You will hurt my feelings if there is any left. No pressure." He chuckled. "So if it is okay with Pastor Bob, please get a plate and load up on some brain food. You are probably going to need it. So dig in."

When everyone had finished breakfast and found a place in the living room, Bob got things started. "Thanks, Walter, for getting this unruly crowd under control and sitting at my feet for the great pearls of wisdom I have prepared for these incorrigible guys." Most everyone chuckled at this, too. "I think I speak for everyone that we appreciate your hospitality and the spread. And the coffee here sure beats the coffee we make at the church. Also, this room is a wonderful meeting place for us to have our discussions. I hope we aren't inconveniencing Donna or the grandkids whom you said were visiting. I hope our conversation doesn't cause them to stir before their usual time."

"It's all good, Bob," replied Walter.

"All right, then. Good morning, guys. I trust you have had a blessed week. I know I have. These Saturday mornings allow me to share with you how I came to embrace topics like the authority of God's Word, which we spoke about last week. This morning I would like to address what the Bible says about living with confidence regarding your salvation. Last week I left James hanging, so let's go back to last week's discussion and add a little bit to what I told you.

"As I said, my first impression of John was that he was a spiritual wacko. However, I couldn't seem to get the PPPD letters out of my brain. I just kept thinking that God had a plan, that my sin caused a problem, that Jesus was the provision for my problem but none of it mattered unless I made the decision to receive Jesus into my life.

"But," Bob continued, "I also kept thinking that this PPPD thing was just too simplistic. Certainly, I thought, those who went to Heaven, if there even was a Heaven, were like Mother Theresa, who accumulated enough good deeds to warrant getting into Heaven when they died. And I was pretty certain I had not done any of that, so there was no confidence of salvation for me.

"Also, as I said last week, what ultimately drew me to changing my thinking was not so much the verses John shared but how those verses of Scripture had affected his life. Now, make no mistake, I did not want to be like John in terms of knocking on dormitory doors on Friday nights and speaking to them about Jesus. No way.

"But I did sort of want to have what he seemed to have in his inner life. He had a blueprint for his life, and that was very attractive to me. His blueprint was the Bible. He had faith to trust God with his life and his future. He had peace in his heart regarding his salvation and his place in Heaven when this life was over.

"And he had a purpose. He truly believed that what mattered was what he called 'storing up treasures in Heaven' rather than giving his life for those things on earth that provide only fleeting pleasure, such as houses, boats, and so on. His calm assurance was in contrast to my floundering around and looking for meaning in my life."

"Amen, brother," Calvin said.

"What was that, Calvin?" Bob asked.

"Storing up treasures. That's what I've been saying. We store up treasures by doing good works, right?"

"Calvin, it is true there will be treasures in Heaven for those who have done God's will here on earth, but if it is okay with you, I would prefer to go deeper into that topic on another morning. Let me just say that you don't buy your way into Heaven with good deeds."

"You're confusing me, Pastor."

"Bear with me, Calvin, okay?"

Calvin threw up his hands. "Okay, I'll bear."

"Knowing that John had what I wanted and knowing that he attributed what he had to having Jesus in his heart, I decided to pray to receive Jesus into *my* heart. This is the story I didn't get to share last time, James.

"One night, in the privacy of my dorm room, with no one there and no prompting from John, I knelt by my bunk bed and closed my eyes and folded my hands and said something like this. 'God, I know that I have committed many sins. And those sins separate me from You because You are Holy. I know I am unworthy to have those sins forgiven. But if You are real, and if You are listening, and if the Bible verses John has shared with me are true, then I ask You to forgive me of my sins and I invite You into my life. Thank You, God. Amen.'

"What do you think happened?"

James said, "Well, based on the way your stories have gone so far, probably not a lot."

"Bingo! Nothing profound happened. There were no angels flying around my room. There was no applause from Heaven penetrating my silence. There was no voice from God saying, *This is my son in whom I am well pleased.* But guess what? Something profound did happen, even if I couldn't sense it or hear it. That night I had what Jesus calls my second birth, or my spiritual birth, even though I didn't feel any different."

George spoke up, "So you didn't feel any different? Nothing?"

"Nope. Nothing. Nada. Not a thing. Anyway, a few days later, I thought I would call John and let him know. His response? John said with great enthusiasm, 'Are you kidding me? You prayed to receive Christ and you waited three days to tell me? Where are you?'

"I told him I was in the student union cafeteria having lunch and waiting for my 2:00 PM class to begin. John said, 'Hang on, don't move. I will be right over.' I honestly did not expect that. I thought he would be pleased but I didn't expect his all-out exuberance. Remember, I didn't feel all that different.

"When John came into the cafeteria, he headed straight for me, and when I stood up to greet him, extending my right hand for the usual handshake, he brushed my hand aside and gave me a huge bear hug and lifted me off the ground about two feet. Remember, he was 6'5" and I was 5'8". I probably should have made an appointment with a chiropractor after that."

Everyone chuckled at that.

"John said something like, 'Bob, welcome to the family! We are now brothers in Christ, and we are going to spend all of eternity with each other. Wow, this is fantastic!'"

I think I responded with something like, 'Yea. I guess if I am now in the family, that makes us brothers in a way. Thanks for taking the time to come say hi to me.'

"'I had to come,' John said. 'I really want to get some time with you. When are you available?'

"I said, 'How about tomorrow morning,' to which he said, 'How about 7:00?' Reluctantly, I agreed.

"When we met the next morning, we spent almost two hours

together. So what did John start explaining to me? Among other topics, he spent most of the time helping me learn about having assurance of my salvation.

"And the verses John shared with me I would like to share with you this morning. There are many more, but let's just look at a few. James, would you look up John 1:11–13. Tony, John 10:27–30; Calvin, Ephesians 1:13–14; Dave I John 5:11–13."

Bob gave them a few moments to find their places. Tony felt awkward but managed to find his assigned verses.

Bob then continued, "Now, before we read these verses, keep in mind that the reason I am sharing these verses with you is so you can do what I have already done. That is, to build your confidence of your salvation on what God has said in his Word, no longer trusting your feelings. I can't tell you how many days every month I still wake up and I do not feel like a Christian. I do not feel like I would go to Heaven if I died that day. Feelings are like shifting sand. They come and go. So let's look at what *God's Word* says about living with the confidence of our salvation. James, would you get us started? What does the Bible say in John 1:11–13?"

Walter interrupted, "Really, Bob. *You* don't feel like a Christian? You even question your salvation? Doesn't sound very pastor-like to me!"

"It's not that I question my salvation. It's that my feelings sometimes get in the way of my beliefs." He put his hands up in surrender. "Yes, it's true, we pastors are human and have issues. Sorry to disappoint you all."

Everyone laughed nervously.

"Thanks for asking, Walter. James can you please read John 1?"

James began to read. "*He came to his own, and His own people did not receive Him. But to all who did receive Him, who believed in His name, He gave the right to become children of God, who were born, not of blood nor of the will of the flesh nor the will of man, but of God.*"

"Thanks, James. Tony, would you read John 10:27–30?" Bob asked.

"Uh, Sure. *'My sheep hear My voice, and I know them, and they follow Me. I give them eternal life, and they will never perish, and no one will snatch them out of My hand. My Father, who has given them to Me, is greater than all, and no one is able to snatch them out of the Father's hand. I and the Father are one.'"*

"Thanks, Tony. Calvin, what does Ephesians 1:13–14 say?"

Calvin responded with, *"In Him you also, when you heard the Word of truth, the Gospel of your salvation, and believed in Him, were sealed with the promised Holy Spirit, who is the guarantee of our inheritance until we acquire possession of it, to the praise of His glory."*

"And finally, Dave, would you read I John 5:11–13?"

"Sure," Dave replied. "First John 5:11–13. *'And this is the testimony, that God gave us eternal life, and this life is in His Son. Whoever has the Son has life; whoever does not have the Son of God does not have life. I write these things to you who believe in the name of the Son of God, that you may know that you have eternal life.'"*

"Thanks, everyone. So let me ask you, do you think God wants you to live with great uncertainty regarding your eternal destiny? Or do you think God wants you to remove that uncertainty so you can live with the confidence that when you die you will join him in Heaven?" All of the guys mumbled something to the effect that God wanted that.

Bob then said, "Guys, just sit back in your chairs and close your eyes. Try to picture Jesus. Listen to the words we just read." Bob recited as follows:

"But to all who received Him—they are children of God."

"They will never perish. No one can snatch them out of My hand."

"You were sealed with the Holy Spirit—the guarantee of your inheritance."

"That you may know that you have eternal life."

Bob waited a few moments before speaking again. Then he said quietly, "Can you see Jesus? Can you hear Him say these words: children of God, never perish, guarantee, know? Okay, open your eyes. It boils down to this. We have assurance of salvation based on the Word of

God. But we live each day with the confidence of that assurance by exercising our faith. To be able to live every day with this confidence, you have to do it by faith. Does this make any sense?"

No one said a word. After a brief silence, Bob just smiled. "Look, it is my responsibility to challenge you to base your assurance of salvation on what the Bible says and to base your confidence on living by faith. But remember, the assurance of salvation is promised only to those who receive the gift of grace we call salvation by asking Jesus to come into their hearts. A verse we didn't read this morning is Revelation 3:20, which says, *'Behold, I stand at the door and knock. If anyone hears My voice and opens the door, I will come into him and have fellowship with him.'* So the real question is this: Do you know with certainty that you have opened the door to your heart and invited Jesus in? Can any of you share the time in your life when you invited Jesus into your life?"

James was the first to speak. "Yes, I can. I was at a church camp in the summer when I was in the seventh grade. On the last night, the speaker was Joe Robinson, a point guard with the Duke basketball team. He shared his story of becoming a Christian and he invited those of us who were listening to follow his footsteps and invite Jesus into our hearts. At the time, I'm not certain that the reason I went forward and prayed to receive Christ was because I wanted Jesus in my life. Maybe I just wanted to get closer to a celebrity athlete. But I have no doubt that Jesus heard my prayer and it stuck. I do consider that moment to be the day I had my spiritual birth."

"Thanks, James. I appreciate your sharing your story with us. Maybe in the weeks ahead some of you might also want to let us in on how you came to know Christ. But before we look at the Lordship of Christ next week, I would challenge you to simply evaluate if you can point to a time when you prayed to receive Christ into your heart. Let's close in prayer."

After Bob offered a brief prayer, and everyone, except Tony, responded with an amen, they all started to get up. Bob looked up and asked, "So who wants to host next week?"

James raised his hand, "I would love to."

"Wonderful," said Bob. "If you could, please send directions to everyone. We will see you all there."

As people were packing up to go, Bob went over to Tony and asked, "How is this going for you, Tony?"

"It's very intriguing, Bob. I'm glad you are teaching us through your own story. That makes it more interesting to me. Don't be offended, Bob, but I'm not the kind of guy who just accepts things because someone in authority presents his case."

"The reason I asked is because I noticed that you were shaking your head there towards the end. What was it that did not sound right to you?"

"I'm not sure you want to hear it."

"I can assure you, there is nothing you can ask about that I'm not willing to discuss."

"Okay, you asked for it. It's this idea that only through Christ can we get to God."

"Yes?"

"Well, what about all the people throughout history, heck, the ones today, who don't accept Christ? More importantly, what about the ones who never even heard of Christ? Seems they would be getting a raw deal. They never heard of Him, so they can't accept Him, so they are screwed. No Heaven for them."

"That is a very good point, Tony. But it will take too long to address right now. Perhaps we can bring that up next week?"

"Sure. I would like an answer to that question."

"Plan on it. If I forget, please remind me when we meet next Saturday to talk about this because what you have asked is very important. Have a great week."

They shook hands and Bob went to bid the others goodbye and to thank Walter for the use of his house.

Tony looked back at Bob. He was a little surprised that Bob was so open to talking about what Tony thought was a key flaw in the whole Christian doctrine. He knew he would have to be ready for that discussion.

CHAPTER 30

Beth was just stepping out of the shower. Tony was standing in the bathroom, clearly waiting for her.

"What's up, honey? You seem to have something on your mind," she said as she wrapped a towel around herself.

"Yeah, I do."

"Okay, spill it. But do you mind if I get ready for work while you do?"

"Of course not. It's about the Life Group."

"Oh, what about it? Are you still enjoying it?"

"Enjoying might be a stretch. Let's just say I'm finding it interesting."

"So, what is it that you want to talk about? You're not thinking of quitting, are you?" She started putting on her makeup. Tony had always thought she didn't need any makeup, but Beth put it on sparingly. She said that the business world expected certain things of women, and she did what she had to do.

"No. Not yet, anyway," Tony replied.

"Okay, so what is it that is on your mind?" She stopped and turned towards Tony. "Are you second-guessing your decision on the St. Louis job?"

"I don't know. Uh, maybe. Darn it, it was such a good offer."

"Yes. It was." She walked over to him and put her arms around him. "Do you want to change your mind? Is it too late for that?"

"Oh, yeah. It's way too late for that."

"Oh, I am so sorry, honey."

"Well, don't get too upset. It's not that bad, really. Quite frankly, I didn't want to move anyway. I like it here. It's just that the whole church experience is not what I expected."

Beth stepped back to her mirror and continued to apply makeup while she waited for Tony to continue.

"And well, you know that we are now meeting at different peoples' homes."

"Yes."

"I guess if I continue with the group, I, uh we, will have to host it on one Saturday."

"I assumed that." She stopped what she was doing and turned to look at him. "Is that a problem for you?"

"I don't think so, but I didn't want to offer without talking to you first. I mean it may be an imposition. You would have to watch the kids and all."

"Tony, I do that now when you leave on Saturday mornings."

"Yeah, but now you would have to keep them quiet and probably help get the house ready. It could be a lot."

She walked back over to him and put her hands on his face in a loving gesture. "Tony, darling, don't you know that I am happy to have you do this? But I think you will have to do most of the cleaning." She giggled a little, then said, "But seriously your willingness to spend time studying the Bible and talking with men of faith is something that I have prayed about for quite some time. Of course, I am happy to support you in this. I just don't want you to regret staying here and not taking the job offer."

Tony looked at her for a moment. "No, I think it was the right decision. For me and all of us, really. It's just that the interaction part, with these men, it's sometimes unsettling. I'm not sure what to make of it all. These guys aren't quite what I expected."

"How so?"

"For one thing, they can't all just quote the Bible. They sometimes seem to be just as in the dark as I am."

"Uh-huh."

"And then there's Bob. For a pastor, he seems, well, pretty much a regular guy."

"Oh, horrors. That must be a shock."

"Aw, quit kidding around. I'm not shocked, just, you know, surprised."

"Yes, I suspect that you will be continually surprised." She finished her makeup and went over to Tony, grabbed his face gently, and kissed him. "And that, my dear, is a very good thing."

"Anyway, the idea of bringing it all into our house, well, it's weird for me. And of course, I don't want to put any more of a burden on you, as I said before."

"Like I said before, it will be fine. Besides," she snickered a little, "I'm kind of curious about what you fellows talk about. Not that I would eavesdrop or anything." She winked at him and went back to her mirror.

"Okay then, I'll volunteer for a meeting." He went back to his mirror and lathered his face to shave.

Boy, he thought to himself. *I've put both feet in it now.*

He shook his head and finished shaving.

CHAPTER 31

Tony showed up at James's house much as he had at Walter's, expecting something big and expensive. Again, while it was nice, it wasn't overdone. Given that James was a doctor, Tony had thought it would be bigger. James and his wife had two children, both in preschool, and the house looked like it. Even as the men were coming in, James and his wife, Judy, were still picking up toys.

"Sorry for the mess," Judy said. "But the kids decided to get up early today and, well, this is usually the result." They continued to stuff toys into a big box in the corner of the great room. "Please go into the kitchen. Breakfast is ready, and there is plenty of coffee. Just leave some for me." She giggled and went back to picking up toys.

Tony went into the kitchen to find George and Bob already eating at the bar. There was French toast, waffles, two breakfast types of meat, orange juice and tomato juice, and what looked like scrambled eggs. *Oh, boy,* thought Tony. *When we host, I am going to have to step it up.* He got some coffee and a waffle and sat down at the bar with Bob and George.

"That was a lovely party for the twins," Bob said. "I really enjoyed myself."

"Me too," said George. "And your dad seems very nice."

"Yeah. He was on his best behavior."

"Oh, is he usually not that nice?" said George.

"Um, it's just that he isn't very fond of church folk."

Bob chuckled. "Oh, is that what we are, 'church folk?'"

Tony was immediately embarrassed. "No, it's just that my mom was a churchgoer, as is my Aunt Susan, her sister. But Dad, not so much."

"Well, I hope we didn't turn him off," said Bob.

"I don't think so. He seemed to think you all were okay."

They continued to eat in silence. Tony felt as if Bob suspected he wasn't telling the full story, but he didn't press him. Slowly the others showed up and got something to eat. As 8:00 rolled around, Bob called everyone into the big living room.

"Well, how is everyone doing this morning?" Bob said rather enthusiastically. After a few responses of "doing well, thanks," he continued. "I, first of all, want to thank James and Judy for opening up their beautiful home to us. And for the wonderful breakfast. I'm guessing you guys are really happy that I'm no longer doing the catering." Everyone chuckled at that.

He continued, "I see everyone has their coffee and most of you appear to be awake. That's great because this morning I want to share with you probably the most important decision you will have to make if you want to have peace with God.

"After you've received Christ into your heart, there are other decisions to make. First, you make the decision to base your assurance of salvation on God's Word and not your feelings. The second is to embrace the Bible as authoritative in your life. These form two of the legs of what I call the 'three-legged stool' of the Christian life. The third leg is making the decision to live your life with Jesus as your boss. All the other issues we face regarding our Christian lives rest upon this three-legged stool."

Tony interrupted, "Bob, forgive me for interrupting, but you asked me to remind you to address the issue of how people get saved who have never heard of Christ. There must be a way to Heaven for them other than through Jesus."

"Oh, right, Tony, thanks for reminding me. Why don't you share with us what it is about 'getting to Heaven through Christ alone' that you would like to discuss."

Tony turned to address the group. "Well, like I said to Bob last week at the end of the meeting, the whole idea that there are millions, no, *billions* of people throughout history who won't get into Heaven because they never even heard of Jesus seems wrong to me. Heck, even today, there are people in the world who won't ever hear of him because of where they live. Are they all doomed to an eternity in Hell because they didn't receive Jesus Christ? Clearly, that isn't fair, and frankly, it doesn't endear me to God."

He looked around the room and realized he had raised his voice a little more than he had intended. "Oh, I didn't mean to raise my voice. Just trying to make a point."

"It's all right, Tony," said Bob. "Anybody want to respond to Tony?"

James raised his hand. "I'll take a crack at it. That is something that bothered me for a long time as well. I'm not sure I have a good theological answer, but what I have come to believe is that God wants everyone to be with Him in Heaven. He says so in that John 3:16 verse, the one that says God so loved the world. I think that means everyone. I think God pursues all of us in one form or another. And everyone has the opportunity to come to Him, as He is trying to reach us."

"You think that God is chasing after us?" Tony asked.

"Yes, because He wants a relationship with each and every one of us. Now, how He does that to people who haven't heard the name Jesus, I don't know. But I believe that He does. The God I worship does not leave anyone out of His grace." James looked around the room then back at Tony. "I know that may not be satisfying, but that's how I answer that question."

Tony said, "You're right, it isn't satisfying."

Bob looked around again. "Anyone else?"

Walter spoke up. "I always just assumed that people who didn't believe in Jesus didn't get into Heaven. I never really thought about your question. I guess I just assumed that they didn't deserve to get in. If they did, God would find a way to let them hear about Jesus, but you're right. Some people in a far-off land will not ever get the opportunity."

Bob spoke up after an awkward silence. "Yes, it's a good question. James, I think you may have something there. And yes, many people do not get to hear the Gospel the same way we have. But the idea that God is always pursuing us is, I think, a valid one. God will find a way to offer each of us the opportunity to let Him into our hearts. That may not be a satisfying answer, Tony, but it may be the best one we can offer at the moment. Why do I believe this? For two reasons, each one of which is found in the Bible. Are you surprised that I would turn to the Bible for our answer?" Everyone but Tony chuckled.

"James, would you please turn to Romans 1:20 and read to us what that verse says?"

"Sure," James replied. He read, *"For since the creation of the world, God's invisible qualities, His eternal power, and divine nature, have been clearly seen, being understood from what has been made, so that men are without excuse.'"*

Bob continued, "Now, I believe that this verse is saying that no matter when a person lived or where a person lived, nature itself is evidence that there is a Creator. There is a Master Designer who put together this world we live in. It is too complex and too beautiful for all of creation to have just been the result of chance. Calvin, would you please find Jeremiah 29:11–14?"

Calvin began reading. *"For I know the plans I have for you, declares the Lord, plans for welfare and not for evil, to give you a future and a hope. Then you will call upon Me and come and pray to Me, and I will listen to you. You will seek Me and find Me when you seek Me with all your heart. I will be found by you, declares the Lord.'"*

"So," said Bob, "what Romans 1:20 is saying to me is that creation itself reveals that there is a Master Designer or a God. And Jeremiah

29 says that God has a plan for everyone. That plan includes 'being found' by anyone who wants to know the God who has revealed Himself through the sunrises and sunsets, through the mountains, through the great seas or the birth of a child. The path to Heaven is still only through Jesus Christ because He is the only One who was God, sent by God, perfectly obeyed God, and became the sacrificial lamb of God.

"But for the person who never even hears the name of Jesus," he continued, "the price for his sins has been paid by Jesus just as it has for you and me. And it is God's promise that if a person seeks the God of creation, he will find God. That is how I live with confidence, and quite frankly peace, that those who never hear of Jesus but who see the evidence of God in nature all around them and seek a relationship with the Creator have the same chance to be in Heaven. All because God has revealed Himself to them through all that God has made."

One thing was certain at this point. Tony didn't necessarily buy everything Bob believed, but it was clear that Bob did know his Bible. And Bob knew a lot of it by heart. And Bob trusted it. But Tony wondered, *If Bob weren't a pastor, would he still live this way? After all, pastors are supposed to know the Bible and they are supposed to live exemplary lives.*

Without even realizing it, Bob was becoming for Tony what John had become for Bob.

Tony looked around at the men and realized that he wasn't going to get any support from them. He sighed and said, "Okay, I guess we can move on then."

Bob said, "All right, but we can come back to this if we need to. I believe it is an important issue for you, Tony, and maybe for others in our group as well. I don't want you to think we haven't fully addressed it. Having said that as an introduction to today's topic, let me start by asking you: what are some characteristics of a good boss?"

The guys chimed in with several answers. Finally, Bob had to stop them.

"Well, those are some good examples of leadership characteristics. These are things that we admire in a good boss, someone who you desire to follow. Thanks for sharing those reflections. What I want to share with you this morning is how I decided to ask Jesus to be my boss.

"Biblically we use the term 'Lord,' but I believe we can use the term 'boss' as well. You hear people say that Jesus is my Lord and Savior. These are two 'titles,' if you will, that the Bible uses to speak of Jesus. Lord and Savior. We have talked about Jesus as our Savior—the one who paid the price for our sins. Now, we need to talk about him as our Lord, the one who directs our lives.

"Now, as Lord, Jesus is the ultimate authority over us. On the one hand, Jesus is kind of like the President of the United States. The President sets policy and direction for the country, but he doesn't call any of us personally and give us direction on a daily basis. He sits up there in Washington, and even though we can see and hear him through the media, there is no personal connection between us."

Bob continued, "But Jesus is also like our boss at our places of work who does give us daily direction. Jesus is both. As Lord, He governs the universe. As boss, He governs us. You see the promise that we have in Jesus is that He does want to be involved in our lives and that He does want to help us make decisions. His primary way of doing that is through His Word. And the challenge for us is to accept that He plays both roles and that we need to embrace Him as our boss as well as our Lord."

Bob took a sip of his coffee and then a deep breath. "While I was at college, John had presented me with the need to have Jesus as my Lord. For Jesus to be my 'boss.' But I never formally made that decision. Why? I had my own plan for my life. I was going to marry Susie. I was going to become a teacher. I would get my master's in counseling and become a school counselor. That was *my* plan. That was a good plan. And after all, who knew better than me what I should do with my life? Right?" Most of the guys gave an affirming nod of their heads.

"I continued to resist turning my life over to God and letting Him run the show. One major reason was this: I was certain if I truly let Jesus be my boss, He would turn me into a missionary and send Susie and me to some godforsaken land where I would never see the rest of my family or friends again. I would have to live in some bug-infested hut and eat grasshoppers. Our kids would suffer, and I would be miserable.

"How's that for a picture of God? Some bony-fingered troll who, once I made Him the CEO of my life, would turn on me and make me miserable. And compared to what my plan was, God's plan was something that I just didn't want to open myself up to. Does that make any sense to any of you?"

"Yes, it does, Pastor," said Calvin. "I too had a career path. I wanted to travel, and I didn't want anyone to get me off onto some other rabbit trail. To be honest, I'm not sure I even knew that God had a plan for my life, but if He did, I also would resist it if it didn't coincide with what I wanted to do myself."

"That's true," Walter chimed in. "As I moved up the ladder in business, I garnered more and more control, or so I thought. I was very reluctant to give up any of it. To anyone else. Even God."

Bob continued, "You guys understand what I was going through. I had been a Christian for a few years by this time. While I was thrilled to have Jesus as my Savior—what a great life insurance policy He had given me—my negative thoughts about having Jesus as Lord, as my boss, were at the center of my spiritual struggle. This struggle was keeping me from having peace with God. One day, John called me and invited me to join him at a Christian men's conference. I signed up for the conference that night. Little did I know the impact it would have on my life.

"Here is how that took place," he explained. "Within the first two days of the conference, John pinpointed the source of my struggle. Based on some of his own experiences, John suggested that I take an afternoon and get away from the conference, hike up the mountain and get some alone time with God. So that's what I did. After hiking for about an hour up the mountain, I found a quiet place and sat down with my Bible to meditate and listen.

"After a brief time of sharing with God my reticence to have Him as my boss, I decided to open my Bible. I read a few passages in the New Testament. I read a few passages in the Old Testament. In my past Bible-reading times, I had rarely been drawn to the Prophets. Their writings always seemed to me to be words that chastised the people of God—pretty negative stuff. Looking back on that time, there is no doubt in my mind that it was the Holy Spirit who took me to a passage in Jeremiah. It was in chapter 29 that the miracle happened. Jeremiah 29:11 to be exact."

Everyone started to open their Bibles. Bob stopped them. "You don't have to read this, just listen. This is what God said to the people of Israel. *'For I know the plans I have for you, says the Lord. Plans for welfare and not for evil to give you a future and a hope.'*

"I went through what I can only describe as an epiphany or revelation. It was almost a physical response. It truly was visceral. My heart was changed. God had a plan for my life that was good for me! That plan was designed by God to give me a future and a hope. I truly believe that if I had read that verse in the confines of my home office, it would not have affected me in the same way. But here, in the grandeur of the mountain, looking out at the vast beauty of creation, it was the perfect place to hear God's voice to me. 'Bob, just as I have created the beauty of these mountains and the beauty of this moment, I desire to create beauty in your life, and turning it over to Me will only bring wonder and joy into your inner being. Stop resisting Me.'

"Where did the thought *If I let God plan my life, I will be miserable* come from? Where did that picture of God come from? To this day, I honestly don't know where that 'stinkin' thinkin' came from. However, it may have been sheer arrogance on my part. I, I, I. It was all about *me*. I and I alone knew what is best for me."

Bob drew a deep breath and went on. "It was on that mountain, that afternoon, that I said something like: 'God, forgive me for wanting You to be my Savior but rejecting You as my Lord. Today I drive a stake in the ground, right here, right now, and I settle the issue that has been plaguing me for years. You will be my Lord. You will be my boss. I will go where You want me to go; do what You want me to do; and I will become the person You want me to become. Today You are my Savior *and* my Lord. I will trust You with the plan You have for my life. Amen.'"

Bob stopped speaking and picked up his coffee. He was clearly emotionally drained. Telling that story had impacted him deeply. Tony watched and tried to decide if it was real or not. He remembered that Bob said he had taught high school drama. *Is this merely a show? Is he doing it for effect?* Tony looked at Bob and decided that if it was a show, then Bob deserved an Oscar. He was so clearly ragged out.

Bob composed himself and continued. "Sorry about that. Didn't mean to get all emotional on you. Anyway, since that time, I have had to get on my knees and say those words many times. As a result of making that Lordship decision, God has fulfilled His promise to me. He has revealed to me His glorious plan for my life and that plan has given me a future and a hope.

Now, making that decision required a huge leap of faith on my part. It didn't come easy for me to live with Jesus in charge of my life. I didn't give up control easily. But once that decision was firmly made and the stake was driven into the ground, it has been a journey of joy following His lead."

"Wow, that's a powerful story, Pastor," said George. "I wish my conversion story was as good."

"George, each of our stories is powerful. God works with each of us as we need. I kind of have an inside seat when it comes to your story. Are you willing to share it?"

"I guess," he said tentatively. "It's just not very dramatic."

"I'm sure it was for you."

"Well, you know some of it. After all, you were responsible for it." Bob remained silent. George continued. "As you know, Pastor, I was in prison. I had done some bad things. This time it was because I had stolen a car and taken it across state lines. Actually, there were several cars. Prison is not a fun place, and you have to do anything you can to survive. I was just trying to keep to myself most of the time. Then you came and started your ministry there." He looked over at Bob.

"Go on," Bob encouraged him.

"Anyway, you would hold these discussion groups, a lot like this one, but I wasn't interested. I will never understand why you singled me out to ask me to come to them, though."

"Me neither." said Bob. "But let's assume it was one of those 'God things.' I just saw you in the corner of the yard trying to be alone and you looked like you needed a friend."

"I did." He turned to look at the other men. "Anyway, I started going to his group sessions, mostly so he would stop bugging me. We studied the Bible and talked about all sorts of things. None of it made much sense to me. It was just a way to kill time.

"Then one day, we were talking about the Scripture in Matthew 22:37. It's where the Sadducees ask Jesus what the greatest commandment is and He replies," George closed his eyes and repeated the verse from memory. Clearly, he wanted to get it right. He recited, *'Jesus replied: "Love the Lord your God with all your heart and with all your soul and with all your mind. This is the first and greatest commandment. And the second is like it: Love your neighbor as yourself."'*

When George finished quoting the Scripture, all the guys spontaneously applauded. George quoted that verse from memory and that was terrific.

Tony was impressed, thinking to himself, *It is one thing for a pastor to quote Scripture—that's expected. But it was great to see George take a shot at it and do it without missing a single word.* It was clear that this was a very important verse to George. Everyone was very focused on him now, and he blushed a little.

Then he continued, "That night in my cell, I couldn't stop thinking about it. The part that got to me was the 'love your neighbor as yourself.' The thing was, I didn't love myself very much then. I had made a mess of my life and was pretty disgusted with myself. But this verse spoke to me differently. If God thought I could love myself, He must love me too.

"Like you, Pastor, I think I had a revelation. I suddenly felt like God was real and a part of my life. I don't know that I 'put a stake in the ground' as you described it, Pastor, that night, but it was the first time in my life that I felt any real peace at all. In a very strange but real way, I just knew the Holy Spirit was in my heart, and I was at peace, even though I was in a very disturbing place. I certainly did not make Jesus the Lord of my life that night, but just having Him as my Savior was the greatest moment in my life up to that point. That night I slept through until morning, something I rarely did in prison."

George finished and looked around the room. Everyone had remained fully focused on him, hanging on his every word. Even Tony was fully engaged. George was mildly uncomfortable, so Bob stepped in.

"Thank you for sharing, George. That *is* a powerful story. I don't think you ever told it to me quite that way."

Bob looked at his watch and said, "Let me close us with kind of an ending to my story. As we have discussed before, the Bible is not just authoritative, it is trustworthy. After my little event on the mountain, I can say to you without hesitation that before I came down from the mountain, I had made the decision to do whatever God wanted me to do. I wouldn't fight Him anymore for control of my life. I would continue to trust Him to guide me—that was His responsibility. My responsibility would be to go where He wanted me to go and do what He wanted me to do and become who He wanted me to become. I confess to you, however, I haven't always been perfect in terms of keeping my word on all of this. But if God had a plan for me and it was a good one, why not see where it took me? And ultimately, of course, He led me here, to this church.

"That is the result of my decision many years ago. And I would invite you all to do the same. I can promise you only good things will come from that decision. I believe peace with God will continue to be a struggle for you until you surrender control of your life to Him."

He took a deep breath and waited. No one spoke. So Bob closed with a short prayer and said, "Okay then, again, thanks to James and Judy for their wonderful hospitality this morning. Who wants to host the next meeting?"

Tony raised his hand. "We'll do it."

"Wonderful," said Bob. "Please send everyone directions. Oh, of course, you all have been there for the birthday party. Great, then we will see each other next week."

Tony picked up his things and walked over to Dave. "You were awfully quiet this morning, Dave. What's up?"

Dave said, "I don't know. I thought I had a really good handle on my faith. But I'm learning some new things here. I guess I'm just taking it all in. What about you? You getting anything out of this?"

"I am learning some things about the doctrine. Not sure I buy into all or any of it, though. But one thing is certain."

"What's that?"

"You guys have a lot of passion about all of this."

CHAPTER 32

When he got to work the next Friday, his boss, Jerry called him into the office. Jerry started very seriously. "Tony, we have a problem with the Sievers' project."

"What's that, Jerry? I'm not aware of any issues."

"You wouldn't be. You see, the client called corporate last night."

Tony was alarmed. "Are they unhappy with my work?"

"N-no, nothing like that."

"Then why did they call corporate? They should have called me."

"Yes, they should have, and they know that. But, they, well, they want to make a change."

Tony looked panicked.

"No, no. Not with you. They are very happy to work with you. But something has come up. It seems as though one of their investors just pulled out."

"Oh, boy."

Jerry put his hands up to calm Tony. "It's not as bad as it sounds. It just means that we have to make a design change. A major design change."

"Okay?"

Jerry took a deep breath. "We are going to have to take two stories off of the building."

"What? That means a new structural analysis. Not to mention the permitting implications."

"Yes, I know."

"Okay, when do they need this? It will impact the schedule by at least two weeks."

"Yeah. That's the thing. They want to maintain the schedule. That's why they went directly to corporate. To put the pressure on us."

Tony sat back and whistled. "I see. And you want me to manage all of this."

"That's right Tony. This is a pain, I know. But it is another opportunity for you to demonstrate to corporate just how good you are."

"It will mean a lot of overtime."

"Sure. Sure."

"Starting with this weekend. I will have to get the team to come in on both Saturday and Sunday."

"I know. Do what you have to do."

Tony stood up. "Okay, boss. You can count on me."

He walked back to his cubicle and started to look at the project schedule. He looked at his calendar and suddenly remembered that he had a Life Group meeting on Saturday morning. He was just beginning to get into those, and they were important. After all, he was doing it for his kids. And for Beth. But this was important too. It was his career after all. What was he going to do? He put that notion aside and went back to working on the project schedule and notifying the team of the change.

That evening at dinner, Tony broached the subject with Beth. "Today we got a change order on the Sievers' project."

"Oh," she said as she was trying to stuff creamed spinach into Joey's mouth.

"Yeah, they want to remove a couple of floors 'cause they lost an investor."

"I gather that's a big deal?"

Tony was busy wiping Christina's face where she had smeared food all over it. "It is. It will require a bunch of redesigns. And they don't want this change to affect the schedule."

"Sounds like lots of fun," she said tongue-in-cheek.

"Well, the bad part is that I, in fact, the whole team, will have to put in a bunch of overtime."

"I see. Too bad you don't get paid overtime."

"True, but that's not why I brought it up. There are two issues. First, I will have to be at the office, and you will be stuck with the kids alone."

"I figured. How long with this go on?"

"Only a week or two. Christina, do *not* throw that fruit at your brother!" He grabbed the food out of her hand. "See what I mean?"

"Yes. I figured," she said, a little annoyed now. "So, what was the second issue?"

"It's just this, I will have to work this weekend for sure."

"Uh-huh?"

"Well, I have Life Group on Saturday mornings. And I will have to miss it. Do you think that will be a problem? I mean I'm just getting to know these guys, and I am kind of getting into it. I don't want to let Bob and the other guys down."

"Tony, you're worried about the Life Group more than about me and the kids?"

Tony looked at her. "No, of course not! I mean I could go to the meeting and get to work a little later than everyone else. Or maybe I could stay at home and go in later?"

"Yes, you could do either."

"So what do *you* think I should I do?" he said sarcastically.

Beth stopped feeding Joey and looked across the table. "Tony Hunter, I am not your mother. Nor am I your conscience. This is something you will have to figure out on your own. What is most important to you, that's the issue."

She turned to Joey. "Joey, this spinach is not a shampoo. Stop rubbing it in your hair!" She commenced cleaning his head with a napkin.

She continued to Tony, "I will make do, but you will owe me. Now, I think these kids are done eating. Let's get them cleaned up." She got up and went to get a damp washcloth. Tony picked Christina up to take her to the bathroom.

"I guess I better call Bob and let him know I won't be there and he will have to have one of the other guys host the group since I had volunteered our home for this coming Saturday. Work is more important than all this Bible study stuff. I can always catch up with everybody else. And I will make this up to you, Beth. I promise!" Even as he said it to himself, he had an uneasy feeling about it all. But in the end, he chose his work.

CHAPTER 33

By now Tony and Beth had settled into a very workable pattern for their Saturday mornings. Beth got up early to read her Bible and do her devotions. Tony began his day by getting breakfast for the twins, which allowed Beth to finish her devotions before he left to meet with the guys.

Tony would come bounding in the door after returning from his Life Group and the kids, who were walking now, would hear his car entering the garage and they would run or crawl to the door, expecting him to walk through it any moment. When he did, each of the munchkins would grab one of his legs and sit on his shoes, and he would walk them into the living room where Beth would be sitting. They would get up and reach their hands high in the air, and he would lift them in his arms, squeeze them as tightly as was wise, and start kissing their cheeks until they begged him to put them down, all the while giggling and squirming.

But this Saturday was different. Tony had decided to skip the Life Group and work from home in the morning on the Sievers' project, then go into the office around noon. Beth had grudgingly agreed to take care of the kids alone after exacting a promise from Tony that they would do something fun after his work crisis was all over. Tony thanked her, kissed her, and went into the office and closed the door.

At around 11:00 AM, there was a knock on the front door. Beth went to the door and saw Calvin standing there.

"Hi, Beth. Would Tony be here, and if so, would it be okay for me to speak with him briefly?" Calvin asked.

"Why, hello, Calvin. Won't you come in?"

Calvin stepped into the front hall. Beth said, "Tony is working in the office. Let me see if he is available." She showed Calvin into the living room and went to the office.

She poked her head in and said, "Calvin Lowe is here. Can you speak to him?"

Tony stood up and said, "Oh, boy. I hope he isn't going to chide me for missing the meeting this morning." He looked at his watch. "I need to get to the office soon, so I hope this won't take long. Well, okay, send him in."

Beth went and got Calvin and showed him into the office and closed the door.

"Hello, Calvin," said Tony. "Didn't we just see each other last week? You know, I explained to Bob why I couldn't be at the meeting today."

"Hey, Tony, thanks for seeing me. Oh, yes, he said you had to work, but I took a chance that you might be working from home. So I'll try to make this brief. It's just that after this morning's meeting, I, well, it just seemed like I needed to talk to you today."

"Oh? What happened at the meeting?"

"It's not that anything happened, really. It was just the topic."

"I see," as he waited for Calvin to continue, then motioned for him to sit down.

They both sat and Calvin continued. "Yeah. It was about eternal versus temporal values."

"Okay?"

"I guess the details are not important now," Calvin began, "but the discussion prompted me to come to see you. I am in a bit of a predicament and I am hoping you can help me. I will try to make this long story short. A neighbor asked me to help him in serving lunch at the soup kitchen downtown a couple of weeks ago. I said I would be willing to help, so I spent a couple of hours there dishing up food. I had never been there before. Have you ever served a meal at the Bread of Life soup kitchen?"

"No, Calvin, I haven't ever been there."

"Well as I said, neither had I. Do you know they serve lunch to about two hundred and fifty persons every single day? Three hundred and sixty-five days a year? It's incredible."

Tony interrupted. "That is a lot of people. So how can I help? You didn't commit to doing that every Wednesday, did you?"

"No, no, Tony. Trust me, I'm not that committed to people I don't even know. But let me get to the point. Lots of these people are homeless, and people give bikes to the Bread of Life ministry, that's the name of the place, so the homeless can get around town. Most of them live in the woods on Washington Street, about two miles from the soup kitchen. They walk those two miles, rain or shine. But if they get a bike, it changes their whole world.

"Now, the bikes that are donated rarely work. They all need some kind of repair before someone can use them. And that's where I come into the picture. Again, I had never been there before, but when I went to the room to get a bike for one of the people, I was amazed at how many bikes there were in that room. So I agreed to take two of them home and bring them back on Monday, if possible. Now, I know that you are good at mechanical things, and I was hoping you might be willing to do whatever needs to be done to one of them and I would do the other one. I have a boy's bike and a girl's bike, and you could pick whichever one you wanted. I impulsively grabbed two and now I am stuck with them. What do you think?"

Tony thought to himself, *Calvin, you don't want to know what I think!* But he responded more politely.

"Calvin, thank you for thinking of me but I am afraid I am going to have to decline. I am buried with stuff, as you can see," he pointed to the pile of papers on his desk. "I am working on a project from work, and I still need to go into the office today and probably do some more tomorrow. I likely won't even make it to church. It's all I can do to free up Saturday mornings for Group, and even that is getting hard for me. So I am sorry, but I can't help."

Calvin was clearly disappointed. "Uh, okay, Tony. No problem. I just thought I would ask. Have a good rest of the day and I hope you get your project done tomorrow."

"Thanks, Calvin, but that's not likely." Tony showed Calvin to the door. Beth came out and asked Tony what Calvin wanted, and he said he would tell her later, as he needed to get back to work.

Having to work on the Sievers' project proved to be a blessing, Tony thought to himself. He had used it as his excuse for Calvin's request, but in truth, his declining had nothing to do with the project. Tony might do a lot of things to help people, but helping the homeless was not on his list. Tony had always been convinced that homeless people were simply lazy. The want ads were full of jobs for people with limited skills, and there was no reason for able-bodied people to need a soup kitchen. In fact, soup kitchens were part of the problem. They were enabling lazy people to get by, and that wasn't helping them at all. So no, he didn't see himself caving into Calvin's request, ever.

CHAPTER 34

Dave and Sarah seemed nervous. Tony and Beth had always enjoyed spending time with them, and the dinner they had prepared that evening had been over and above their usual high standards. It was almost as if they were trying to impress Tony and Beth. Tony was perplexed. Finally, over a dessert of cherries jubilee, he could stand it no longer.

"Okay, what's with you guys tonight?"

"Whatever do you mean, Tony?" Sarah said innocently.

"You guys have been on pins and needles all night. Something is up."

Beth chimed in, "It's true. You guys do seem a little off tonight. Is there something wrong?"

Dave and Sarah looked at each other. Then back at them. Then back at each other.

Dave turned to them and said, "Yeah, there is something. Not something wrong. Just something that we wanted to talk to you both about."

"Okay, what is it then?" Tony said.

Dave looked at Sarah and said, "You want to do it or me?"

Sarah looked a little sheepish, "Will you, please?"

Dave took a deep breath and said, "Okay." He turned back to Tony and Beth. "So here's the thing. Sarah is pregnant!"

Beth jumped up. "Oh, my, that is wonderful!" She ran around the table to hug Sarah. "You all have been trying for so long." She took a step back. "Is there a problem? I mean this is great news, so why the hesitation?"

"No, no problems. Everything is fine," Sarah said.

"So what are you guys nervous about?" Tony asked.

"It's this,'" Dave began. "We want the two of you to be the godparents."

"Oh, that is wonderful, too," exclaimed Beth. "Isn't that wonderful, Tony?"

Everyone looked at Tony. He was not smiling. Dave said, "Look, Tony, you don't have to agree if you don't want to."

Beth interjected, "Why wouldn't we accept, Dave? It's a great honor. Right, Tony?" She looked at him and then at Dave. They were looking at each other very intently.

Dave said, "Tony, I will understand if you say no."

Beth said, "Understand what? Will someone please explain why you are all bound up about this?"

Dave looked at Beth then back to Tony. Tony was deep in thought. Dave said, "Tony, I know that you take this very seriously. We have talked about this before. And we didn't ask you to be the godparent of Katie because you didn't feel like you could do the job."

"Right, I remember when you asked me. I told you then that I was not the right guy for this," said Tony.

Beth was confused. "The job? What job?"

Sarah turned to Beth, "The job of helping us bring up a godchild in the faith."

Beth was taken aback, "Oh!"

Tony said, "Right. And as much as I love you guys, and Katie, I'm still not the right man for that job. Beth can do it, but not me."

Dave leaned over the table to look directly into Tony's eyes. "We think differently."

"Oh? What has changed? I'm still not *a believer.*"

"Perhaps," said Dave. "But I, we, have seen a change in you these last several months."

"Uh-huh. Oh, you mean because I'm part of your Life Group?"

"Our Life Group. And yes. You have committed to learning about the faith. You are committed to teaching it to your children. I know you would have that same commitment with our child, our children. And, Tony, when you commit to something, you follow through."

"And perhaps, even more importantly," Sarah said, "We love you and know you love us. And will love our child, children that same way."

Beth had now sat down next to Tony and was holding his hand. "They're right, you know."

Tony looked at all three of them in turn. "You think that I'm going to convert, don't you?"

"I have prayed that you will. We all have," said Dave. "But even if you don't, you will be the best godfather that I can imagine. I truly believe that. And we both want you to be a part of our family in that way."

"Why were you so nervous to ask me?"

Sarah said, "Because we did not want to pressure you. We are not saying that we expect you to *convert,* as you put it. You will come to God in your own way and own time. Either way, we wanted to link our families even closer, because we love you, both of you." Sarah reached out her hand to Beth. They all looked at Tony.

"Let me get this straight," Tony said very carefully, "you are both willing to have me, a non-believer, be responsible for helping teach your child about God?"

"Yep," responded Dave. "And to be in his or her life in whatever way that you choose to be. And yes, if you teach him or her with the same commitment that I know you will have for your kids, they will be well served. Besides," he chuckled, "we'll still be around to correct the mistakes you make."

"Oh, so now I'm going to make mistakes, am I?" Tony said with a smile.

"Kidding, just kidding. Look, we know this is a big decision for you, so take some time and think it over, okay?"

Tony paused for a moment. *What's different?* he thought to himself. Somehow this felt different.

He wasn't quite sure how or why, but suddenly he found himself saying, almost as if someone else was talking, "No, I don't need to think about it." He reached over to grab Beth's hand. "We would be honored to be your child's godparents."

Beth almost squealed in delight. "Oh, yes. Yes. We would!" She jumped up, as did Sarah and they hugged each other.

Dave jumped up as well, "This is wonderful! Let me get us all a drink to seal the deal." He looked over at Sarah, "Sorry, dear, it's non-alcoholic for you." He went into the kitchen along with Beth and Sarah, leaving Tony to sit alone at the table. He looked down at his dessert and played with his fork.

What have I done? he thought. *Is this the right thing? It feels right yet seems wrong.* He looked up at the ceiling and thought, *Maybe Dad is right, I'm getting brainwashed. But if I am, I'm not feeling bad about it.*

He got up and followed the others into the kitchen.

CHAPTER 35

Tony felt very comfortable here in Dave and Sarah's house. After all, he spent a lot of time here. He even showed up first so he could help them get ready for the meeting. But they had it well in hand. Even so, Dave seemed more nervous than usual.

Tony asked, "What's up with you this morning, Dave? You have hosted lots of things here and, as usual, you appear to have all the i's dotted and the t's crossed."

"It's not that, Tony. It's the topic."

"Oh?"

"Yeah, it's on stewardship."

"What's that?"

"It's about money."

"Oh, crap! Are you afraid I'm going to lose it?" asked Tony.

"Something like that."

"Well, not to worry, I think I can be civil. Besides, I think Bob already knows how I feel about that. I won't say anything that will surprise him, or you."

"Good," Dave responded. He went about making the coffee, and Tony put out the cups and dishes. Then the guys started arriving and there was no more time to talk.

When Bob called the men together after breakfast, he started with, "Thanks to Dave and Sarah. That was quite a spread."

Tony spoke up, "Hey what about me? I helped!" Tony loved making the guys laugh.

"Of course. Thank you, Tony." Bob bowed deeply in his direction. Dave just rolled his eyes.

Then Bob turned to the group. "All right, we have come to the place where I hoped we would be, the last of the decisions that are essential if we want to have peace with God. This morning's focus is very much related to last week's discussion, but it is the most radical of the decisions that we must wrestle with. Don't say I didn't warn you. And before I forget, Tony, we missed you at our last Life Group. It's good to have you with us this morning."

"Remember that last week I challenged you to make another crucial decision to live with an eternal value system. To summarize our discussion, that means we are not so wrapped up in the things of this world as we are dedicated to the things of God's kingdom. There are only two things that will last forever: God's Word and people. In reality, the key to living with an eternal value system boils down to investing time in God's Word and investing in people. And that leads right into the decision I want to discuss with you this morning. We each need to decide to live our lives as stewards, or trustees of *God's resources* rather than as owners of *our own resources*.

"Let me try to explain by first focusing on the concept of ownership," he continued. "To do so, I want to start with another one of Jesus' parables which reveals how owners feel about their resources.

"In the Parable of the Vineyard, recorded in Matthew 20:1–16, a landowner chooses to hire workers for his vineyard. He hires some early in the day and they agree to work all day in the vineyard for one denarius.

"Then a few hours later, he hires some more workers and tells them he will pay them what is right. Two more times in the day, the landlord hires more workers.

"At the end of the day, the landowner tells his foreman to call the workers together and pay them. So the foreman begins by paying the workers who were hired last, the ones who worked the fewest number of hours. He gives them one denarius.

"The workers who were hired early in the morning and who had worked significantly more hours than the ones who were just paid thought to themselves, *Since the ones hired last are getting one denarius for their work, certainly we who were hired first and worked the longest will get more than one denarius.* But that is not what happened.

"Those who were hired first also got one denarius just as the landowner said. So they complained to the landowner that he wasn't being fair, and this was his response, '*Friend, I am not being unfair to you. Didn't you agree to work for a denarius? Take your pay and go. I want to give the man who was hired last the same as I gave you. Don't I have the right to do what I want with my own money? Or are you envious because I am generous?*'"

Bob then said, "Let me stop here. What do you think of the owners' statement, 'Don't I have the right to do what I want with my own money?'"

Walter spoke up first. "Honestly, I think what the owner did stinks. The workers have a valid point. They worked longer than the others. They should get paid more for their efforts."

"I agree," said Calvin. "A fair day's wage for a fair day's work. That's assuming, of course, that the workers he hired in the morning actually worked all day. I mean, that they didn't slack off."

"On the other hand," mused James, "they did have an agreement when they started. Did the landowner make the same agreement with all the others? The landowner apparently doesn't tell them how much he is going to pay them when he hires them. It does seem a bit unfair, though."

Bob said, "Those are all valid points. The point I want to focus on, however, is what the landowner's perspective was because he *was* the owner. Remember, he said to the workers, 'Don't I have the right to do what I want with my own money?'" Bob paused for effect. "Well, doesn't he?" He looked around the room. There were some general head nodding. "I would certainly say he does," Bob continued. "And that is why church members deplore sermons that address the topic of money from a biblical point of view."

Tony spoke up. "You lost me there, Bob," he said.

"You see, most folks believe they own what money they have, and retain the right to use it any way they want. So when I share with them they need to develop the habit of being generous with their money, if they could, they would shout out at me, during my stewardship sermons, 'Hold on a minute. Who are you to tell me what to do with *my money*, Mr. Preacher man?' *And they are exactly right.* I have no business telling anyone, not the least of which are my church members, what they should do with their money."

"You're talking in circles here, Bob," Tony responded.

"Ah, let me finish. Unless . . . unless the money they have is actually *not* theirs. What if the money they have, in fact, belongs to someone else?"

"Like who? They earned it. They own it," Tony said emphatically.

"Like God. If it is God's money, then, according to the parable we looked at, God has every right to tell us what to do with His money. It all boils down to this. The money you have in your wallet. The money you have in your bank. The money you have in your 401K. Whose money is it anyway?"

Tony sat back and thought, *Okay, here it is, finally. Dad was right. This whole thing has always been about money. My money. They just want my money. Hah, they were starting to suck me in.*

Bob continued, "Before I address that penetrating question, let me ask you a more important question. If I give you my opinion, and it doesn't agree with your opinion, are you bound to live your life based on mine? 'Heck no,' you might say. But, and this is huge, if you have declared that God's Word will be authoritative in your life; and if you have said God would be the boss of your life; and if you believe that the boss has the right to give you directions that you have the responsibility to follow; then what do you plan to do when you discover that the Bible says everything you have belongs to God? That He is the owner and you are the trustee, or steward, of His resources? But before you answer, let's take a look at what God's Word says about ownership and stewardship. Who would be willing to look up Psalm 24:1, 2?"

Calvin raised his hand.

As Bob was dishing out Scripture references, Tony thought *I don't care what the verses say about money. I would have to be crazy to think the money I make, and the money Beth makes is actually God's. No Bible verse is going to change that.*

"And who would be willing to look up Leviticus 25:23? You might need to use your index to find this one." James took this verse.

"Would one of you look up Psalm 50:10–12?" He looked at Tony, but Tony had closed his Bible and was sitting back in his chair. He was clearly disengaging, so Bob didn't press him. George raised his hand and Bob thanked him.

"Dave, would you look up Deuteronomy 8:17–18. Thanks." After pausing until it looked like everyone had found the passage assigned to them, Bob continued.

"Calvin, let's hear Psalm 24:1." Calvin read, *"'The earth is the Lord's and all it contains, the world and those who dwell in it, for He has founded it upon the seas and established it upon the rivers.'"*

"James, please read the Leviticus passage?"

James nodded his head, *"The land, moreover, shall not be sold permanently, for the land is Mine."*

"George, what does Psalm 50:10–12 say?"

George read, *"'For every beast of the forest is Mine, the cattle on a thousand hills. I know every bird of the mountains, and everything that moves in the field is Mine. If I were hungry, I would not tell you; for the world is Mine and all it contains.'"*

"So, guys," Bob asked, "What is there that God doesn't own according to the Bible?"

Tony piped up, "It seems like God thinks He owns everything. But I just can't agree. I worked pretty damn hard to get where I am today and I'm not buying this stuff that God owns my house. If that's the case, let Him cut the lawn and pay the mortgage."

With that, Tony sat back in his chair and folded his arms across his chest. Everyone could see the flames coming out of his ears. And it seemed he spoke for most, if not all, the guys sitting around the table. Seemed to them that Pastor Bob had crossed the line from teaching to meddling.

Bob sat for a minute before responding to Tony's anger. To be honest, it wouldn't have surprised Bob if Tony had gotten up and headed for home. Bob had not only touched a nerve, he had stomped on it.

Bob continued a bit more gently, "I understand how radical this is, Tony. But all I ask is that you let what the Bible says about ownership and stewardship be put on the table. Then we will all have a chance to hear what each of us thinks about it and listen to what we might be feeling about this."

Tony shrugged his shoulders and nodded assent. He wanted to say, *Do I have a choice?* but he kept his lips sealed, partly so he wouldn't embarrass Dave any more than he already had.

Bob continued, "Dave, would you please read the Deuteronomy passage?"

Dave looked down at his Bible, trying not to catch Tony's eyes, and started to read. *"Beware lest you say in your heart, 'My power and the might of my hand have gained me this wealth.' And you shall remember the Lord your God, for it is He who gives you the power to get wealth that He may establish His covenant which He swore to your fathers, as it is this day."*

When Dave had finished, he put his Bible down and looked at Bob, again trying to avoid Tony's gaze.

"What do you think the author of Deuteronomy is saying to us in this passage?" Bob asked.

There was a pretty long period with no one wanting to break the silence. The answer to Tony's tirade was contained in these verses, but no one was willing to say anything. After a time, Bob spoke up.

"The author of Deuteronomy fully comprehends the thoughts and feelings that Tony expressed. For those of us who have worked all our lives and have achieved a modicum of financial stability, it can be very offensive to say we don't own what we possess.

"But these two verses stand out in Deuteronomy. I ask you to think about them and see if they don't ring true. Here is how I interpret them. Sure, I, like all of you, have worked hard over many years to have what I have. No disagreement here. But without God making a path for me, opening doors for me, keeping me in good health, and giving me the ability to do what I do, my life would have taken a very different turn. And the resources I currently have would probably be significantly less."

He paused and looked around the room. There was still no response from the group.

"Let me explain what I mean by telling you something else about me. When I was in fifth grade, I was one hundred percent illiterate. I could not read 'Run, Spot, run.' In middle school, my parents moved to an incredible school district in the suburbs and I took a special reading class every day through my senior year in high school. In essence, I was a 'special ed' kid, with all the stigma that comes with that.

"If we had never moved to the suburbs," Bob continued, "I probably would never have learned to read. If I had never learned to read, I never would be a pastor today. What I choose to believe is that because God had a plan for me and it was based on my ability to succeed in school, it was God who led my parents to move and thus, turn me from an illiterate into a person who could read. Would my parents say it was God who caused them to move? No, absolutely not. But I believe it was God who was behind the move. So it was God who was the one allowing me to become the man I am, one who is able to read, work, and earn money.

Bob stopped talking and sat waiting for the others to comment. He knew he had opened a can of worms, but he was prepared for the backlash.

Walter started it, "You know, I've heard most of this before. And it is always a difficult discussion at best. But the context of what we have been discussing over the last several weeks seems to have it sit differently with me."

"How so?" asked Bob.

"Well, the context of the authority of the Bible makes a difference. Oh, I've also heard all that before, but I've been thinking a lot about it since we discussed it. And what I think is different, at least for me, is this idea that I might get different messages from reading the Bible, at different times in my life. That the Bible may speak to me differently depending on my needs or circumstances."

"How does that make it different for you?" George asked.

"It's just this. If that is true, then God really is speaking to me directly through the Word. I don't necessarily need someone like a priest or pastor. No offense intended, Bob."

Bob raised his hand, "None taken."

"It means that I need to interpret the message each time I read it as if I'm listening to God. And when you all read those last verses, it rang differently to me than it ever has before. And more importantly, the idea that God owns my stuff doesn't offend as much as it did before."

"You know," Calvin said, almost to himself, "I had a job in a bank once. I was just a security guard, but I remember going into the vault and thinking, *All that money, and none of it is mine. I've got to make sure that it is safe for the people who do own it. Not like what happened to my father's money.* That's kind of like this, isn't it?"

Tony looked around at the group. *They are actually buying this crap*, he thought. Bob looked over at him, and even though he knew it was fraught with danger, he asked, "Tony, do you have something you would like to share?"

Tony didn't want to make a scene, but Bob had opened the door. So he walked through it.

"I guess so, Bob. I've been coming to these sessions for weeks now. And by and large, I have enjoyed them. I have learned some things and I have even shared some things. But to be quite honest, this is what I had feared all along would happen."

"You feared what would happen?" Bob asked.

"That you would ask me for money. I'm kind of disappointed, Bob. I had thought, well hoped, it wouldn't go that way."

"I'm sorry you feel betrayed, Tony, but in response, let me ask you this; have I asked you for money?"

"What? Well, isn't that what you are doing? Asking me to give you, or the church, my money? Because it all supposedly belongs to God?"

"No, I'm not. I am not asking you to give one penny to me or the church."

Tony sat there with his mouth open. He didn't have a response. He looked around the room to get help from someone else, but they all seemed confused as well.

Bob then said, "Let me say it again. Tony, I am not asking you to give one penny to me or the church. Do I need to make it any clearer?"

Tony responded, "If you're not asking for money, then what are you doing, exactly?"

"I am merely pointing out that if you, or anyone, understands and accepts that the Bible is God's Word and it has authority over their lives, it clearly states that everything—money, possessions, land, you name it—is God's. We merely manage it for Him. And given that, we should look to Him for direction on how He wants us to manage it. If that means that God leads us to give some of it to the church, so be it. If it means that God is asking you to support a homeless ministry, or the Salvation Army, or a missionary that you know, or a relative that has fallen on hard times, that you be faithful to do that. God is the owner, not me. All I'm saying is that you let God direct you as to how *He* wants you to manage *His* money. We must look for that direction and follow it when we receive it.

"It goes back to what we talked about on the retreat—receiving

God's grace, which leads us to be grateful, which leads us to be generous. The 3 G's. The only new thing I have proposed here is that what we are being generous with is God's and not ours."

He continued, "But, Tony, let me be bold here. The reason you are having difficulty with this is you have not settled the issue that the Bible has authority in your life. And therefore, you will just pick and choose what you want to believe and apply. As soon as you don't like what the Bible says, you reject it. And you, my friend, are like 90% of people in the church. And that is why pastors often do not teach what the Bible says on this issue—they value harmony more than truth."

Tony looked at him for a long time. "So you don't want my money, then?" he asked.

"What I am saying is, I want you to do what God leads you to do with the money He entrusts to you. If God leads you to support our church, then I want you to be faithful to do that. If He leads to give it somewhere else, then I want you to do that."

Tony sat there, dumbfounded. There was something different here. Tony couldn't quite grasp what it was, but despite his initial resistance, Bob's response to Tony's accusation disarmed him. For the first time in his life, he seemed willing to listen. He wasn't buying into all of this, but he was more open to hear the arguments.

James interrupted the discussion between Bob and Tony. "Bob," James said, "I have a question about giving that isn't related to whose money it is, ours or God's. It is related to the amount of money that should be given. Do we have time to deal with this?"

Bob looked at his watch and then said, "James, it looks like we have about fifteen minutes left. Is that okay, guys?" Everyone seemed very thankful to James for diverting the discussion away from Tony, so all were nodding, almost in perfect unison.

"Okay," said James, "let me be clear. I believe that one of the reasons why people don't like sermons on giving is that so many pastors, who are generally very grace-centered and not usually legalistic on most issues, seem to morph into legalistic Pharisees when it comes to the tithe. These pastors, when they encounter people who don't quite meet the moral standards of the Bible, extend love to them as they are, with no problem. But when it comes to giving money, these same pastors dig their heels in and become almost tyrannical with those same people when they don't give the magical number of 10 percent."

He paused for a moment and looked directly at Bob. "Bob, please don't take offense at this, but I have left church on some stewardship Sundays believing you are very legalistic about this ten percent tithing thing and frankly, it is like you become someone else on those Sundays. Those of us who love you dearly are just happy to get past the 'Stewardship Tithe Sledgehammer Sunday Bob.'

"Having said that," James continued, "let me say what I have said before about this issue. In fact, I think I presented some of these ideas on the mission trip: the idea that statistically speaking, ten percent of anything is considered significant. Therefore, I believe that God is more interested in a *significant* amount of giving than some legalistic amount that is rooted in a very different culture and a very different time than we are living in today. I think that's what God was, uh, *is* telling us in the Scripture.

"But how much is a significant gift? I define a 'significant level' as one that causes a person to have to make some sacrifices to attain that level of giving. That's what 'significance' means to me."

James paused for a moment, thinking that Bob or one of the guys would jump in. When no one did, James continued. "Forgive me for going on, but let me wrap up my thoughts. For some people, giving two or three percent of their income to kingdom work is absolutely significant for them. For these folks, listening to a sermon where you or any other pastor berates them for not giving ten percent only leaves them feeling judged and inferior.

"For others, their giving wouldn't be called significant until they were giving beyond the 10 percent. Ten percent is nowhere near a significant level of giving for them. And quite frankly, sermons that let them off the hook are doing them a disservice. Far more would be accomplished if these affluent followers of Christ were giving at a truly significant level, significant for them, that is. Bob, I hope that I haven't offended you, but I would like to hear what your thoughts might be on this issue now that I have opened up Pandora's box."

Wow, thought Tony. *Where the hell did this James come from? I can't wait to see how Bob tries to squirm out of this one.*

Bob responded to James' mini-sermon with grace, reflective of his class and character. He leaned forward in his chair and looked around at the group. "James, you certainly have caused me to want to pause and consider everything you have said. I don't think of myself as being one of those pastors who hangs on to some legalistic doctrine like a pit bull with a steak bone. However, I always welcome challenges that come to me from sincere, grace-centered people like you. Even though my head and my feelings might not be in the same place right now, let me try to respond to your ideas and questions as best I can."

Bob took a deep breath, sipped his coffee, and then began to speak. "Let me start with the issue of tithing. Here is what I believe deeply about this practice. The principle behind tithing is giving God the first portion of your income and then managing to live on the remaining portion. That idea of what we call the 'first fruits' is very key to all of this. It's not the leftovers at the end of the month that you give to God; it's the first and best of what you have.

"Regarding the amount, let's look at this from Scripture. The first time we see this sort of thing is in Genesis. Abraham, after a battle, comes to the King of Salem, Melchizedek, who was also a priest connected with Jerusalem. Melchizedek blesses Abraham and in return, Abraham gives him a gift, *one-tenth of everything he had taken away from the battle.*"

Bob continued, "Now, the first time we see the term 'tithe' used in the Bible is in Leviticus Chapter 27 31–33, where God tells us that the tithe represents a tenth of what the Lord has entrusted to us.

"Therefore, we see that the word 'tithe' in the Bible means ten percent. That is the definition of the word. In that sense, you can't say the word 'tithe' and not mean ten percent because that is what the word *tithe* means. So I am inclined to be legalistic about a tithe being ten percent. But the issue you raise about being legalistic about the practice of tithing is very much open to debate and discussion. James, I like the idea of encouraging people to give at a significant level and letting them determine what that means for them."

He paused for a moment and seemed to gather himself. "And I have to admit that my initial knee-jerk reaction to what you said about my stewardship sermons, was to say, 'Hold on, here, James, *I'm* not legalistic. I'm *grace-centered!!!*' However, upon more somber reflection, albeit a short reflection, I am deeply thankful to you for raising this issue with me. I promise you that I will take a good look at what I say and how I say it from now on when it comes to challenging people in their giving. I will also pray that those who have sat through my teaching on stewardship and who were offended or hurt, feeling judged or inferior, that they will be able to forgive me for any way that I may have wounded them."

He sat back and looked around the room. There was a general relaxing of body tensions, and for that, Bob was grateful. "Guys, this has been exceptionally good for me, in spite of it being a bit difficult. I hope there is something in our discussion that has been helpful to you as well."

Tony wasn't sure that anything that was said about the issue of stewardship versus ownership was very helpful to him. But the biggest takeaway for Tony was his appreciation for the way this group of men challenged each other without giving the slightest impression that they were upset with each other. James had given Bob a pretty good shot to the midsection, and Tony was pretty sure that hurt. However, Bob had not gone on the defensive. He liked that about Bob.

Bob looked at his watch. "Wow, it looks like we have gone over our time. I apologize. But I do have a question for all of you. When we started, I said I wanted to go through several critical decisions, and we have done that. The question is, do you all still want to continue to meet and continue to discuss what it means to live the Christian life in today's world?"

"What would we do, Bob?" Tony asked.

"Well, that would be up to us, but we can continue to do Bible study. We can do specific books, or we can simply start at Genesis and work our way through, all the way to maps." That drew a welcomed chuckle from all present.

Much to Bob's surprise, Tony said, "I would like to do that, start from the beginning. I said when I started with you all that I am willing to do this so I can make sure my kids know what the church teaches, so I would like to continue."

Everyone else nodded in agreement. Bob was pleased. "Well, then, we just need a place to meet next week." Tony raised his hand to volunteer since the week he and Beth were supposed to host, Tony had chosen to go into work instead.

"James, would you close us in prayer this morning?" Bob asked.

James said a short prayer and then Bob said, "All right, then. See you guys tomorrow at worship."

They all got up and brought their dishes into the kitchen. Bob touched Tony's arm and said, "I hope that I didn't make you too uncomfortable, Tony."

"No, I hope I didn't come across as too angry."

"No, I understand, these are very hard concepts."

"Yes, they are, Bob. Very hard indeed." He paused and looked Bob directly in the eyes. "But I will tell you this: you have given me a lot to ponder."

"As have you all for me," replied Bob.

CHAPTER 36

C harley's was full that night. Beth, Tony, Sarah, and Dave were in their favorite booth. They had just ordered their food and were enjoying their drinks. Dave proposed a toast, "To us, the best blended family in town." They all clinked their glasses and drank.

"So how is the morning sickness?" Tony asked Sarah.

"Tolerable. It was worse the first time. But no fun in any case. It should be over soon, I hope."

"Let's hope there are no complications," offered Tony.

"Let's hope you are right, Tony," she responded. There was silence for a few moments, then Sarah asked, "How is it going in the Life Group? Are you getting all you need to teach our son the Word?" She giggled a little. Tony gave her a nasty look. "Oops, sorry, I didn't mean to bring up a sore subject."

"It's all right," he said. "I'm sort of enjoying it, I guess."

"Sort of?" Sarah asked. "You've been doing it for what, almost three months now, right?"

"Yeah," Dave chimed in. "You have been awfully quiet the last few meetings. Not like when we first started. What gives?"

"I've just been listening a lot, you know?"

"That's not like you, brother. What's on your mind? Are we not studying what you want? We're started from the beginning, as you asked. We've been doing that ever since Bob finished his big major lesson."

"Yes, we are, and that's been good. I'm learning stuff I didn't know, especially the history and all. That's not what's been on my mind, though."

"What then?"

"It's the tithing thing."

Beth chimed in, "What about it, honey?"

"Ever since Bob finished his talk about stewardship versus ownership and generosity and giving, you know, the last of the big major lessons, as you put it, I can't seem to stop thinking about it."

"What about it?" asked Sarah.

"Well, the whole idea that everything we think we own is God's just rankles me. I mean, I work hard. You work hard, Beth. I've always felt that all that work entitled me to control what I want to do with it."

"Yeah," said Dave. "However, I sense a 'but' here."

"As I said, I've been thinking about it. And I have been listening to the guys in the group. And, perhaps, most importantly, I have been watching people. People at the church, people at work, people in general. And it's a funny thing."

"What's a funny thing, honey?" Beth asked.

"Well, first of all, I fully expected that Bob or somebody else in the church would be asking me for money. Bob made it very clear that he was not. My dad always said that that's the agenda of all pastors and church people in general. But I haven't seen that."

"And?" said Beth.

"And the other thing I have noticed is there seems to be a connection between, how do I say, this giving thing and happiness."

"Go on," she encouraged him.

"Like, take a look at you guys," he pointed to Sarah and Dave. "You seem to actually enjoy giving your money away. And you do it even when you seemingly can't afford it. Like the time you told me you were

getting ready to go to church and realized you didn't have the money
in the checking account to cover the tithe check?"

"Oh, right," said Dave.

"And what did you tell me? You stuck your offering in the offering
plate anyway and on Monday you got an unexpected refund from
your insurance company that more than covered it?"

"Right, right. That was pretty much a 'God Thing,' as Bob might say."

Tony said, "Yeah. I would have said it was just a coincidence."

"And now?" asked Sarah.

"Well, it's just that I have been noticing coincidences all over
the place. Things I never gave much thought to before. Ah, who am
I kidding? I still think they're just that."

At that point, Jimmy showed up with the food and served
everyone. There was general silence as they ate. Tony ordered
another round of drinks and they finished their food.

"Anyone for dessert?" asked Tony. "My treat."

"I'm stuffed," said Dave.

"Me too," piped Beth.

But Sarah said, "Heck, I'm eating for two now and that carrot
cake in the display looked awfully good! And I am supposed to eat
lots of veggies, so I'll have some carrot cake, please."

Tony ordered the carrot cake for Sarah, and so as not to leave her
to eat alone, he got a key lime pie for himself. As they were waiting for
the dessert to arrive, Tony said, "Let me ask you all a question. When
you tithe or give money to the church, how does it make you feel?"

"How do you mean?" asked Dave.

"I mean, is it a burden? Like, 'Man, here I am giving my hard-
earned money away.' Or is it just out of a sense of obligation? Or do you
get pleasure from supporting 'kingdom work,' as Bob would call it?"

"For me, it's not that exactly," said Dave. "I think I speak for Sarah
as well."

She nodded.

"Okay then, let me ask this. Do you expect something in return?

Like the time you gave when you didn't have the money. Do you expect to get more back?"

Sarah said, "Nothing like that."

"Then what?" Tony was frustrated.

"Easy, dear," said Beth putting her hand on Tony's arm to calm him down. "You don't need to get excited about it. It's just us here."

"Uh, sorry. I'm just trying to understand the motivation."

Dave stepped in. "Let me try to explain it this way. Remember when Bob was talking about the idea that we have gotten what we have because of God? You know, because of God's grace?"

"Yeah?"

"And that makes us grateful?"

"Right."

"Well, if you buy into that, and we do, then giving becomes something you just do because it feels right." Beth and Sarah nodded their heads. "We give *back* because we have received. It never feels like we are giving anything away. And quite frankly, it has become sort of a habit."

"A habit?"

"Yeah. We do it because we should do it. It feels bad if we don't. Tony, let me ask you a question. Are there days that you don't necessarily feel like running but you run anyway?"

Tony didn't hesitate, "You bet. Lots of times I don't feel like running."

"But you often run anyways?" Dave asked.

"Usually. I rarely give into my 'I don't want to run' feelings."

"And how do you feel on those days after you have finished running?"

"I feel really good," Tony said.

"Why?" Dave asked.

"Because I know that my running is good for my health and that feels good," Tony replied.

"And that's exactly how Sarah and I feel when we don't base our giving on our feelings at the time, but we faithfully give our tithe.

We know we are investing in the well-being of others and that gives us real pleasure."

Tony was silent for a while. The desserts came, and Sarah immediately began to eat. She was eating for two and was enjoying not being on any sort of diet.

Finally, Tony said, "It's one of those 'church things,' isn't it?"

Beth looked up at him. "You mean one of the things you've said you might have to do to have the full 'church experience'?"

He looked at her and said meekly, "Maybe."

They all sat in silence for a while.

"Sooooo?" Beth asked.

"So I guess I'm going to have to experience it." He quickly put up his hands. "But I'm still not convinced that I'm not giving *my* money away. And I'm not prepared to give a whole 10 percent of *my* money."

"Okay, honey. Take it easy," Beth said.

"Right. So I guess what I'm going to do is to give a little bit, maybe 10 or 20 dollars a week. Then I'll see what happens."

"That's fine, dear. Whatever you want to do," said Beth.

Dave raised his glass. "Well, then, here's to you learning something new, Tony. And to God being good to you as you do it."

They all raised their glasses. "To learning," said Beth.

CHAPTER 37

I t was a Friday morning several weeks after Tony had decided to start giving money to the church. He was still undecided as to how he felt about it, but he was committed to experiencing the "church thing" to the fullest.

Tony had gotten up for an early morning run before going to work. It was dark when he started and there was a little fog, so his visibility was limited. He stayed to the path in the park to stay away from the roads. He couldn't see very well, but he attributed that to the fog. But it was annoying.

When he got home, he walked into the house and noticed his vision was still foggy. He rubbed his right eye. It didn't go away.

He walked into the bathroom where Beth was getting ready for work. "Look at my eye, will you, Beth?"

"Sure." She looked at his eye, he opened the lids with his hand so she could see better. "I don't see anything. What's wrong?"

"I don't know, it's just not right."

"Does it hurt?"

"No. It's just as if there is a sort of sheer curtain over everything. The vision isn't right."

"I'm sure it's nothing. But just in case, why don't you call the eye doctor and get an appointment?"

"Right. I'll do that when I get to work. They don't open until 8:30 anyway."

It was about 9:00 when he called the eye doctor and explained what was going on. The receptionist said she had a 1:30 appointment that had just canceled, so he said he would take it. He worked through the morning but found his vision very annoying. So he took an early lunch at 11:30 and went to the daycare center to see the kids. They were having too much fun to be bothered with him. He watched them for a while and then went to get lunch.

When he got to the doctor's office, they got him right in and did all the usual up-front procedures. Then the doctor came in.

"How goes it, Tony?"

"It's okay. Just have this weird thing going on in my right eye."

"Can you describe it?"

"It's like someone has pulled a sheet or something across it. It doesn't hurt, I just can't see very well."

"Okay, let's take a look." The doctor put one of the devices up to Tony's eye and looked in.

After a moment he sat back and said, "Okay, here's what we have. You have a detached retina."

"What?! That's serious, isn't it?"

"Yes, Tony it is. What you need is an ophthalmologist."

"Okay, when can I get an appointment?"

"No, you don't understand. You need to go now. I am going to call Dr. Beamus and you are going over to his office immediately."

"Uh, okay. Can I drive myself there?"

"Uh, yes. It's only about half a mile down the road. The nurse up front will give you the directions. Now go and don't make any stops."

Tony got out of the chair and went to the front desk. The receptionist gave him the directions, and he got in his car and drove to the office. When he got there, they were waiting for him and immediately showed him into a room. He sat in the chair, and almost immediately, the doctor walked in.

"Hello Mr. Hunter, I'm Dr. Beamus. I understand we have something to look at here."

"Hello. Yeah, I guess."

The doctor didn't waste any time but pushed the chair back so that Tony was essentially laying on his back. The doctor then pulled out an instrument and looked into Tony's eye. He sat back and said, "Okay. Here is what is happening. The retina is kind of like a piece of plastic wrap around the back of your eye." He cupped one of his hands inside the other to demonstrate what he was saying. "Yours has started to detach or move away from the back of your eye. If it continues, it will stay detached and you will lose the vision in that eye."

Tony was becoming frightened. "I see. Is there anything we can do?"

"Yes. First, we need to get the retina to move back in place. The way we are going to do that is by injecting a small bubble of CO_2 into your eye. Based on where this is happening in your eye, you will need to lie on your left side for twenty-four hours. Hopefully, the bubble will push the retina back into place."

"Whoa, isn't that going to hurt? And that will solve the problem?"

"No. And it won't hurt. I will use a topical anesthetic first. But it won't solve the issue by itself. Tomorrow you will come back, and if everything has gone well, I will weld the retina back to the back of your eye."

"WELD?"

"Yes, that's the best description of it. Oh, don't worry. I'm not going to use a blowtorch. I will use a laser. It will sort of spot-weld the retina to the back wall of the eye."

"I see."

"You will need someone to drive you home. Can you call someone now?"

"Uh, sure. Yeah. I'll call my wife."

"Good. I will have the nurses get ready for the procedure and be right back." He walked out of the room. Tony was left alone. He pulled out his cell phone and called Beth at work.

"Hello, Beth Hunter, how can I help you?" she answered.

"Hey Beth, it's me."

"Oh, I didn't look at the Caller ID. What did the doctor say?"

"It turns out I have a detached retina."

"What?!" she exclaimed.

"Yeah, surprised me too. Anyway, they sent me off to an ophthalmologist, a Dr. Beamus. He's going to do some sort of procedure on me and then I have to go home. He said someone is going to have to drive me home."

"Of course! I will be right there. Where are you?"

"I'll text you the address. See you soon."

"Okay, yes. I'll be right there."

They both hung up. Tony almost forgot to text her the address, then remembered. He put his phone away and laid his head back. He was scared. This did not sound good. Maybe he should call someone else. Maybe he should have called Dave and not worried Beth. While he was thinking all of that, the doctor and a nurse came in.

"All set then?" Dr. Beamus asked.

"Uh, yeah, my wife is coming to pick me up."

"Good, good. Any questions?"

"No, I think you explained everything to me pretty well."

"Okay, then let's get started."

The doctor went through the procedure as he had described it. It didn't hurt, but Tony was very deliberate about not moving unless told to do so.

When the doctor was done, he said, "There, that should do it. Now, I can't be clearer. Keep your head in that position as much as you can. When you return tomorrow, we will see if what we have done today has worked. If everything looks good, I can finish the welding procedure. See you tomorrow."

He walked out and the nurse cleaned up after the doctor. "Has he done this a lot?" Tony asked her.

"Oh, not to worry, Dr. Beamus is very good. You are in very capable hands. Now, you rest while we wait for your wife to pick you up. I'm going to dim the lights for you." She did just that and walked out of the room, closing the door behind herself.

Tony was left alone with his thoughts. *How could this have happened?* he wondered. It didn't matter really, but he was glad he had come to the doctor's when he did. He had almost dozed off when the door opened and Beth walked in.

"Oh, Tony. Are you all right?"

"I guess. But I have to sit like this for twenty-four hours."

"I know. They gave me all the instructions when I got here. Let's get you home." She helped him out of the seat, and they walked to the lobby.

"Wait a minute," he said. "What about my car?"

"Don't worry. I'll call Sarah and they can come to pick it up."

"Oh. Okay."

He let her lead him to her car. He got in the back seat so he could lie down.

"I feel so terrible," she said as they started off.

"Why do you feel bad?"

"I feel like I didn't take your issue seriously enough this morning."

"Aw, don't worry about it. You're the one who suggested I call the doctor. Let's just get home."

They rode the rest of the way in silence. When they got home, as Beth was helping him out of the car, she said, "Don't you worry about the kids. I will take care of all of that. You just get undressed and hop into bed. And keep lying on your left side!"

Tony went into the bedroom and got out of his clothes. He crawled into bed and lay down.

It wasn't until then that it hit him. He could be blind in one eye! He almost started crying. He curled up into a fetal position, being sure to stay on his left cheek, and started shivering. He had always taken his vision for granted. Now, not so much. Finally, he dozed off . . . more from emotional exhaustion than anything else.

That night was mostly a blur in Tony's memory. He dozed on and off. Dave came in to see him but didn't stay long. But long enough to say a prayer over Tony. In the morning, he woke up to the sound of the kids. He almost forgot that he had a problem and started to get up to help Beth, but then laid back down. Beth came in and said, "Ah, I see you're awake. Good morning. How do you feel?"

"Okay, I guess. I don't think I slept very well."

"You didn't. Look, I'm going to take the kids to Dave and Sarah's so they are not underfoot, and then I will come back. Will you be okay?"

"Yeah. Sure. I'm just going to go to the bathroom, and then I will get right back in bed. I promise."

"Okay, be sure you do." She kissed him on the forehead and walked out. Tony got up, went to the bathroom and then brushed his teeth, as his mouth felt like it was made of cotton. It was hard to do that while keeping his head tilted to one side. Then he decided he had had enough of bed and went to lay down on the couch. That's where Beth found him when she got home.

"What are you doing out here?" she asked with a stern voice.

"I just got tired of being in the bed. As long as I keep my head tilted, it should be okay. But I'm also hungry. Can you get me something to eat?"

"Sure, I'll make you something." She went into the kitchen and brought back some toast with jam. He ate slowly then closed his eye. The morning went very slowly. He was afraid to open his eyes or move about much. Finally, it was time to go to the doctor. They loaded up into the car, and Beth drove them.

Beth had to wait in the reception area, even though she wanted to be with Tony. The doctor put Tony in the chair and looked into his eye.

"Well, it seems as if the CO_2 has done its job. The retina is back in place. What we are going to do now is use the laser to reattach it to the eyewall. This will likely be uncomfortable. I will be using pulses of light to weld the retina. When it hits your eye, it may hit a nerve, and when that happens, you will feel a sharp pain. You must do your best to not move during the procedure. If you do, I may hit the wrong place, and that will damage the eye, and you will lose vision in that part of the eye. Do you understand me?"

"Yes."

"Okay, then."

The doctor set Tony up in the chair and put the apparatus in place.

"How long will this take?" Tony asked.

"No talking now," the doctor said sharply. And he began.

It was painful. It was like the doctor was shooting bullets into his eye. And it was loud. It hurt almost every time he zapped the laser. Tony took a deep breath.

"No moving!"

Tony did his best to not move, but it was hard. After what seemed to Tony to be an eternity, the doctor sat back and pulled the apparatus away from Tony's face.

"Is that it, Doc?"

"I'm afraid not. But that is enough for today."

"We're going to do this again tomorrow?" asked Tony.

"No, not this. There is a part of your eye that needs to be reattached that I cannot see with the laser. I will have to use another technique. But I need to give your eye a rest before I do that. So you are to go home, stay in a darkened room, and rest. No TV or reading or anything like that. Then come back tomorrow morning, at 9:00 AM."

"On a Sunday morning?"

"You have something better to do?"

"Well, we usually go to church."

"I think God will be happy to have you here. And if I can be here, so can you. See you then." He got up and walked out.

Tony sort of blinked after him. He got up and went into the front of the office. There, a nurse handed him a sort of blindfold. The kind people use to sleep with.

"Here," she said, "wear this when you sleep."

On the drive home, Beth asked, "How was it?"

"Very uncomfortable. It's like little shots into your eye. And every once in a while, it really hurt."

"I'm sorry. Why are we coming back tomorrow?"

"Apparently he couldn't get it all with the laser. He's going to use some other technique then." He stopped and then said, "I hope it's not a needle and thread."

They both shivered at the thought.

The rest of the day was not difficult. Mostly it was boring for Tony. Beth had the burden of the kids and cooking after Dave had dropped them off in the evening. Sunday morning came, and Sarah came over. She offered to take the kids to church with them, and Beth gladly accepted. When they got to the doctor's office, they found only the doctor and none of his staff.

"All alone this morning, Doc?" asked Tony.

"Yes. Hard to get good help. I'm kidding. I don't need any help today."

"Okay, what are we doing then?"

"I'm going to use a freezing technique to finish the 'welding.'"

"How does that work?" asked Beth.

"I'm going to inject an anesthetic into the eye. Then I will use this tool," he picked up a device with a handle and a prod that stuck out at an angle. "This tip is very cold, and I will apply it to the outside of the eye where the retina needs to be reattached. The cold will act much like the laser and 'weld' the retina back to the eyewall." He looked at Tony. "Now, if at any time you start to feel pain, you tell me, all right?"

"Yes, sir," Tony replied.

Dr. Beamus brought Tony back into the examining room and shut the door on Beth, who went to sit in the waiting area. Dr. Beamus injected Tony, who was getting quite used to having things poked into him, and they waited for the anesthetic to take effect. Then Dr. Beamus poked at Tony and asked, "Do you feel that?"

Tony acknowledged that he felt nothing.

The doctor began. It was different than the day before. Tony didn't feel anything except the fact that Dr. Beamus was pushing his eye around. He was apparently having trouble getting his tool in the exact place he wanted it. Finally, it was over, and Tony took a deep breath.

"Did you get it all, Doc?"

"Yes, I believe I did."

"Great, so I'm fully cured?" asked Tony.

"Well, we hope so." Dr. Beamus opened the door and called to Beth to come in. He said, "Here is the deal. I have reattached the retina to the back of your eyewall. If those welds hold, you should regain full vision in that eye. We will have you come back in a week to take a detailed look. In the meantime, you can resume your normal activities, but no heavy lifting or any strenuous activities. And try to limit your use of a computer screen."

"Ah, Doc, I'm a runner. Can I do that?"

"Not for a while. Let's see how your eye is healing first."

"Okay," Tony said, "Anything else?"

"I don't think so. Just nothing that puts a strain on your eyes."

He got up and led them to the door. "Call tomorrow for an appointment time. See you next week."

When they got home, Sarah and Dave were there with all the kids. "How did it go, buddy?" asked Dave. "Everything all right?"

"I guess so. He said he was able to reattach the retina. I have to take it easy for a week and then go back to see him. Say, Beth, did he say that I could drive?"

Beth walked over to him and stared him straight in the eye. "Tony Hunter, you are going to stay home this week and take care of yourself. No going to work, they can get along without you. I will call them myself if I have to. And you are going to follow the orders the doctor gave us. Got it?" She poked him in the chest.

"Yes, ma'am," he replied putting his hands in the air in surrender.

"Good. Now, let me get some lunch for all of us."

No one argued, and they all helped get the food, except Tony, who sat on the couch. After lunch, as Dave and Sarah were getting ready to go, the doorbell rang. Beth went to the door, and when she opened it, she found Pastor Bob standing there.

Hi," he said. "Is it all right to see the patient?"

"Of course, it is. Come on in, Pastor Bob." She ushered him in, and Tony got up to greet him.

"Hello, Bob. What are you doing here?" asked Tony standing up.

"Oh, please, don't get up for me. I just came to see how you were doing. We missed you at group yesterday. But I suppose you had a valid excuse," he said kiddingly.

"I didn't know I needed one. I can get a doctor's note if you want," he joked as he sat back down.

"No, we'll let it pass this time."

Everyone sat down. "What did I miss at church, today?" Tony ventured.

Bob replied, "Just another brilliant sermon, that's all. But it's your loss. The podcast is never as good as being there in person." They all laughed. "But seriously, how are you doing?"

"I guess I'm okay. The doc said he was able to repair the damage. I have to take it easy for a while and go and see him again next week."

"I see. How do you *feel?*"

"I never actually felt bad. Just had some foggy vision."

"Well, God is good, then," said Bob. "John does tell us that Jesus is the 'light of the world.'"

Tony thought for a moment then said, "Funny you should mention Scripture, Bob."

"Not that funny. It's kind of my job, you know?"

"Yeah, yeah. I get that, but," Tony got up and said, "wait here a minute." He went into the bedroom and came out with a five-dollar bill in his hand.

"I put this in my wallet a while back. But I never looked up the reference. I guess I forgot all about it. But, can you tell me what it is?"

Bob looked at the bill. It had *ACTS 9:10* written on it. He looked startled.

"What is it, Bob?" Beth asked.

Bob smiled and said, "This is the story of Saul."

"Saul," asked Tony?

"Yes, that was Paul's name before his conversion. You see, he was struck blind by Jesus and this set of verses is where God sends a messenger to Saul who places his hands on Saul's eyes and cures him of his blindness."

Everyone was silent. Bob smiled again and said, "Tony, you first went to the doctor on Friday, right?"

"Yeah?"

"That was three days ago."

"Yeah."

"Saul was blind for three days before he was cured."

Again, there was silence in the room. Tony went over to Bob and took back the five-dollar bill and looked at it. He looked up at Bob, "It's a coincidence, right?"

"What do you think, Tony?"

"Quite frankly, I don't know what to think." He turned around and walked into the bedroom, looking down at the bill the entire time.

Beth got up and said, "Would you like a glass of iced tea, Pastor Bob?"

Bob looked up at her and smiled, "Yes, I would, Beth. Yes, I would."

CHAPTER 38

It was Friday, two weeks after his procedure. Tony rose early, and, while still a bit groggy, he went to his cell phone, unplugged it, and checked to see if he had received any messages during the night. Some of his customers were in different time zones, and it wasn't uncommon that one of his customers would leave a message after he had gone to bed. He was pleased to see that no one had called. Then, as usual, he checked his calendar to make sure he remembered all the things he had scheduled for that day. And there it was: Lunch with Calvin, 11:00 AM. Ah, yes, he remembered. *This should prove interesting*, he thought.

Beth had also risen early and was already in the shower. Tony went into the kitchen and started the coffee pot and headed back to the bedroom.

"Good morning, honey. Did you sleep okay last night?" Beth said.

"Good morning, love. Yes, I did. How about you?"

"I sure did."

"So, have anything interesting on your calendar today?" Beth asked.

"Actually, I have that lunch thing with Calvin today," Tony replied.

"Oh, yes," said Beth. "Are you looking forward to it?"

"Going to that soup kitchen place for lunch? I don't think so. But Calvin is still trying to get me to work on that bike and he said this would inspire me. So I guess I have to go. It kind of makes me uncomfortable, you know? Anyway, after Calvin created such a guilt trip in me over saying 'no' to helping him with the bike, and finally saying 'yes' just to appease my guilt, he has been bugging me to finish it. I just haven't had the time to work on it. It hasn't been on my priority list. It's just sitting in the garage taking up space."

"Yes, I noticed."

Tony wrinkled his nose at her. "Maybe this is his way of pushing me, I don't know."

"Well, good luck," she kissed him on the cheek and went to finish dressing.

After tending to all the morning details, both Beth and Tony headed off for work. Today, Tony offered to drop the kids off at the daycare, and he rather enjoyed doing that. It felt good to get hugs and kisses just before the kids dashed into the daycare center.

The morning flew by, and before he knew it, the "clock struck midnight." Well actually, it struck 11:00 AM, and sure enough, Calvin appeared in the lobby of Tony's building. The receptionist rang Tony and told him that Calvin was here to see him.

Tony replied, "Tell him I will be right there."

Tony straightened up some papers on his desk. He put a couple of confidential files in his desk drawer and locked it. He then proceeded to come down from his second-floor office and he greeted Calvin with a hearty handshake.

"Calvin, thanks for your promptness. Why don't you say we head out?"

Tony was a little nervous about this lunch plan. First, he wasn't dressed to go to a homeless shelter or soup kitchen or whatever it was. Even though it was casual Friday at the office, and he had on jeans, he still felt overdressed. Second, he had never been to one of these places and wasn't sure how to act. Finally, he didn't relish the idea of eating with or even being around homeless people. He had a sense they were all dirty and crude and that he didn't have anything in common with them. But he had promised Calvin, if for no other reason to get Calvin off of his back about that bike!

As they approached a section of downtown that seemed a bit run-down, Tony was surprised that Calvin was pulling over to the curb in front of a fairly large building that appeared to be new. It stood out as the only attractive building in a rather blighted area. As they got out of the car and walked towards the building, Tony could see a pretty large gathering of people who were certainly not dressed in sport coats and ties. With few exceptions, they all looked pretty "worn out." When he got close enough to read the sign over the front door, he could see he was at the "Bread of Life" soup kitchen. He was becoming more uncomfortable but didn't say anything. He just dutifully stayed close to Calvin and walked through the crowd, most of them looking up at the two of them.

Inside the building, there was a decent-sized lobby with a person sitting behind a glass window and a bell sitting on a ledge. Calvin went immediately to the window and told the lady who he was and that he was supposed to meet with Juan Rodriguez. The lady behind the glass said she would "buzz him in" and when Calvin heard the door to his left start buzzing, he motioned for Tony to join him. They both went through the door and they could hear it automatically lock behind them when it closed.

The lady behind the glass met them in the hall and escorted them to Mr. Rodriguez's office. She poked her head into the office and said, "Mr. Rodriguez, Mr. Lowe is here to see you." She then motioned for them to go in, and she started back down the hall.

Mr. Rodriguez was a large man and paunchy, with a Tom Selleck mustache. He immediately got up from his desk and came around and extended his hand towards Calvin. Calvin took his hand, and when he did, Juan immediately drew Calvin toward him and gave him a big bear hug.

"Calvin, I am so pleased to see you. Thank you for coming, it means a great deal to me."

"No problem, Mr. Rodriguez. You would be surprised at what I will do to get a free lunch." Everyone but Tony smiled.

"And who is your friend, Calvin?" asked Juan.

"Oh, forgive me for not introducing you. Juan, this is one of my best friends. This is Tony Hunter."

Again, Juan reached out his hand and shook Tony's hand vigorously, but he didn't draw Tony into a hug. Maybe he could sense the stiffness within Tony.

"Pleased to meet you, Mr. Rodriguez," Tony muttered.

"No, the pleasure is all mine," replied Juan. "Have a seat, and maybe we can have a little visit before we go out on the food line and serve some wonderful people the best lunch in town."

Go out on the serving line? Is that what I heard him say? Tony thought to himself. But before he could even think of any objection he had as to why he was at a soup kitchen, Juan started in.

"Well, Calvin, I know you know most of this, but for Mr. Hunter's sake, let me tell you why you are here and what we will be doing. I will try to be brief, but a little background might be helpful.

"Bread of Life feeds about 240 people a very substantial lunch three hundred and sixty-five days a year. Although many of these folks are homeless and have no employment, many are simply the working poor. They have jobs, some of them work two or three jobs, but the level of their employment keeps them unable to sustain themselves at even a modest way of life.

"The jobs they have are mostly part-time, and that is by design. Employers do not want to give them benefits, so they hire them for part-time work. So having one really good meal a day means the world to them. You will see all kinds of people come through the line. They all have stories. They all have feelings. They all have needs. But don't be surprised by the single moms who are bringing their two or three children with them. Looking into the eyes of those wee ones can pull on your heartstrings. But that doesn't explain why you are here."

Calvin piped up and said, "Right." He turned to Tony. "I thought it would be a great thing for you to meet some of the people that we are trying to help. You know, with the bicycle ministry."

"Right," said Tony.

Juan continued. "So, Tony, about a year ago our board of directors determined that one of the things that many, if not most, of these clients lacked was transportation. Very few, if any of them, have the means to have a car. And without transportation, they can't do a lot of things they need to do.

"At first, we tried to help them by arranging volunteers to drive them to places. After about three months of that, we gave up. It just wasn't working. The people were still dependent on others to help them and for many, they already felt badly about imposing on others. Also, many of the volunteer drivers became concerned about the liability and stopped volunteering.

"So within the last six months, we have taken a different approach. We started the bicycle repair ministry, and that's where you guys come in.

"When we instituted this ministry, we recognized that we had no budget for it. However, we went out on faith and since we serve a *can-do God,* we asked him to send us people who would donate used bicycles and if a bicycle needed to be repaired, hopefully, God would lead us to a team of people who, at their own expense, would take the bicycles, get whatever parts were needed, repair them, spruce them up, maybe paint them, and bring them back to us so we could give them to needy clients. And that is exactly what God has done. We now have about thirty bicycles in a storeroom just waiting for people like you to restore them. And we probably have fifty clients waiting to get a bike."

He paused to let all that sink in. Then he continued, "So why are you here over a lunch hour? Our board, in its wisdom, believed it would be a real blessing to the folks who donated a bicycle and to those who repair a bicycle to meet the person who gets the bicycle. But we wanted them to remain anonymous at the same time. You see, we didn't think it was a good idea for the two persons to meet because that might complicate things down the road. The person getting the bike might feel shamed by meeting the person who donated or fixed it. So we wanted this to remain simple but personal.

"For the past two months, we have had the bike ministry people come and serve one meal to our clients." He noticed Tony's discomfort. "Now don't worry, I will be standing next to you. The person who received the lady's bicycle that you repaired, Calvin, should be here today. Her name is Mary. And when Mary comes through the line, I will probably say something like, 'Wow, look who's here. It's Mary, Mary, quite contrary! How's Mary today?' That way, you will meet Mary, but there is no connection after that. But you will have a name and a face to put with the bicycle you repaired. And if you choose to pray for Mary, you will have a picture of her in your mind.

"Now, we only do this once. Tony, I understand that you have a boy's bicycle to repair, and the recipient of that bicycle will surely go through the meal line today as well. I will point him out to you when he does. His name is Jonathan. All we want today is for you to see that your labor of love will have an impact on a real person, and we hope this gives you joy for giving so generously of your time, talent, and treasure. So that is why you are here. And let me add one more thing. It may seem simple to you that a grown woman or man now has a bicycle. It is way more than that. It is every bit as significant as when you got your first car. Do you remember that day, Calvin?"

"You bet. 'Course I had to buy it on my own, but sure, it changed my life," replied Calvin.

"How 'bout you, Tony? Do you remember that day?"

"Yes, sir, I do."

"Well imagine living your whole life since you were sixteen without a car. Many of these people have had lots of cars. Nice cars. But they have fallen on difficult times and now all they have is semi-worn-out

shoes. But now Mary has, and Jonathan will have, 'wheels'. Mary guards
that bicycle like it was a Rolls Royce. We also make sure every bike
has a combination lock, so they don't have it stolen. Any questions?"

Tony spoke up, "Okay, Juan, I do. How did you acquire this
building?"

"Oh, Tony, I am so glad you asked. I should have shared that
earlier in my 'history lesson'. We had a very inadequate building on
this site for forty years. It only had a room big enough inside to
seat about thirty people. It had one shower for the clients to use,
but we desperately needed more. Long story short, a man on our
board knew a person who had the means to start a building fund, so
the board member approached him and shared with him our need
for a new facility. That man thoroughly checked us out, and after
vetting us, he responded with a gift of one million dollars on the
condition that we could overcome the objections of the politicians
and the local residents. If we could get a go-ahead, he would donate.
It took us three years of fighting City Hall and some of the neighbors
before we broke ground. Many other generous gifts came through
once we started construction and, well, here we are. This building is
completely paid for. God is so good.

"That's the technical answer to your question, Tony. But let me
tell you the real story. How were we able to tear down the old building
and build this one? We serve a big God, that's how. And he's a God
of unlimited resources. Did you know that the Bible says he owns
the earth and everything in it? Even the cattle on a thousand hills?"

Tony simply nodded his head but thought to himself, *Yeah, I have
heard that one before.*

And so the three of them went into the great hall and took up
their places behind the serving line. Tony stood next to Calvin, who
stood next to Juan. For over an hour, they served the people who
came through the line. And Juan was right. Tony's heart was touched
by the children pushing their trays down the line, following their
moms close by.

Tony thought Juan was incredible. He knew almost every person by name, and he was clearly in charge. The clients didn't mess with him in terms of the rules. Juan even had to leave his post for a moment to usher out a couple of guys who were trying to cut in line. But the regulars who knew the rules were in no way going to allow that.

And just like Juan had said, Mary came through the line. When she came to where Juan stood, Juan said with a huge smile and arms reaching across the food station, "Mary, Mary, quite contrary. How the heck are you today?"

Mary replied with a big smile, "I'm great, Mr. Rodriguez. How are you?"

"I'm more than great. I'm blessed! Have a blessed day, Mary."

"You too, Mr. Rodriguez."

Calvin was elated to "meet" Mary and to be standing right next to Mr. Rodriguez. And deep within, he was filled with joy that Tony was standing by him. He believed that Tony had become a true "friend of the heart" and he felt great all over.

A short time later, Jonathan came through the line, and Juan was able to point him out to Tony. Before all the people had been fed, three replacements took their places in the serving line, so Calvin and Tony each got a tray and sat at a table with some of the clients.

Both of them thought they just might be having the best lunch anyone in town could be having. Which surprised Tony. When they were finished, Juan let them peek into the bicycle room, and sure enough, there appeared to be about thirty bicycles waiting to be restored. After thanking Juan for allowing them to "meet" Mary and Jonathan, they headed for Calvin's car.

After pulling away from the curb, Tony didn't hesitate to start questioning Calvin. "Calvin, have you ever been here before?"

"Yes, but not quite like that. I mean I have served in the food line before, but not to 'meet' a person I fixed a bike for."

"Okay, I'll accept that. But why did you ask me to go along?" asked Tony.

"Well, when I asked you a month or so ago to help me repair one of the two bikes, I chose you instead of the other guys because I knew you were pretty mechanical and you could probably do it in half the time it would take one of them. I didn't have any grand plan. But when you weren't able to help me at that time, I thought that maybe if you saw what was going on at the Bread of Life ministry that you might join me in fixing up a bicycle. Now we know that the bike I gave you is for Jonathan. Like I said before, I thought I could get you to work on it if you met some of the people. You know, inspire you? I had no idea that Juan would point out a specific person."

"Yeah, that was weird."

"You know, I had hoped that if I could get you involved, then maybe some of the other guys in the group might want to be part of it too. We could have a, you know, little team from our church and it might turn into a whole thing. Pastor Bob doesn't talk about the way the church helps people in our community and literally around the world because he just isn't the type of guy who wants to sound like he is 'tooting his own horn,' but I don't mind telling you that our church is incredible in the way it gives its money to help people in our community. Bob has led our church board to commit to being a 'double tithing' church, which is so very rare. That means that 20% of every dime that comes into our church is used to meet human needs for people who may never step foot in it, as well as to meet real financial needs when some of our members fall on hard times. Frankly, I wish Bob wasn't so quiet about it.

"So maybe I did have an ulterior motive. Lest you think I am some sort of saint, let me tell you why I chose the bike ministry. I don't want to make a firm commitment to do anything regularly. That is why I wouldn't agree to serve meals at Bread of Life every Friday, or even the first Friday of the month. That's a commitment I'm not willing to make. I don't want to have a 'have to' on my schedule. I only want 'I desire to's' on my schedule. But to help out by taking a bicycle now and then, on my terms, I think I can do that. And you know what?"

"What, Calvin?"

"Not that long ago, I would have been doing this to get more brownie points in Heaven, you know?"

"Yeah?"

"But not this time. I just want to do it. Does that make any sense?"

"Yes, Calvin, I think it does," Tony replied.

When Tony got home that evening, Beth asked him at dinner time, "So Tony, how did it go today at the soup kitchen?"

Tony replied, "Differently than I thought it would."

"Oh? How so?"

"Well, for one thing, our meal today was very good."

"And?"

"And I met some very interesting people."

"I see. Will you go back?"

"You know, I just might. I just might do that."

Once again Tony had this eerie feeling that something was happening that he couldn't put his finger on, but like other times when this happened, he would usually choose to just sleep on it. But tonight, after the kids were put to bed, he went out into the garage and started working on the bike for Jonathan.

CHAPTER 39

Dave looked very serious as Tony slid into the booth. Charley's wasn't crowded yet, so it was relatively quiet. That was the usual case for a weeknight. But it seemed to make Dave uncomfortable. He kept looking around as if to make sure no one was listening.

"What's up, Dave?" Tony asked.

"I, uh, wanted to talk to you, Tony," he stammered.

"Well, okay. I'm here, so talk."

"Yeah. This is a hard one, Tony."

"Dave. How long have we known each other? How hard could it be?' He stopped for a moment, then, suddenly alarmed, reached across the table to grab Dave's forearm. "What a minute! It's not Sarah, is it? I mean the baby is all right, yes?"

Dave looked up. "Oh, no, no. Nothing like that. Sarah and the baby are just fine. Everything is going well there."

Tony sat back, clearly relieved. "Whew. You had me scared there for a moment. So what has your panties in such an uproar, brother?"

Dave took a deep breath. "It's like this. And let me start by saying I know you don't believe in this sort of thing."

"What sort of thing?" Tony interrupted.

"Let me just say this. I had a dream last night."

"Uh-huh?"

"It was about you and your dad."

"Okay?"

"You and your dad had a big fight. I mean a really big fight."

"You mean like we hit each other?"

"No, nothing like that. But it was about something important to each of you. I don't know what it was, but the outcome was that you and your father, uh, split."

"Split?"

"Yeah. Basically, you broke up. Decided that you didn't ever want to see each other anymore."

"Okay?"

"See, and here's the part I don't think you will like. I think it was a message from God."

"A message from God," Tony echoed.

"Yeah. Remember a few weeks ago in the group, we talked about how God speaks to us?"

"Yeah. No one could agree on how that happens."

"Right. It's just that He speaks to each of us in different ways. Sometimes He speaks to me in dreams," Dave said.

"I know. You have told me about this before. What makes you think this particular dream was a 'message from God?'" He did air quotes.

"It's hard to describe. But when it happens, I just know it. And I'm usually right. Like last year, I dreamt that my Uncle Leo got hurt, but I didn't know how. I woke up and told Sarah that we had to pray for him. And sure enough, the next week, he fell in his yard and broke his ankle."

Tony was very skeptical, and it was clear from the look he was giving Dave.

"I know, I know, you're not buying into it."

"Just a coincidence, Dave."

"Maybe, but haven't you been having some *strange coincidences* lately?"

That brought Tony up short. It was true. He was starting to see things he never saw before. He shook his head as if to shake off the notion.

"All right. If this is some sort of message, what does it mean? And why did you get the message and not me?" Tony responded.

"Tony, I can't answer that. I only know that you and your dad are on a collision course. And that it is going to hurt you. *And* that I had to tell you about it."

They were both silent for a long time. Each sipped his drink and just sat there. Tony didn't know exactly what to make of this revelation, but he knew Dave well enough to know that he fully believed what he was saying. And that Dave was worried about him. Dave was looking at Tony with all the heartfelt concern that Tony knew he had. He decided to ease Dave's fears.

"Okay, then, Dave. You have done your duty. You have given me the message. I will take it under consideration."

"I'm sorry about this, Tony. I know that you love your father very much."

"Yeah. I do. So whatever happens, we will work it out."

"I hope so, Tony. I certainly hope so."

They clinked their glasses together and finished their drinks.

CHAPTER 40

The baptism was a lovely event. Sarah was absolutely glowing over Jacob, her new son. The delivery had been textbook, even though Jacob had come a couple of weeks early. It seemed like the whole church had attended the ceremony and now had come to the party at Dave and Sarah's home. There were people everywhere in their house and backyard.

Tony and Beth were busy trying to keep all the food and drinks flowing. They had volunteered to help manage the party. Tony was mostly having a ball, as he was the main chef, but now he was a little overwhelmed and was rethinking why they hadn't just catered the whole thing. Beth was the perfect hostess and seemed to be enjoying herself.

All of the Life Group men were there with their spouses and children. All of the kids were running around the backyard, causing some confusion. But as Tony continued to man the grill, he watched how the guests interacted with the children. There was no annoyance or negative reaction to anything the kids did. Even when they caused someone to spill a drink or almost trip, there was laugher and joy.

George came over to Tony and said, "Hey, brother. Do you need any help?"

"Sure," he replied as he was loading up another platter of burgers. "You can take this into the kitchen."

"Love it," said George. He picked up the platter and started to go, then turned around. "Tony, did I ever tell you how much I appreciate having you in the Life Group?"

"No, not really, George."

"Well, I don't know if I can say it enough. I like some of the questions you raise and how you are willing to discuss anything. It really makes me think, sometimes."

"George, I'm glad about that. I enjoy listening to you and your stories as well. And how you have reached out to others, like that young man from prison, what is his name?"

"Jason."

"Jason, that's right. It's very inspiring."

"Oh, well, it's nothing really. Anyway, I just wanted to tell you."

"Thank you, George."

George took the platter, turned, and walked away. Tony was a little taken aback. He didn't know what to make of it. However, George's heartfelt sentiment struck a chord somewhere inside Tony. He shrugged his shoulders and went back to cooking.

As he cooked, he listened to the various conversations going on. There was the normal chitchat about what was happening in everyone's lives. But occasionally, and especially when they were interacting with either Sarah or Dave, there were discussions about the new baby. And all of them were focused on how people could help them. There were offers of childcare, food to be brought to the family, and other helpful actions. There were even offers of money.

Tony was brought back to when the twins were born. How the church had rallied around him and Beth with the same offers. But then, there had been a real need. Beth had been sick, and Joey had issues. They had benefited from all the outpouring of support. But here, now, there was not that need. Everything had gone well for Dave and Sarah. Yet these people were in the same place. And, most importantly to Tony, they didn't ask for anything in return. They all seemed to do it naturally.

Bob walked up to Tony at this point. "Hey, Tony. How are you doing here? Great burgers, by the way."

"Thanks, the secret is in the special ingredients."

"Ah, yes. And I assume that it is a secret recipe handed down from generation to generation?"

"Naw, I just got it off of the back of a Lipton soup package." They both laughed.

Bob continued after a pause, "I was glad to see that you and Beth are the godparents."

"Yeah, we are happy to do it, uh be it. You know what I mean."

"Yes. It is somewhat of a responsibility, I mean having to teach the child and all," said Bob.

Tony paused to look at Bob. "It is. I'm not sure how good a job I will do at it. Good thing Beth will be there to help. She is a good teacher."

"Oh, I think you will be too. If you are as committed to teaching Jacob about the faith as you are with your children, you will do very well." He patted Tony on the shoulder. "You are one to follow through on the things you set out to do."

"Uh, thanks, I guess. But you know I still don't buy it all."

"Yes, I know." Bob paused and took a drink of his beer. "But you know, you have been very diligent in your studies. And you ask very good questions. You know more than you think. And I believe that God is working in your life. You have been so deliberate about doing all *the Christian things*. Even giving money to the church." Tony gave him a 'look' and Bob raised his hands in surrender. "Okay, perhaps not the time for a sermon. But I will say this, I see God chasing after you all the time. And someday, you will catch Him."

Tony had heard this before from Bob, so he let it slide. It wasn't the right time to get into a theological discussion. But Bob was correct. Tony had tried to immerse himself in the life, to understand it. He was even giving five percent of his income. Not quite tithing, but doing it, anyway. He was so surprised that it didn't feel bad to him. Beth, of course, had supported him in all those decisions.

Tony laughed and said, "Okay, I will watch out for Him on my runs."

They clinked bottles and Bob went off to speak with other folks. The party finally wound down and people left in small groups. Sarah was exhausted and went to her bedroom, leaving Tony, Dave, and Beth to clean up. The twins were sleeping with Katie in the living room. Dave was still running high on adrenalin.

"Tony, you guys sure throw a great party! Thanks for everything, brother," said Dave.

"Aw, it was nothing. Happy to do it. It was fun."

"Yeah. Of course, now the hard work starts."

"You mean the cleanup?" asked Tony.

"No. The raising of the kid." They both laughed.

"It shouldn't be that hard. I mean you've got soooo much help."

"What do you mean?" asked Dave. "You mean you and Beth?"

"Well, that too. But to hear everyone talk today, you'd think that the entire church will be here to raise Jacob."

"Yeah, I guess it's 'cause it's what we do. It's that whole generosity thing that Bob talks about. You know, we receive grace, we are grateful and want to give back."

"Yeah. Right." Tony was thoughtful for a while as they continued to clean up. "I guess that is right. I have seen that a lot recently."

They finished cleaning and Tony and Beth packed up the kids into the car and said goodnight to Dave. They were silent pretty much the whole drive home. When they got home, they put the kids to bed and went into the bedroom to get ready for bed themselves. Finally, Beth said, "You've been quiet since we left Sarah and Dave's. What's going on?"

"What do you mean?"

"I know you. When you are like this, there is something on your mind," she said.

"You got me. There is something."

They sat on the edge of the bed together and Beth waited.

"Here's this thing, and I can't explain this," he began.

"Okay."

"I need to fully tithe."

Beth was silent.

Tony continued. "I can't explain it. It's just that somehow, I *know* that I need to tithe. To give ten percent. It's been nagging at me for a couple of weeks, and, well, there it is."

Beth looked at him for a long moment. "Are you sure about this?" she asked gently.

"No. I'm not sure. It's just this feeling that won't go away. So I think I'm supposed to do it."

"Well, I will support you, of course. However, let me ask you one question. Have you already figured out what we need to cut out of the budget to increase our giving to the church?"

Tony acknowledged he had given this some thought but didn't have a firm idea of what needed to be reduced. But, he said, they would figure that out.

Beth hugged him. He hugged her back and they stood up to get ready for bed.

Tony then said, "Beth, come sit down again. I have another question to ask." Beth sat back down. "Beth, as best you know, does the full tithe have to go to the church?" he asked.

"I don't think so," Beth responded. "Why?"

"Well," Tony said, "I have been thinking that I've been upping my giving over the last months and if I am already giving five percent to the church, maybe I would give the other five percent to Mr. Rodriguez down at the soup kitchen. I liked him a lot the day I was there and supporting him and his work would be just as much a part of doing *kingdom work* as Bob would say. And I'm now kind of part of the whole Bike Ministry thing. Would that be okay with you?"

"Absolutely, honey," Beth said with a huge smile.

"Okay, then. I'll start the first of next month." Tony said with a clear sense of conviction.

Then Tony sighed, looked up at Beth, and said, "Man, oh, man! What would my father say about this?"

CHAPTER 41

I t had been some time since Tony had finished repairing the bicycle that he had reluctantly taken from Calvin. On and off for those weeks, he kept thinking of "Mary, Mary, Quite Contrary." When he and Calvin had encountered her going through the meal line at Bread of Life, he couldn't stop thinking about what Juan had said in his office. "Everyone who you will see coming through the line today has a story." He wondered what Mary's story was.

Tony often frequented a mom-and-pop restaurant not far from his house and one of the waitresses was an elderly woman who tugged on his heart. *A woman her age shouldn't have to be carrying those heavy trays or be standing on her feet all day. It's just not right. At her age, she should be taking it easy,* he always thought. When she waited on him, he made sure he left a hefty tip.

But now that Tony had fixed up a boy's bicycle, he just had the yearning to see if he and Calvin were right and Jonathan was the one who received it. And what was his story? So on this particular Saturday, before he headed off for his men's Life Group, he asked Beth if he could stop by the soup kitchen on his way home.

"Ever since I took that bicycle back to that soup kitchen, I have been thinking about the guy who has it now. Juan said his name was

Jonathan. I know we are not supposed to have a relationship with the person who gets it, but I can't get this Jonathan off my mind. If it's okay, I would like to stop by there today after Life Group and see if I can strike up a conversation with Jonathan and learn a little bit about his story. I won't stay too long, and maybe when I get back, I could take you and the twins out to lunch. Would that work for you?"

"Sure, Tony. That would work for me. I have been having a yen for a foot-long chili dog at DQ with a small hot fudge sundae, so would that work for you? I know the kids would love some ice cream, also."

"Absolutely. Consider it a lunch date."

After a better-than-normal Life Group meeting, Tony headed down to the soup kitchen. As it was only 9:00 AM when the group finished, and they started serving lunch at 11:00 AM, Tony stopped by the office first to do some work. Then at 10:30, he left for the soup kitchen. Upon arriving, he maneuvered himself through the crowd, into the lobby, and approached the lady sitting behind the glass window.

"Good morning. How can I help you?" she said with a pleasant countenance.

"Good morning. I was wondering if I might have a moment with Mr. Rodriguez," Tony asked?

"Well, you could have a moment with Mr. Rodriguez, but just not today. He took a day off, so he will be back Monday. Would you like me to leave him a note to call you?"

"No, that's not necessary. But let me ask you. The last time I was here he mentioned that among the many jobs I could volunteer for, one was to just hang outside in the courtyard and let my presence help the clients not get out of line. Would it be okay if I just hung around there for a while?"

"Of course, that would be fine. When you need to leave, you don't have to check back in. But you are always welcome to grab a tray and have a nice meal."

Tony replied, "No, that won't be necessary. I'm having a special lunch date with my bride and my twins. But I'll just hang out for a while. Thanks."

This was working out perfectly. Tony didn't want to break the rule about developing a relationship with the person who received the bicycle; he just wanted to confirm that Jonathan really did get the bicycle that he repaired. But now that Juan was not present, maybe he could have a conversation with Jonathan and come to know "his story." Tony thought that if he could just "hang out" in the courtyard, he might see Jonathan riding the bike he fixed up, and then when he went through the line he could take a seat at his table and visit with him. So that's what he set out to do.

After a while, he began to think, maybe this wasn't such a good idea after all. *Maybe Jonathan isn't the person who received my bicycle. Maybe whoever got the bicycle just took the bike and sold it and spent the money on who knows what.* But no sooner did he get that "Old Tony" idea into his head, there it was. There was Jonathan, riding the bike that Tony fixed up into the courtyard, and he got off and walked it straight to the bike rack. He was just as Tony remembered him, a small man and pretty thin. He looked like he was in his late fifties or early sixties. He wasn't ragged, but he wasn't clean-shaven, either.

Soon Jonathan disappeared into the building, but it wouldn't be long till he appeared again at the other end of the line. Tony decided to move into the large hall so he could see where Jonathan would sit. Tony saw him sit down at a table where there was only one other person sitting. So when Jonathan sat down, that was the optimum time to just go and sit next to him and start up a conversation.

Tony casually walked over to where Jonathan was sitting and said, "Good morning. Mind if I sit down for a bit?"

"Don't mind at all. Are you going to go get some food? As always, it looks very good," replied Jonathan.

Tony replied as he was positioning himself directly across from Jonathan, "Thank you for asking, but not today. I have eaten here before, and I agree with you, they do serve a wonderful meal."

"They sure do."

Feeling some pressure to make this quick so Beth and the kids didn't have to wait too long for their lunch date, Tony decided to be fairly bold and just jump in. "Let me introduce myself. My name is Tony, what's yours?"

"Glad to meet you, Tony. My name is Jonathan. Not many people ask me my name. Are you one of the board members? You don't look like one of the regulars." Jonathan sized Tony up and down as he spoke.

"No, Jonathan. I'm not one of the board members. I just come every once in a while, to help out, you know? Tell me, if I am not being too pushy, have you been part of the lunch bunch for some time?"

"No, I don't mind your asking. I think I know what you are trying to get at. For years, I drove past this location and I thought those who were here were bums. Too lazy to work. Take every penny they get from holding up signs at expressway exits trying to get handouts and then running off to get booze or drugs with the money they had in their pockets. So I understand your preconceived notions about me."

Wow, Tony did not expect that. That hurt, and Tony thought this might go badly. "Uh, I didn't think anything like that," Tony blurted out.

"Oh, it's all right, I know you did, but I don't hold it against you. But if you are interested, I will tell you what happened to me. Are you interested?"

"Why yes, Jonathan, I am interested. But first, let me say I hope you can forgive me and every other middle-class snob who carries around that judgmental attitude. I'm sorry."

"Tony, it's okay. That's exactly what I thought too when I was working and living that middle-class life."

"So you had a family and a career?" Tony asked.

"Yes, I did. I didn't have any children, but my wife and I were married for twenty-eight years. I had a two-year associate degree and ran a CAD program for over twenty-one years at a five-person engineering office here in town. When my wife was forty-two years old, she was told she had contracted ALS. Do you know what ALS is, Tony?"

"Yes, I believe I do. That's the Lou Gehrig disease, isn't it? Jonathan, go ahead and eat your lunch while it is hot. Meatloaf and mashed potatoes aren't all that good when they get cold."

"Tony, until I started eating here all I knew were cold meals. I don't mind." But Jonathan did start shoveling food down in a bit of a hurry and Tony just sat quietly. Jonathan finished most of his meal and said, "Well, back to my story. As I said, when she was forty-two, she took sick. ALS is the cruelest disease on the planet. It is a long, slow death where you can't control any of your muscles. Believe it or not, when some folks get the disease, their spouses can't take it anymore and they just leave. Not me. I loved Marge and when I said, 'For better or worse, in sickness or in health,' I meant it." He paused for a moment, clearly remembering something.

Then he continued, "Anyway, let me get to why I'm here. We had about $200,000 in our 401K at the time of her illness, but when she died, that was all gone. The medical bills completely wiped us out. For the last two years of her life, she needed someone to do everything for her. I couldn't afford to pay someone to give her that care and besides, I wanted to be the one helping. It took a toll on me. I think I aged ten years those last two. I had to stop working and was living off that 401K, trying to be as frugal as I could while paying a little on all the medical bills. My employer said he couldn't keep me on the payroll forever, so he let me go and that is when my income stopped. He said, however, that when I was ready, he would hire me back, as I was very much appreciated. Well, I think he meant it but some of his accounts chose to take their business to larger firms and he not only couldn't hire me back, he had to let one other guy go too.

"So when Marge passed, there I was. No job. No money. I lost the house. The car was repossessed, and I started searching for employment. At the age of fifty-eight, with only an associate degree, I didn't stand a chance of getting a decent job. So now, Monday through Friday I get to the day work office early and sit and wait to see if anyone is hiring a day worker for that day. I probably get work, on average, two days a week. They pay us in cash, and it is for minimum wage. Have you heard about the tent village just up the road about two miles?"

"A friend of mine told me where it is, but I don't know much about it," Tony replied.

"Well, you have gone by it a thousand times, but you never knew it. Some thick woods block a clearing, and in that clearing, many of us homeless folks live. I have a small tent I purchased with my day work money, and it's a place to sleep."

"Well, if you don't mind me asking, without a car, how do you get around? I mean, walking to the day work office five days a week and walking here for lunch, how do you manage?" asked Tony, knowing that Jonathan had just received a bicycle. But Tony was surprised at what came next.

"Oh, my, thank you, Jesus. Several weeks ago, I got a very nice bicycle from the center here. You have no idea what a difference that makes. It allows me to get here every day for a good meal. Before I had my bike, there were days that I just didn't have the energy to walk the two miles, so I went hungry, just staying in my tent. Now I get to the day work office earlier than most anyone else and now I am getting day jobs more like three or four days a week.

"But Juan also told me about other government offices I can go to and apply for aid, and I am following up on some of those suggestions. I just couldn't do that before when I was totally on foot. Honestly, Tony, that bike is starting to open up a whole new world to me and I believe something will change and maybe I can get back on my feet. Maybe wishful thinking for a sixty-year-old bum, but maybe it isn't too far-fetched. At least I pray that is the case."

Tony was completely taken aback. He had no idea that his little bit of work on an old broken-down bicycle could have such an effect on another human being. Juan was right. Jonathan had a story. He didn't have much of a life at the moment, but he had a story. And the overwhelming thought that kept rattling around in his brain was *This could be me.* He had not expected this reaction for sure, but there it was. *This could be me.*

After Tony thanked Jonathan for the visit, Tony started to get up and leave. That's when Jonathan asked if he could pray with him. Tony answered, "Sure, that would be nice."

To Tony's surprise, Jonathan said a prayer that wasn't about himself, but for Tony. He prayed that Tony would have a great day and that he and his family would be healthy and safe. Tony was again blown away. Here was a man with essentially nothing, not asking for anything for himself but praying for a man he had just met, who was obviously more affluent than himself. Tony excused himself, anxious to get home to Beth and the kids. Tony was not one to cry, but before he got to his car there was a tiny tear emanating from his right eye.

Beth greeted him as he came through the door from the garage and into the living room. As often was the case, the twins rushed to greet him. Beth had been waiting patiently for Tony. She gave him a big hug, put her arms around his neck, and asked him, "Well, Tony, was your time at the kitchen what you wanted it to be?"

Tony thought a minute and then replied, "No, it wasn't. It was far more than I wanted it to be. Actually, it was what I needed it to be."

CHAPTER 42

I t was Friday evening and Tony had just finished his run. The past several months had been very full. The twins were walking everywhere now, and that changed everything in the house. Christina especially was into everything. Tony and Beth had done their best to make the house "child-proof," but she seemed to be able to bypass every safeguard they erected. Tony often thought, *How can this little minx outsmart us every time?* As a consequence, Tony's runs had become shorter.

The Life Group had been moving through the Bible, starting from the beginning. Tony had slogged through some of it. Some of it had been very interesting to him. The Old Testament had some histories and stories that were tedious. Yet others were fascinating. But one thing was clear: he wasn't sure he always liked the God depicted there. He sometimes seemed to be a mean and vengeful God.

Tony often used his runs to process these kinds of thoughts. But he kept up with the readings and participated in the discussion, mostly questioning rather than accepting. And he had enjoyed getting to know the other guys. They were all real people, even Pastor Bob, and that continually surprised him.

As Tony ran up to the house, he was surprised to see George

sitting on his front steps. His head was hung low, and he seemed to be on the edge of crying. Tony walked up to him and said, "George, what are you doing here?"

George looked up and there were tears in his eyes. "Hello, Tony. I . . . I . . . I'm not sure."

"Well, why don't you come in?"

"Okay," George replied, and he got up and followed Tony into the house.

"Hey, honey," Tony called out. "We've got company."

Beth came in with Christina in tow. Christina had a toy in her mouth she was actively chewing on. "Oh, hello, George. How are you this evening?"

George just looked at her with a distressed look on his face and shrugged his shoulders.

"Uh, can I get you anything? A cup of coffee, perhaps?"

He looked at her and said, "Maybe a beer?"

"Uh, sure," she said surprised. "Why don't you two go into the family room and I'll get that for you."

Tony led George into the office instead and sat him down on the love seat they had in there. Then he brought the office chair around from the desk and put it in front of George and sat down. He waited for George to compose himself. He heard Beth walking around and called out to her, "We're in here, Beth."

Beth came in with two bottles of beer. She asked George if he would prefer a glass, to which George replied, "No, Beth. A bottle is just fine."

She then handed them to Tony and said, "I'll leave you two alone. Don't worry about the kids, honey. I've got that covered." She backed out of the room and closed the door.

Tony handed a bottle to George, who took it and downed half of it in one gulp. Then he sat there looking at the bottle.

Finally, Tony said, "George, what's going on? What is on your mind?"

George looked up and spoke slowly, even for George. "I got some really bad news today."

"About what?"

"About Jason."

"Jason?"

"Yes. Jason, the young man I've been counseling. You know, the one I met in prison."

"Oh, yes, of course."

"Well, he was found dead this morning. A drug overdose."

"Oh, my God. I'm terribly sorry, George."

George broke into tears again. "I thought he was doing so well. But apparently, he's been back on drugs again for a while."

"I see."

"They found him in an alley. *Next to a garbage dumpster.*" George almost shouted it. "He had been using all this time and I didn't even notice it."

"George, it's not your fault."

"Yeah? Then whose fault is it?"

"You can't be responsible for the actions of others."

"Then what was I doing all this time? Talking to myself?"

Tony didn't know how to answer that question, so he remained silent. Finally, he said, "How can I help, George?"

"Aw, you can't help. I'm not even sure why I came here. I'm sorry to bother you and your family." He started to get up to leave. Tony gently pushed him back in his seat.

"Sit down, George. I don't want you to go in this state."

George sat down, put his beer on the end table, and buried his head in his hands. Tony sat with him and let him finish crying.

"You know, Tony, I wonder if it's all worth it. If it all makes any sense."

"What's that, George."

"Believing in God."

This surprised Tony. George was one of the more devoted

members of the Life Group. He never seemed to question the Word of God or his existence. To hear him say anything negative about God was astounding.

"What do you mean?" Tony asked.

"I mean, how could God lead me astray like this?"

"Astray?"

"Yeah. I've been working with Jason for a long time. I've been teaching him about God and Jesus and the Bible. He seemed to be getting it, to be catching on. I thought he was becoming a believer. Turns out he was faking it the whole time."

"Faking it?"

"Yeah! If he believed in God, then how could he do this to himself?"

"I don't know, George."

"And how could God let *me believe* that I was making a difference?" He paused for a moment and looked at Tony and said, "I'm starting to think that maybe you're right."

"About what?"

"That maybe we're all fooling ourselves and there is no God. Maybe it's just something we make up to help ourselves feel good. 'Cause like you said a few weeks ago, maybe Man created God rather than the other way around. 'Cause how could a God who loves us let this happen to me?" He buried his head in his hands again and sobbed.

Tony sat silently. This was indeed a crisis. Not only for George but for Tony. He had always prided himself on his logic and ability to communicate. During their weekly meetings, Tony had put forth many logical arguments to refute the Bible. Those arguments had been met with open and honest discussion, but never had George sided with Tony. Now, from way out in left field, Tony was confronted with George's declaration that there might not be a God. And the weird part was that Tony felt bad about it, almost as if his objections to God and the Bible and living by faith had converted George to the dark side. That had never been Tony's intention.

"Uh, I'm not sure that is what this means," Tony found himself saying.

George looked up. "Aren't you the one who is always saying none of this makes sense? How a God who loves us wouldn't do such bad things as we read about in the Bible?"

"Uh, yeah. But . . ."

"But what?" George looked at him expectantly.

"But, heck, I don't know what, George."

George looked at Tony. He wanted something from Tony. Tony realized he wanted solace. Affirmation. An explanation. Something that Tony didn't have for him. Tony was at a complete loss. He downed his own drink and put the bottle down. Then words came out of his mouth that he didn't seem to have control over.

"George, look. I'm certainly no expert, but I do know this. You tried your best with Jason. You spent a lot of time with him. You poured your heart out to him and I'm sure he was listening. But someone like Jason, someone with an addiction like that, isn't always responsible for their own actions. But certainly, other people *can't* be responsible for someone else's actions. You can only show them the way. It is up to them and only them to walk on that path. Now, I don't know if there is a God, but I do know this. Your faith in Him has always been an inspiration to me."

"It has? But . . ."

"Yes, I know. I don't believe in God. But the fact that you do, regardless of the circumstances, has always impressed me. The idea that you believe in God and try your best to follow His direction without facts or proof that He is out there somewhere, is, how can I put this, attractive to me." Tony almost couldn't believe that these words were coming out of his mouth.

"It is?"

"Yeah. I would like to have that kind of faith in something. I don't, but you do. And I don't think you should be questioning it now."

"You want to have faith like me?"

"Well, let's just say that I sort of envy you. You know Bob has had an impact on me in many ways. But, and this may sound crazy, in a lot of ways, you have impacted me more. Bob's a pastor and he's supposed to say and believe the things he does. But you are a regular guy—like me. And I have seen you have struggles, but they never seem to get the best of you. You have relied on your faith to get you through those times. That has had a profound impact on me.

"This may be one of the worst times you have ever encountered, so, understandably, you came crashing down. But I suspect that tomorrow, you will again draw on what you believe deep down and your feelings will be different. George, you do believe in something that sustains you in bad times. I don't have that. So in some ways, I'm sort of jealous of that."

George sat and thought about it for a while. The door opened a little and Beth stuck her head in. She looked at Tony questioningly. He shook his head and motioned for her to close the door. Which she did.

"But Jason . . ."

"I'm sure that Jason was better for all that you did for him. But the fact that he messed up is not your fault. And it shouldn't shake your faith. I see that you are angry, but didn't Bob say the other day that one of the things about God is that His most important desire is to affect our spirits? That He is most interested in our spiritual well-being?"

"Yes."

"Well, I'm sure that your ministering to Jason improved his spiritual well-being. Even if his physical well-being was not as good."

"You think?"

"I'm sure of it."

They were quiet for what seemed to be a long time. Each was deep in his own thoughts. Finally, Tony spoke up and surprised himself again with his own words, "Can I pray with you, George?"

George looked up, "Yes, please."

They bowed their heads and Tony said, "God, we know that George is troubled and asking for help. He doesn't understand why this thing has happened to his friend. He is looking for answers and not finding them. I, uh, we pray that you will help him understand what has happened." He paused, searching for the right words. "Uh, he wants to keep believing in You but is having trouble now. Help him to understand. Amen."

George said, "Amen." He looked at Tony for a long time. "Thanks, Tony. I feel a little better."

"I'm glad, George." They both stood up and hugged each other for a long time. George finally, disengaged.

"I'm sorry to have just come over like this," George said.

"No. No. It's fine. You come over anytime you need to talk. That's what friends are for, right?"

"Friends. Right. We are friends. Well, let me get going. I will see you on Saturday."

"Right. Saturday."

He walked George to the front door and let him out. "You will call me if you need to talk some more, right, George?"

"Yes. I will. Thanks again, Tony." He turned and walked slowly away. But his step seemed a little lighter to Tony.

As Tony closed the door, Beth came up to him. "What was that all about? It seemed rather heavy."

"It was. I will tell you all about it."

"What did he want from you?"

"I'm not sure. I don't think he knew. But the funny thing is, I believe that I may have been able to give it to him. And that feels good."

CHAPTER 43

Tom was playing with Joey in the back yard. Joey was running around trying to catch the bubbles that Tom was blowing. Tony was watching through the kitchen window as Beth came up behind him.

"Your dad is having fun, I think," she said.

"Yeah, he really is enjoying being a grandfather. I wish he would come and visit more often, though."

"Yes, that would be nice. You'd better start the grill. The guests will be arriving soon."

"I can't believe the kids are two already. It seems like just yesterday that they were born."

"I know." She paused, "Do you think your father will be okay with all of the *church folk?*"

"I'm sure he will be on his best behavior. After all, he has met a lot of them before."

"True. Um, have you thought about inviting him to church tomorrow?" she asked.

"Ooooh noooo. That would be a disaster! It works better if we don't talk about church. He still thinks I'm crazy for being involved."

"But you are having such a good experience. Don't you think you should share that with him?"

"Nope. I think that would be bad," he said with a note of finality. Beth dropped the subject and went back into the kitchen. The guests started arriving and they all had birthday presents for the twins. Tony was always surprised at their generosity.

The party went very well. At one point Tony looked up from the grill and noticed Bob in what appeared to be a deep discussion with his father. No sparks were flying, so Tony went back to cooking and didn't think much more about it. However, after the guests had all left and they were about done cleaning up, Tom tapped Tony on the shoulder and said, "Can we talk, son?"

"Sure Dad. What's up?"

"Not here. Let's go out on the back porch. Beth can handle the kids." Tony looked over at Beth and she shrugged her shoulders and nodded her head. Tony followed Tom out onto their patio and Tom closed the sliding door.

"What did you want to talk about, Dad?"

"I had a long talk with your Reverend Bob today."

"Oh, yeah. I saw you two were talking," Tony said hesitantly.

"He says that you have become pretty involved in the church."

"Yeah, I suppose."

"You suppose?"

"Well, I do go to services on Sunday mornings, and I help out a little around the church."

"He made it sound like you're a regular member of the church," Tom said.

"No, I haven't joined or anything like that."

"But you're in some sort of Bible study with him and some other men?"

"Yes. We meet on Saturday mornings and discuss the Bible, among other things. I told you about this."

"And you're doing some sort of ministerial work? At some soup kitchen?"

"Oh, yeah. It's a bicycle repair ministry. We get old bikes and fix them up for the homeless folks. It helps them because otherwise, they can't get around as well. It's fun, actually."

"I see. Sounds like you are liking all of this."

"I guess I am enjoying myself. Why?"

"Son, what have I always told you about church people? They want to get their hooks in you and drain you dry."

"It doesn't feel like that, Dad. These are good people. Hell, you've met a lot of them. They don't ask that much of me. And besides, remember why I'm doing all of this."

"Oh, yes. Please remind me," Tom said sarcastically.

"It's so I can learn enough to teach the kids about religion and when they are old enough, they can decide about God and all that."

"And it requires that you do all the religious stuff to be able to give them that background?"

"Yes, Dad. It does. I need to have enough information to answer all of their questions."

"It looks different from out here. You are spending way too much time with those people. They are doing just what I warned you about. They are brainwashing you, slowly. They are sucking you in. I don't like this, Tony. I don't like this at all."

"I gather you got all of this from talking with Bob today?"

"Him and some other people. They talk about you like you're a full-blown member of their church, for crying out loud!"

"Well..."

"And that priest..."

"Uh, pastor. What about Bob?"

"Right, *pastor*. He is so *proud* of you," said Tom.

"Beg your pardon?"

"He spoke in glowing terms about how you are *coming along*. You are intense in your Bible study. You are generous with your time. You are a good role model. I'm telling you; he's grooming you for some job in the church."

"Don't be silly, Dad. We have had some really good conversations and all that. And this church has been very supportive of us, me and Beth and the kids."

Tom frowned and said, "One of the things he told me about is how you are doing all of the things that Christians do so you can experience them?"

"Yeah, but there are some things that I won't do. Like communion. I think that you have to believe to do that and it's a ritual that I won't do just for show."

"He said that sometimes *you pray* at their meetings?"

"I do. I'm trying to understand what that is all about. I still don't quite get it, but I try."

"Son, they are really getting to you. Pretty soon they will start asking you for money if they haven't already."

"They haven't ever asked me for money. But there is this thing called tithing."

"Oh, yes. The *You have to give so much percent of your money to the church.* Your mother and I argued over that a lot."

"Yeah, well, it turns out that's one of those Christian things," Tony said.

"Wait a minute! Are you telling me that you are giving them money?!" He stood up.

"Yes," Tony said hesitantly.

Tom started pacing around the patio. "I can't believe it. I have failed. That's the bottom line. I have failed as a father." He stopped in front of Tony and pointed a finger in his face. "How much are you giving them?"

"Uh, five percent. And I give five percent to the soup kitchen."

"So a total of ten percent! Ten percent of everything you make?"

"Uh, yes."

Tom sat down and put his head in his hands. "Tony," he said, "this is very bad news. You are on a very dangerous path here. And I can't condone it. You can't see it, but you have gone off the deep end."

"I'm sorry you feel that way, Dad. But I'm not asking for your permission here."

Tom looked up in shock. "I don't know who you are. When you married Beth, I didn't say anything about her being so religious."

"Oh, you didn't have to, Dad. Everybody knew you weren't happy about it."

"And this is the reason why. I thought she might drag you in this direction. Don't you see, son, this is wrong. This will lead you and the kids into a cult."

"This is not a cult, Dad. These are good people and they have me and my family's best interests at heart. And Bob is a good man. He has never asked me to do anything that I would consider bad."

Tom was silent for a long time. Finally, he stood up. "I'm going to bed. I will be leaving in the morning."

"But I thought you were going to stay the week?"

"I was. But I cannot, in good conscience, stay and watch you throw your life away like this."

"Oh, come on Dad. That's kind of overreacting, don't you think?"

"The fact that you think that I am is proof enough. You have gone over to the dark side and I won't be part of it." He started to leave, then turned back to Tony. "Don't worry about getting me to the airport. I will get a cab in the morning. And don't bother calling me. I won't be answering."

"Aw, Dad. Come on, don't be like that."

"Son, I don't know any other way to be. I went through the *church* being part of my life when your mother died. I won't do it again."

He turned and walked into the house. Tony followed him, but he just went up to his room and closed the door. Tony went into the bedroom where Beth was getting ready for bed.

"What was that all about?" she asked.

"Dad is a little upset."

"About what?"

"About my church activities. And about the people we are hanging out with. You know, *church people*. Apparently, he spoke with Bob today and Bob told him about all the things I'm doing to understand the faith. He is upset about it. In fact, he's leaving tomorrow morning, or so he says."

"He's not staying the week?"

"Apparently not."

"I see. Are you going to take him to the airport?"

"No, he says he's going to get a cab."

They were silent for a while. Beth came over to Tony and hugged him. "I'm sorry about this, Tony. I'm sure that after he has time to think about this he will come around."

"I'm not so sure. He also said he doesn't want to talk to me anymore. Says I have gone over to the dark side and wants to break contact with us."

"Oh, my. Well, let's hope he changes his mind."

"I'm not sure he will."

And he didn't.

CHAPTER 44

It had been over a month since Tom and Tony had had their fight. Tony had continued to try and contact Tom but to no avail. Tom was being stubborn, as he always had been. Tony had concluded that his dad was just trying to make a point and that he would eventually come back. But that had not stopped Tony from calling and leaving messages.

On this particular evening, Tony and Beth had finished dinner and Tony was on the floor playing with the twins. This was always a fun time for Tony. He marveled at how much he enjoyed being a father. It was something that constantly surprised him. The phone rang, and Beth answered it. She spoke for a moment and then brought the phone to Tony.

"It's your Aunt Susan. And she doesn't sound good."

"Okay, I'll take it in the office. Could you watch the kids?"

"Of course," she said and sat down on the floor. Tony took the phone and got up and walked into the office.

"What's up, Aunt Sue?"

"I'm afraid I have some very bad news for you, Tony."

"What is it?"

She said, choking back tears, "Your father had a heart attack this afternoon. He's gone, Tony."

"What?"

"Your father died, Tony. I'm so sorry."

Tony sat down heavily in the chair. He had no words. It was as if a hammer had been smashed against his chest. He just sat there.

"Tony? Are you still there?"

"Yes, Aunt Sue. I am. What happened?"

"I know this is sudden, but he had a massive heart attack. I guess they got him to the hospital, but there was nothing they could do. They just called me a few minutes ago."

"Uh, I see." Tony was at a total loss for words. He just sat there looking at the phone. Finally, he blurted out, "Uh, well, thanks for calling me. I'll call you later, I guess."

"We can talk later about arrangements. Again, I am so sorry, Tony."

"I know. We'll talk later." He hung up the phone and just sat there. His father was gone. And he hadn't spoken to him since their fight. He thought he might throw up. Beth saw Tony through the glass in the door just sitting there so she poked her head into the room. "What's going on, honey?"

He looked up at her. "Dad had a heart attack. He's gone."

"Oh, no!" She immediately came into the office and leaned over and put her arms around Tony. "I'm so sorry, honey. Oh, my!"

She just sat there hugging him for a long time. Finally, she stood up. "What can I do, Tony?"

"I don't know. I just don't know. I think I need to be alone for a while."

"Are you sure?"

"Yeah, I'm sure."

She kissed him on the head and said, "Okay, I'll get the kids ready for bed, then come back to see you."

"Okay."

She left and closed the door behind him. *What does it all mean?* he thought. *How can he be gone?* Tony was lost. What was he to do? He stood up and paced around the room. His stomach was in a giant knot. Then he walked over to the bookshelf and picked up his Bible. He couldn't have told you why he did. He went over into the corner of the room and sat on the floor with his back against the wall. He opened the book randomly, searching for he didn't know what. He ended up in the book of First John. He began to read.

He got to the fifth chapter and read, *"Anyone who believes in the Son of God has this testimony in his heart. Anyone who does not believe God has made out to be a liar because he has not believed the testimony God has given about the Son. And this is the testimony: God has given us eternal life and this life is in His Son. He who has the Son has life; he who does not have the Son does not have life."*

Tony was suddenly brought up short. It was as if someone had punched him in the gut. He suddenly "knew" that his father was not with God! He started crying. That deep sort of crying that involves one's whole body. He was wracked with sobs. His dad was not with God! It was a horrible prospect! Yet he didn't believe in God. How could he care about that? He couldn't make heads or tails of it. He just knew that he was filled with unbelievable grief! It was perhaps the worst prospect he had ever contemplated.

Just then, Beth opened the door. "Are you all right, honey?"

Through the tears, he blurted out, "Dad is not with God!"

"What?"

"Dad's alone! I can't explain it!" He continued to sob.

"Oh, well, I'll tell George to call back."

Tony looked up. "What?"

"George is on the phone. He said he wanted to speak with you. But I'll tell him you will call him later."

"No. No. I'll talk to him," Tony said. He couldn't explain it, but he knew he should take the call. "I'll pick it up here," he said as he picked up the receiver.

"Uh, okay," she said as she left and closed the door.

"Hello," said Tony.

"Hello, Tony," said George. "I hope I am not interrupting anything. I'm not even sure why I called. But I just had this sudden feeling that I needed to, so I am calling. It sounds like it's a bad time."

"It's all right, George. I just found out that my father died today."

"Oh, no! I'm so sorry, Tony. I don't know what to say."

"It's okay. You don't need to say anything."

"Uh, okay." He was silent for a while. "If there is anything that I can do . . ."

"I don't think so. Just the fact that you called helps."

"It does?"

"Yeah, I don't know why, but it does. You say you don't know why you called?"

"Uh, yeah. I just sort of felt like I needed to. I can't explain it."

"That's okay, you don't have to. Look, I will have to call you later. But thanks for calling. I really appreciate it."

"Uh, sure. I'm sorry about your dad, Tony. Uh, bye."

"Yeah, thanks, George. Bye."

Tony hung up the phone. That call had hit a chord with Tony. What had made George call? Could it have been God? Tony shook his head. He was being ridiculous! There was no God! How could there be if He let this thing happen to his dad? To him! Yet there was this hole in his heart. His dad was not with God! It hurt to even think it.

At that point, Beth came in. She sat down on the floor with Tony and put her arms around him. "What did George want?"

"He didn't know."

"Pardon?"

"He just felt like he needed to call."

"Oh." She was quiet and just held him. He started sobbing again. She rocked back and forth with him.

Finally, he stopped and said, "Dad is not with God."

"What do you mean?"

"I'm not even sure. But I was reading my Bible and it came to me that Dad is not with God. Beth, I'm not even sure there is a God. So why should I be bothered by the thought that my father is not with Him?"

"I don't know, honey."

"Not only do I know it, but it also hurts to think that it is true. Oh, God, it hurts." He started crying again. Beth just held him. Finally, he slowed down. "I don't know what to do, Beth."

"What can I do to help?"

"Will you pray for my father. Pray that he is with God?"

"Of course." She took a deep breath. "Dear Father in Heaven. We are so saddened by the loss of Tom. We know that You are a gracious and loving Father. We pray that You have taken Tom to be with You and that he will be safe and happy. Please give Tony this assurance as well. In the name of Jesus, we send this prayer to You. Amen."

She looked at Tony and he smiled weakly back. "Come to bed, honey," she said as she tried to help him up.

"No," he said. "I think I need to be alone for a while."

"Are you sure?"

"Yeah. Thanks."

She kissed him lightly and got up and left the room. He sat there, feeling completely lost. Finally, he spoke out loud, "God, if You are up there, please take my father. Don't leave him alone. Please let him be with You. Please!"

He curled himself up into a ball on the floor and finally fell asleep. And that's how Beth found him in the morning.

CHAPTER 45

It was evening and Tony was running. He was running hard. It was the day after he had heard of his father's death. He was heartsick. Beth had tried to comfort him, but it didn't help, though he appreciated the effort. He was so conflicted.

On the one hand, he had understood his father's position. After all, Tom had driven into Tony's head that the church was out to get you. On the other hand, in the time he had been spending in Bob's church, Beth's church, he had not experienced that sort of attitude. Quite the opposite, in fact. He had come to like many of these people. And maybe even love some of them. But that whole thing had split him and his father apart. And now he could never reconcile with him. He simply didn't know what to do anymore.

He stopped to take a breather. He had been running very hard and fast and hadn't been paying much attention to where he was going. As he stood there, trying to catch his breath, he looked up. To his great surprise, he was only a few houses from Bob's home. What had brought him here? He was about to start running again when he started walking, almost without his own volition, towards Bob's house. And before he could stop himself, he was ringing the doorbell.

Bob opened the door and smiled. "Hello, Tony. What a pleasant surprise. How are you?"

"Not so good, Bob."

"Oh?"

"Yeah. I'm, uh, my father died yesterday."

"Oh, my. I'm so sorry to hear that. Would you like to come in?" Bob asked and stepped back to invite him in.

"Uh, sure." Tony stepped inside and Bob closed the door. Then he led Tony to his office. They stepped in and Bob closed the door.

"I hope I'm not interrupting anything. Quite frankly, I don't even know why I am here. I was just running and when I stopped, well, here I was." Bob offered him a chair in which to sit, but Tony resisted, saying, "I've been running pretty hard, and I am kind of sweaty. Do you have a towel that I could sit on?"

Bob replied, "Don't worry, Tony. That's not much of a chair. It'll be fine. Is there anything I can do for you?" Bob sat down across from him and waited.

Tony didn't know where to start. He searched for the right opening and finally blurted out, "I don't know what to think about God!"

"Okay, what does that mean?"

"Look, I've been coming to your Bible study sessions for months now. I still don't believe in this all-knowing and all-seeing God. And my church involvement broke my relationship with my dad."

"Oh, how so?"

"Right after the twins' birthday party, Dad and I had a big fight."

"I see."

"Yeah, he talked to you at the party and got really mad."

"Oh, my. I'm so sorry. What did I say to make him mad at me?" asked Bob.

"No, no. He's not mad at you, he was mad at me."

"I don't think I understand."

"Well, you told him about all the things I've been doing to understand the faith, and he didn't like that."

"Uh-huh."

"I guess I need to give you a little background. I don't know if I ever told you all of this, but my mom was a believer. Actually, she was more than a believer. She was a very committed follower of Christ. She went to church faithfully, was a tither, volunteered in Vacation Bible School, and so on. And she had me going to church as well. My dad never believed but tolerated it in her. When she got sick with cancer, she relied on the church and her church friends to help her. They prayed a lot and all of that. But in the end, she died a painful death."

"I'm sorry to hear that."

"The point is, all of that praying and stuff did nothing to ultimately help her. And it made my dad angry. He knew what the doctors were telling him, and he could see the writing on the wall. She was going to die. My dad thought that what would have helped her the most from her church was helping her prepare for her death. But they just gave her false hope."

"I see," said Bob. "That is a very difficult story, Tony. And I am sorry the church let you and your dad down. Often people don't recover from experiences like that, and I am sorry to admit that it happens more than I would like to think."

"Yeah, and after she died, he pulled me out of anything related to the church and taught me that the church is just some sort of cult that wants to control your life. And when you told him that I was doing all these things with and for the church, it just put him over the top. He walked out of the house and now he's gone, and I won't ever be able to talk to him again." Tony put his head in his hands.

"Oh, Tony. I am so sorry. I had no idea. I never would have said anything if I had known."

Tony waved him off. "I know that, Bob. I'm not upset with you. It's just . . ." He couldn't seem to find the words.

"It's just what?" Bob prompted him.

"It's just that, I haven't experienced that from you guys. Especially from you. Dad always told me that you pastors were just out for our money. But you have never asked me for a dime. And when I told him that I was tithing, I mean fully tithing, boy, that sent him into orbit. And then there's . . ." Again, he was at a loss for words. Bob just waited patiently. Tony finally said, ". . . what happened last night."

"So what happened last night?"

"After I heard about Dad from my Aunt Susan, I opened up my Bible. I'm not sure why. And I ended up in the first book of John. And as I was reading . . ."

"Go on," Bob gently encouraged him.

". . . as I was reading it came to me."

"What came to you?"

Tony choked up and could barely speak. Finally, he croaked out, "That Dad is not with God." He burst into tears.

Bob let him cry it out. Finally, Tony composed himself somewhat and looked up at Bob. "What does it mean, Bob?"

"I'm not sure. Uh, can you give me any more detail?"

"No! It's just the feeling, no, the knowledge. I just *know* that Dad is not with God. And for crying out loud, I don't believe there is a God! So why would that bother me? I ask you why?" Tony was pleading at this point.

"I don't know, Tony. I honestly don't know. I wish I did." They were both silent for a while. Then Bob said, "Could it be that your experiences with us, you know, in the Life Group and at the church are the reasons?"

"Yeah, uh, maybe. I've been experiencing things that I didn't expect, and I don't know what to make of it."

"Go on."

"Well, things that I would have thought were coincidences before. Now I'm not so sure."

"Such as?"

"Well, Dave told me some weeks before the kid's birthday party that he had a dream. He said he believed it was a message from God, that I would have a big fight with my dad. And here we are. Then there is the whole bike ministry thing. You know the one that Calvin got me into?"

"Yes, of course."

"I mean, I can have a positive impact on other people in ways that I never understood before. And it feels good. It feels right. Even the tithing I'm doing doesn't feel like I'm losing something. Though that is what really put Dad over the top."

Bob waited for Tony to continue.

"Then there's this feeling."

"Feeling?"

"Yeah. I can't explain it. But it's like there's something, someone nudging me. I seem to 'know' things that I didn't know before. Like this thing with Dad. Oh, I'm not explaining this well."

"It's okay," Bob assured him. "Take your time."

"Okay, it's like when I try to pray. I never before took any stock in that, especially since as a young child I saw the church women praying over my mom, and then she died. You know, when I did try to pray, I felt like I was talking to thin air. There was no one listening. But lately, I pray, and I feel sort of, I guess, heard. Does that make any sense?"

"Yes, it does, Tony."

"I just don't know what to do with all this. I am beginning to think differently from the way I used to think. But now my dad is gone, and I just don't know what to think, Bob." He stopped and looked at Bob as if to say, *Please just give me the answer and make it better.*

Bob looked back at him for a moment. Then he said, "Tony, I am truly sorry about your father. I know that must be very hard on you, as you two have always been very close. Having said that, I have seen a change in you over the last several months."

"What do you mean?"

"Well, in the group, you are less combative. Almost as if you are beginning to understand some of the concepts. Perhaps even accepting some of them. And you have started to pray. I have seen you pray in a real way during the group. And all of these changes are very hard for you. You come from a very strong, negative position and some of what you are experiencing is shaking those beliefs. That is not easy. It probably even felt like you were betraying your father."

"That does sound right."

"But it is part of the process. You see, I believe that God is working in your heart. God, the God that I worship, is a God who wants so much to be part of our lives. He pursues us relentlessly. He chases after us, just like the father in the Prodigal Son story where he leaves his front porch and runs to his son. He wants us to catch Him so He can be with us. And that is what I have been seeing in your life. Tony, you have been so diligent in your studies and your questioning. I think that you are now experiencing the fruits of those labors. What you are describing is an awakening. An awakening to the presence of the Lord in your life. And it is hard because it is so different."

"But if God is so good and wants only the best for me, how can He abandon my father?"

"I don't have an answer for that, Tony. However, I believe that God uses both the good and the bad for His purposes. But I believe that if you ask God to give you an answer, He will."

"And what about until then?"

"Tony, I see you as a person who never gives up. God knows this about you. But God never gives up on us either. Just ask Him into your life and He will be with you. And you will know peace."

"Sounds so easy."

"Oh, it's not. And it is scary. To give your life up to God is to give up control. And most of us don't want to do that. But once you do, well, you have to experience it to truly understand it. I can tell you, it is better."

Tony sat there for a long time trying to take in what Bob had said. He had heard it all before, but somehow it felt different at this moment. He closed his eyes and tried to picture God. What did He look like? He couldn't do it. He opened his eyes and looked at Bob but had no words.

Bob said, "I know this is a hard time for you. Is there anything I can do for you?"

"No, I don't think so, Bob, but this has been helpful, somehow. I kind of feel a little better. I've got a lot to think about. Will you, uh, pray for me?"

"Of course." They both bowed their heads and Bob prayed, "Gracious Father in Heaven. We come before you in pain. Tony has had a difficult time. His father has been lost to him, and it breaks his heart. I pray that You will put Your hand on Tony in a way that he comes to know that You are real and that You are with him and with his father. He has been searching so hard for You. Please watch over him in this difficult time. We pray this in Jesus' name. Amen."

Tony looked up. "Thank you, Bob. I do feel better. I better get home. Beth will be worried about me." He stood up.

"Not at all, Tony. Anytime you need to, you can call on me. Anytime!"

They walked to the door. As Bob opened it up, Tony turned and looked Bob in the eye and said, "Bob, you have been a good friend to me. That means more to me than you have just been a pastor. Thank you." He hugged Bob without actually thinking about it.

Bob hugged him back. "Of course, Tony. I feel the same way."

Tony turned and ran down the driveway and started for home. He couldn't explain it, but his spirit was strangely lifted.

CHAPTER 46

Tony and Beth flew in on Thursday, the day before the funeral. They left the kids with Dave and Sarah. Tony's Aunt Susan had insisted on making the funeral arrangements. There would be a full Catholic Mass and then internment at the gravesite of his mother's grave. Tony was sure that his father would have been furious about that, but he wasn't about to fight with Aunt Susan.

Susan picked them up at the airport and hugged both of them for a long time.

"I can't tell you how sorry I am for this. Tom was a pain sometimes, but we all loved him," she said.

"Yeah, he could be difficult," said Tony. "Are you sure you want to do this church service and all? Dad would not have wanted it."

"Well, you're right, Tony. But as they say, funerals are for the living, not the dead. And this is the right thing. Besides, your mother would have wanted it this way."

"I suppose."

Beth chimed in, "So what is the plan?"

"First we will get you settled in at my house. I thought you wouldn't want to stay at your father's place. Then we can go to the funeral home and you can see your dad. After that, I suppose you will want to go to the house and look through some of the papers. Your dad did have a will, and you will have to start figuring out what to do with everything."

"Yeah, I'm not looking forward to that," said Tony.

"Then there will be a viewing tonight. And the funeral service is at 11:00 tomorrow," Susan continued.

"Right. We, uh, have a flight out on Saturday morning. I will plan to come back next weekend. I don't think I can deal with all that right now," said Tony.

"I understand. It can wait."

They piled into Susan's car and drove to her house. They unloaded their stuff in the spare bedroom and got back into the car and drove to the funeral home.

When they went in to see Tom, Tony almost lost it. He looked so small to Tony. He had always been larger than life and now to see him laid out like this . . . It was almost too much for Tony to bear. After a while, when Tony had calmed down, they left and went out to get a bite to eat before the viewing.

That evening, there were many who came to pay their respects. Tony had no idea so many people liked his father. Most of them Tony didn't know. Tony's dad and mother had moved to where her sister Susan lived so many years ago that they had a life that Tony was not that familiar with. He was grateful for their condolences, but very glad when it was all over.

The next morning as they were getting ready for the funeral service, Beth said, "You know, I'm not used to a Catholic service. I think I've only been to one in my whole life."

"Oh, they're not that different from our church. But it will be a full Mass, so it could be fairly long," replied Tony.

"Okay, but you will have to tell me what to do."

"Sure. You can follow my lead, if I can remember everything."

When they got to the church, there was a row reserved for them in the front. They sat there with Susan and her husband Andy and waited for it to start. The priest came up to greet them first and asked if there was anything special that they wanted in the service. Tony assured him that whatever Susan had arranged would be fine. As Tom had been a veteran, they had arranged for a bagpiper to play "Amazing Grace" and military honors, but that would be at the end of the service.

As the service started, Tony looked around at the people there. Many of the ones who had been at the viewing were there, but there were some other faces he did not recognize. All in all, Tony decided it was very well attended. The service went through the normal Catholic Mass ritual. There were several hymns sung and the usual liturgy.

Then the priest began his sermon. It was obvious to Tony the priest did not know Tom personally. That made sense, as Tom would never have willingly set foot in the church. But he did his best, undoubtedly basing his talk on the information Susan had given him.

Somewhere in the middle of it all, the priest said, "I would like to turn your attention to a Scripture reading. It is Luke Chapter 24, verses 13 through 32." He read:

"'Now that same day two of them were going to a village called Emmaus, about seven miles from Jerusalem. They were talking with each other about everything that had happened. As they talked and discussed these things with each other, Jesus Himself came up and walked along with them; but they were kept from recognizing Him.

"'He asked them, "What are you discussing together as you walk along?"

"'They stood still, their faces downcast. One of them, named Cleopas, asked Him, "Are You the only one visiting Jerusalem who does not know the things that have happened there in these days?"

""'What things?" He asked.

""'About Jesus of Nazareth," they replied. "He was a prophet, powerful in word and deed before God and all the people. The chief priests and our rulers handed Him over to be sentenced to death, and they crucified Him, but we had hoped that He was the one who was going to redeem Israel. And what is more, it is the third day since all this took place. In addition, some of our women amazed us. They

went to the tomb early this morning but didn't find His body. They came and told us that they had seen a vision of angels, who said He was alive. Then some of our companions went to the tomb and found it just as the women had said, but they did not see Jesus."

"'He said to them, "How foolish you are, and how slow to believe all that the prophets have spoken! Did not the Messiah have to suffer these things and then enter His glory?" And beginning with Moses and all the Prophets, He explained to them what was said in all the Scriptures concerning Himself.

"'As they approached the village to which they were going, Jesus continued on as if He were going farther. But they urged Him strongly, "Stay with us, for it is nearly evening; the day is almost over." So He went in to stay with them.

"'When He was at the table with them, He took bread, gave thanks, broke it, and began to give it to them. Then their eyes were opened, and they recognized Him, and He disappeared from their sight. They asked each other, "Were not our hearts burning within us while He talked with us on the road and opened the Scriptures to us?"'"

The priest continued, "I know that was a long reading, but here is what I want to say. The Lord our God is a God who wants to be in communion with us. He pursues us relentlessly. Just as He did those two apostles. The fact that Jesus was willing to chase after them, to walk with them, and to stay and teach them, is the point of the story. God wants all of us to know Him and He will go to any lengths to be with us. So we pray that God will pursue Tom so that Tom can have everlasting life with Him."

There was more to the sermon, but Tony didn't hear most of it. The idea that God would pursue his father and himself was the message that he had been hearing for over a year now. How could this priest know that? And how did that jibe with this *knowledge* that he had that his father was NOT with God? Tony felt sick. He almost got up to leave but couldn't get himself to move. Then the sermon was over, and they were moving into communion. As the priest went through the ritual, Tony sat there numb. Then as the people started to get up from of their seats to receive communion, Tony grabbed Beth's hand.

"What are you doing?" she asked, a little panicked.

"We're going to take communion," he said.

She whispered, "What? I can't. I don't know how to take communion in the Catholic church."

"It's like any other church. You'll be fine. Now come on!"

He dragged her with him to the front of the church. They both received the host and went back to their seats. Both Beth and Susan looked at Tony as he sat there with his head bowed, clearly praying. They looked at each other and shrugged their shoulders. The service concluded and after the flag ceremony was finished, the casket was wheeled out of the sanctuary to the tune of "Amazing Grace" by the bagpiper. There was a limo for the family, and they all piled in.

As it pulled out to follow the hearse, Beth turned to Tony and asked, "What was that all about?"

"What?" asked Tony.

"The communion thing. You don't do communion."

"I know."

"So?"

"It's hard to explain." Tony took a deep breath. "Well, it's kind of like a baseball game."

Susan spoke up, "A what?"

"You see, when you called me to tell me that Dad had died, I got this sense that he wasn't with God."

"Uh-huh. But you don't believe in God," Susan replied.

"Well, yeah, that's true, but believe it or not, I have been praying that he was, uh, is, uh, with God, that is."

Susan shook her head, "I'm still confused."

"You and me both. I still don't get the baseball game thing," said Beth.

"It's like this. If you have a favorite team, you like to go to their games, right?"

Everyone nodded.

"And you want them to win."

"Right," said Beth.

"Now, as a fan, you can't really affect the outcome of the game directly. See you're just a spectator."

"With you so far," said Beth.

Tony continued, "So what can you do to help the team win?"

Everyone shrugged their shoulders.

"About the only thing you can do is to get seats right behind home plate. From there you can yell at the umpire."

"I'm not following. How does yelling at the umpire help your team?" asked Susan. Beth and Andy nodded as well.

"Yeah, well, maybe you can influence his calls at the plate. You know, shame him into making the right calls for your team."

Everyone looked dumbfounded.

"So by taking communion today, it's like I'm sitting behind home plate, closer to God so He can hear me better. And that lets me shame God into bringing my dad to Him." He paused and looked around the car. "At least that's what it felt like in there."

Nobody said anything. They just looked at each other. Finally, Beth patted Tony's arm. "That's all right, dear. Just next time, give me a little warning."

"Right. The next time this comes up, I'll be sure to let you know."

They rode the rest of the way to the cemetery in silence, each with their own thoughts.

The committal service went fine. They finished and went back to Susan and Andy's for a quiet meal. Then Tony went to his father's house and collected some papers and other things that he needed to work on the estate. That night, they all went to bed early. They got up the next morning and went to the airport.

Susan walked them to security and kissed them both. "I will see you next weekend. Is there anything I can do for you between now and then?"

"Yeah," said Tony. "Pray for Dad."

CHAPTER 47

They got home rather late Saturday evening. They were both exhausted and Dave and Sarah offered to keep the twins overnight. Beth gladly accepted. They got ready for bed in silence. When they were both under the covers, Beth reached over to Tony, "I'm so sorry, honey."

"Thanks, Beth. I will miss him. He will never get to know the kids, or they him."

"Yes, that is sad."

"Yeah."

Beth turned over and fell asleep, but Tony stayed awake for a long time. He couldn't put his finger on it, but something was different. He finally dozed off and slept fitfully. In the morning, they got up early and got ready for church. Sarah and Dave would bring the kids there. When they got to the church, they found where Dave and Sarah were sitting and plopped down beside them.

"How did it go?" Sarah asked.

"As well as could be expected," replied Beth. "The funeral was well attended, and the service was, well, interesting."

"How so?"

"I'll have to tell you later."

Dave, who was sitting next to Tony, put his arm around him. "I'm sorry, brother. I know this is hard. I liked your dad."

"Thanks, Dave." The service was beginning, so they turned their attention to the front of the Sanctuary.

In many ways it was a normal service, so Tony wasn't paying much attention. Then James stood up and went to the lectern. He was there to pitch a new children's ministry to the congregation. The idea was to develop a new outreach to grade-school children, which made lots of sense, as that was the age of his children. As he began talking, Tony was only half listening. Then James did something that caught his full attention.

James said, "For us to reach out to as many children as we can, we are going to need lots of help. So we want some of you who are not involved in any other ministry to get into the game." At which point he reached under the lectern and pulled out a baseball glove and baseball. He put the glove on and started throwing the ball into the glove.

Tony sat bolt upright in his seat. James continued, "Now, for those of you who have never been involved in the children's ministry, we want to assure you that we will equip you with everything you need. Just like on the baseball field, you need equipment, and we have that for you. So do not be afraid to join us. With God's help, we will give you the tools you need." He raised the glove high to show it to everyone. "Please make the decision to be part of this new ministry. Judy and I will be in the lobby after the service if you want more information. Thank you." He went to his seat, playing with the baseball the whole way.

Tony followed him with his eyes all the way to his seat. Then he looked at Beth, who was staring at Tony with wide eyes. They stared at each other for a long time. Beth put her hand gently on his forearm. Tony looked blankly back at the front of the room. Bob was starting his sermon.

"Thank you, Dr. Callahan," he began. "We will pray that some of you hear the call. Now today, I want to talk exactly about that.

Hearing the call. The call of Jesus. You see, Jesus is calling you because He wants to have a relationship with you. That's each and every one of you. But sometimes it is difficult to hear that call. Or it is difficult to recognize that Jesus is the one calling us. I would like to refer us to the Scripture reading for today. It comes from Luke Chapter 24, what we call 'The Road to Emmaus,' and we start on verse 13: '*Now that same day* . . . '"

This time both Tony and Beth sat upright in their seats. Their movements were so abrupt that both Dave and Sarah turned to look at them in surprise. But they only had eyes for Bob, who read the entire passage just as the priest at the funeral had. Then Bob proceeded to explain that God was always pursuing us. That He wanted a relationship with every person and would chase us until we acknowledged and accepted Him. To Tony, it was as if he was hearing the same exact sermon that had been given at his father's service.

He sat there until it slowly dawned on him. There *was* a God. These could not be mere coincidences. God had been chasing after him all this time. God had been hitting him over and over again with the proverbial Holy Two-by-Four. Tony could see more clearly than he ever had before. Jesus was real. He, God, was real! All the things that had happened over the last two years had led to this. In a blinding flash of clarity, Tony had come to believe there was a God. Yes, there was a God!

He was overwhelmed. He didn't know what to do with himself. He wanted to get up and shout, but he was frozen in place. Then the sermon was over. He heard Bob say, "Today is our week for holy communion. We will be blessing the elements and . . ." Tony had heard it all before, he knew the words, but today it was different. Before, he would always just sit there as the others got up to take the bread and wine. But today . . .

Bob finished the ritual blessing and invited the congregation up. Tony grabbed Beth's hand and stood up. Beth looked at him, and then she grinned. Dave looked up, somewhat shocked. Tony looked over at him and smiled and proceeded to walk to the front. Dave looked at Sarah who stared back with a questioning look. Then Dave smiled because he knew what it meant. He knew that Tony would not take communion lightly. This was different. Tony had changed and Dave followed him and Beth to the front, with joy in his heart.

After the service, the four of them and the kids all went to breakfast. Dave could hardly keep still. Finally, after they were all served and the kids were busy eating, he said, "I can't stand it anymore. What happened?"

Tony smiled and looked at Beth. She shrugged and said, "It's your story, honey. You tell it."

And he did. Tony went through all that had happened at the funeral and how it mirrored the service today. He ended with, "I guess God needed a two-by-four for me. I'm a tough nut to crack."

Dave said, "Praise the Lord. I always thought that you would get here, right, Sarah?"

She nodded enthusiastically. "Yes, I can't tell you how much Dave has prayed for this day."

"Yeah. I guess you all have."

Beth reached over and gently put her hand on Tony's and said, "Not me. I already knew this day would come."

CHAPTER 48

O ver two weeks had passed since Tony laid his dad to rest. It had been a whirlwind for him. Nothing had been normal. He had only gone into the office a few days, and he had had much less sleep than normal. He had been back to his father's house and disposed of much of his dad's belongings with the help of his aunt and uncle. He had made the arrangement to put the house on the market.

It was Wednesday evening as he walked into Charley's after running there. He found his normal booth vacant and slipped into his normal seat. Just as he did, he saw Bob walk in the door. Tony waved him over and Jimmy showed up just as Bob was slipping into his seat across from Tony.

"Ah, Mr. Hunter, Pastor Angler. Good evening, gentlemen. I am so sorry to hear about your father, Mr. Hunter," said Jimmy.

"Thank you, Jimmy. That's very kind of you to mention it," replied Tony.

"You're welcome. So, what can I get for you two?"

"Two beers, please, Jimmy." He turned to Bob. "Is that all right with you, Bob?"

Bob replied, "Sure, Tony, no problem."

"And put that on my tab," said Tony.

"Just as you say, Mr. Hunter." Jimmy put down a couple of coasters on the table and walked away.

"You don't have to pay, Tony," Bob said as Jimmy was walking away.

"It's the least I can do after I dragged you away from your family on a weeknight."

"Oh, it's no worry. You seemed like there was something important to talk about. And as I haven't talked to you since your father's funeral, I figured we should talk now if you needed to."

"Yeah, I have been busy trying to settle my father's estate and all. I haven't been able to attend the Life Group since. I do appreciate you coming out this evening, Bob. I really do. You have become a really good friend."

At that point, Jimmy returned with the drinks, set them down, and said, "If there is anything you need, let me know." He walked away.

Bob raised his glass and said, "To friends, then."

They clinked their glasses together and drank, then put them down. Bob waited for Tony to speak.

Finally, Tony looked up and said, "I wanted to explain a couple of things to you."

"Okay."

"Like what happened last Sunday at church."

"Oh, you mean about the fact that you took communion?"

"Yes. You noticed that, huh?"

Bob smiled. "Yes, I did. I figured you would tell me what that was all about in due time."

"I guess it's 'due time' then," Tony said.

Tony took a deep breath and proceeded to relate the events of the past several weeks. The call from his aunt. The revelation from reading 1 John. The call from George. The trip to the funeral. And finally the service where Bob used the same Scripture as the priest at the funeral service. He ended with, "And that is when it became clear to me that there is a God and that He has been chasing after me. And

the obvious thing for me to do at that point was to take communion."
Tony sat back and finished his beer in one swallow.

Bob also sat back, as he had been on the edge of his seat the whole time Tony had been talking. He also took a long drink of his beer. He looked up at Tony and said, "Wow. That is one powerful story. I don't think I've ever heard anything like it."

"Yeah and then there's the thing with the five-dollar bill, the prediction from Dave. Just too many coincidences. I can't do anything but believe that there is a God behind all of this." He paused and looked at Bob almost pleadingly. "But here's the thing . . ."

"What's that?"

"I don't know what to do with it."

"With what?"

"With the knowledge. Knowing that there is a God. What do I do with it? Where do I go? I am just very confused."

"And you want me to resolve your confusion?"

"Look, I have had issues before in my life, and I always seemed to get them figured out pretty quickly on my own and move on. But right now, my head seems to be on vacation, and my heart is pretty much in the driver's seat. That's why I wanted to speak with you. Maybe *your head* can make sense of this since mine isn't functioning very well."

"Well," Bob said. "I am happy you called on me to help you. Maybe I can bring some clarity to your mind. But possibly what you are calling your 'heart' is really your spirit. For some time now, I have seen you struggling with everything we have been talking about on Saturday mornings, and I have sensed a tug-of-war going on inside you. It may be that the peace you are seeking won't come through intellectually putting everything in its place. Maybe the unsettledness you are feeling is an indicator that it is time to settle some faith issues once and for all. I use the word 'faith' very intentionally. Faith issues are settled, quite frankly, by exercising faith."

Tony looked at him quizzically.

"Let me clarify. That means there are always still some questions and uncertainties, but when you choose, by an act of your will, to put your trust in what God says rather than in what your brain says or your heart feels, then the peace of God will come." Bob could see Tony was not fully following him. "Let me just share one passage of Scripture with you that speaks to what I am saying. In Philippians 4:6 and 7, Paul says, *'Have no anxiety about anything, but in everything, by prayer and supplication, with thanksgiving, let your requests be made known to God. And the peace of God, which passes all understanding will keep your hearts and minds in Christ Jesus.'* What Paul is trying to say, is that some things just have to be turned over to God before a person's heart and mind can come to peace. Does that make sense?"

Tony replied, "I'm not sure. I think so, but I'm not sure. What you said earlier is true. For months now, ever since I joined the Life Group, I have been wrestling with this whole God thing. And not just whether or not there is a God, but if there is, and I become a Christian, the stuff you have said I need to do scares the bajibbies out of me. It doesn't make sense and it scares me."

"I know," replied Bob. "That is why it is called a step of faith. It means you act first and understand later. You act on faith, not on scientific, proven data. But that comes down to your picture of God. What kind of God is He? I told you before that I had a horrible picture of who God was. I truly thought that if I gave my life to Him, He would make me miserable and His plan for me would make me poor, friendless, and eating grasshoppers. Only when I read that God had a plan specifically for me and it was a good plan that provided me with a future and a hope was I willing to take that leap of faith and say to Him, 'I will go where You want me to go, and do what You want me to do, and all of that.' All I can tell you today, Tony, is I would never have come to a place of understanding nor a place of peace unless I had simply said to God, 'Okay, I surrender.'"

Bob waited for all of that to sink in before he continued.

"Tony, that's why Ephesians 2:8 and 9 says, *'For by grace you have been saved through faith.'* Becoming a Christian is the result of God extending grace *and* you accepting it by faith. And until you fully accept God and His grace, you probably won't attain the peace you are so desperately seeking. That's about as directly as I can say it, Tony. And I say it because I love you and I want you to have God's best."

Tony sat there for a long time, trying to process all Bob had said. Finally, he looked up and said, "Bob, thanks for speaking so directly. I think you may be right. Only in my case, I think it is more than a step. It feels like a giant leap." He paused and then said, "I want to ask you something, but I don't want to throw anyone under the bus."

"You can ask me anything and I will keep it in confidence," Bob replied.

"No, it's nothing like that. It's just something I observed about Calvin that I would like an answer for."

"Okay, shoot."

"You know how Calvin is doing this bike thing down at the soup kitchen. And he's got me involved as well."

"Right."

"Well, the reason he is doing the bike thing instead of serving in the food line is because he doesn't want to commit to having to do anything when he doesn't want to do it. He wants to remain in control. If he had signed up to do the meals, he would have to commit to every Friday, or the first Tuesday of the month, or something like that, whether he feels like doing it or not at the time. If he does the bike thing, he can do it whenever *he* wants. So my question is, is it right to do God's work on your own terms like Calvin is doing?"

"Why do you ask?" replied Bob.

"Well, I think my major hesitation to giving my life to God—uh, to Christ, I guess I may have to get used to saying that—is that I will have to give up all control and I will have to do things I don't want to do when I don't want to do them. But Bob, Calvin is doing a really good thing, but he hasn't given up control. Can I do the same?"

Bob chuckled a bit and put on a pretty large smile. "Tony, trust me when I say that that will all work itself out. There are times when we do God's will and it isn't convenient. But most of the time what God wants from us is in harmony with what we enjoy doing. For right now, I believe that God is very pleased that Calvin is living with an eternal value system. He is investing in people who have needs and he is using his resources, time, talent, and treasure, to meet those needs. This pleases Calvin, and it very much pleases God. It's a win-win situation. And it will be with you also. Oh, and by the way, last week after group was over, Calvin shared with me that he will be serving food at the kitchen every Friday. Of course, he did say that he wanted all of us to come too." Bob chuckled to himself.

"Wow," said Tony.

"So Tony, what do you think your next step is now that you believe there is a God and that God has been chasing after you? Do you think it is time that you catch Him?"

"Bob," Tony said. "I think my next step is to do what you call 'receiving Christ into my heart.' Can you tell me how a person does that?"

Bob leaned forward in his seat and said, "Tony, let me make sure that you know what you are asking. You want me to give you a step-by-step process for becoming a Christian?"

"Yeah, I guess that's it."

"All right then. The Gospel can be explained in a very simple way. Remember the PPPD plan of salvation that I told you guys about in the Life Group?"

Tony responded, "I vaguely remember that, but could you refresh my memory?"

Bob picked up a clean paper napkin and pulled a pen from his shirt pocket. He wrote on the napkin as he spoke. "The first P—Plan. God had a plan for all humanity when He created Adam and Eve and put them in the garden. They had a great relationship, and everything was perfect.

"The second P—Problem. A problem interrupted God's plan

and that problem was sin. Adam and Eve sinned and that caused a separation between God and man. They hid from God and people have been hiding from God ever since.

"The third P—Provision. God said that because there was sin there had to be consequences and those consequences were death. However, God chose to kill unblemished animals for Adam and Eve's sin and God took away their shame when He clothed them with the animal skins. The animals paid the price for their sin. Centuries later Jesus became the provision for our problem, for our sin. Jesus became the sacrificial lamb who was slain on our behalf.

"The D—Decision. God said each person has to decide to embrace God's provision or reject God's provision. The way to a relationship with God is to decide to receive God's gift of grace and trust Him with your life. P-Plan, P-Problem, P-Provision, D-Decision." Bob held up the napkin with the words on it for Tony to see.

"Okay," Tony interrupted. "So how I do this?"

"Tony, you simply say a prayer that acknowledges that God has a wonderful plan for you, acknowledge that you are a sinner and that your sin separates you from Him and ask for His forgiveness. That's when you tell Him you have made the decision to receive Jesus into your heart as His provision for your sin and you will live to the best of your ability following His plan."

"So you're saying that I have to do what you did back in that dorm room when you were in college."

"Exactly! And one more thing. The PPPD plan tells you *how* you become a Christian. But then you have to know how to *live* the Christian life."

Bob picked up the napkin again and wrote the words, *The 3G Lifestyle.* "It's the 3G lifestyle. All you need to know now is that you will start to see all of life through the lens of Grace. And the more you see God's Grace in your life, the more your heart will automatically be filled with Gratitude. And in time, that Gratitude will overflow in being more and more generous with people, in terms of the time you are willing to give them, the talents you are willing to use for their benefit, and the treasure you are investing on their behalf. Grace, Gratitude, and Generosity." He finished writing and handed the napkin back to Tony.

Tony picked up the napkin and stared at it as he sat back in his seat and took a deep breath. "That is one tall order, Bob."

"It is. But you asked me what you have to do? That is what you have to do," he said pointing to the napkin.

Tony sat there for a long time. Bob waited patiently.

Tony looked up, "And I start all of this by saying a prayer?"

"That's how we communicate with him. Would you like to say that prayer now?"

Tony thought for a moment and part of him wanted to pray with Bob. But then something nudged him in a different direction.

"Bob, thanks for offering to pray with me right now, but I think I would like to head home and pray that prayer with Beth. She has been waiting for this since before we were married. Something tells me she is the one that I need to say that prayer with. Is that okay with you?"

"Tony, absolutely!" He reached across the table and put his hands on Tony's forearms. "She has been praying for you for so many years, and it is only right that she be part of when you are going to be born spiritually. You were there when she gave birth to the twins. How cool is it that now that she will be there when you have your spiritual birth! So what are you doing sitting here? You need to get home and drive that stake in the ground. Just remember, Plan, Problem, Provision, Decision."

Bob pointed to the napkin in Tony's hand and Tony looked at it long and hard. Then he said, almost to himself, "PPPD and the 3 G's. Got it." He folded the napkin and put it in his pocket. Then he looked up at Bob and said, "Thanks, Bob, you're the best."

Tony put some money on the table and they both got out of their seats. They embraced for what seemed like a long time. Tony stepped back and grabbed Bob by the shoulders. "Bob, you have become such a good friend. You have slogged through all my discontent and doubts. How can I ever thank you?"

"Tony, there is no need. This transformation I see in you makes me happier than you can know."

They walked out of the pub, Bob went right towards his car and Tony went left. Bob turned back and the last view he had of Tony was him running down the street toward his home. And Bob thought he could hear Tony singing "Amazing Grace."

REFLECTIONS

Now that you have read about Tony and his journey towards God, perhaps it has caused you to reflect on your own life and how God may be involved with you. If you wish to explore this further, we offer some thoughts and questions that might help you in your contemplations. You can use these on your own or have them be part of a discussion with someone with whom you feel close. Either way, we encourage you to think about your journey with God and how your life has and will continue to be affected by him.

At the beginning of the story, Tony did not believe there was a God. Do you believe there is a God? If not, would you like there to be a God?

Do you have a friend who has a different belief system than yours? What allows you to remain friends even though you believe differently?

Many people see a dichotomy between science and faith. James had a perspective on this that allows for both schools of thought to live together. What is your position on this matter?

Tony's father influenced his beliefs about God. Who has influenced yours? How?

Tony and Beth had conflict regarding having children. How do you resolve conflict in your significant relationships?

When you have a crisis in your life, are you willing to ask others for help? Who or where do you turn for comfort, advice, and counsel? What is it about them that allows you to trust them?

Do you believe that you have to do "good works" to get into Heaven? Why do you think this?

The father in the Prodigal Son story is radical in extending grace to both his sons. The Pharisees, and most of the guys in the Life Group, thought the father was foolish. How do you feel about a God who is extravagant in extending Grace to everyone?

The Bible teaches that Jesus came to save us all and His sacrifice was and is a free gift. Why do you think people choose to say no to this gift?

Bob teaches that Generosity is the result of Gratitude, which is the result of accepting Grace. What level of giving would be significant for you and therefore be generous?

Living with an eternal value system means you invest your time, talent, and resources in people rather than stuff. Who are the people who have invested in you? Who are the people in whom you are investing? What are the rewards of investing in others?

Do you feel that people who are "down on their luck" are responsible for their own situation? Do they deserve your support? If not, why not?

Do you think that Tom was right when he said that the church is always asking for money? What is your experience in terms of the church asking for money? How do you feel about that?

If you belong to a church, is it a good steward of the money that is given to it?

Bob teaches that the Bible is and should be the authoritative book for living life even though it was written very long ago and for a different culture. What do you think about this idea?

Do you believe that everything you have and worked for is yours and you have the right to do with them as you please? Have you ever thought about the idea that God owns all that you have? How would believing this change your use of your resources?

Bob taught the Life Group that Jesus is both the Lord and "boss" of us as Christians. He also explained Jesus has a plan for our lives that gives each of us a future and a hope. How do you feel about giving control of your life to Him?

George was devastated when Jason died from a drug overdose. He felt responsible for Jason. Are you carrying the weight of responsibility for anyone? Who might that be?

Have you ever thought about the coincidences in your life? Could it be that they are not coincidences at all or that they may be evidences of God chasing after you?

Tony does not believe in prayer at the beginning of the story but learns to pray later. Do you believe in prayer? If not, why not?

At the conclusion of the book, Tony returns home to Beth to pray to receive Christ into his heart. If the Spirit is leading you to say such a prayer, the following is offered to provide you with guidance. It is Mario's and Hoyt's hope that you might take this step for yourself:

Dear God, thank you for being a God who extends Grace to all. I recognize that I have sinned against You and this has caused us to be separated. I ask for forgiveness of my sin and I desire to open my heart and invite You in to be my Savior and Lord. Thank You for listening to my prayer and for sealing me with the Holy Spirit which is the guarantee of my salvation. Amen.

ACKNOWLEDGMENTS

MARIO BUSACCA

I would like to thank my dear friend and co-author, Hoyt Byrum. His vision of the 3G Lifestyle is what has made the concept of this book possible. I would also like to acknowledge Dr. Gary Spencer, pastor and counselor to me in my times of doubt and searching. Jeff and Janice Clift, the people who patiently allowed me to question everything and who aided me in my studies and my spiritual journey without judgement. My two beautiful daughters, Taylor and Logan. They were the inspiration for me to seek out religious truth for myself. My life has been all the better for their presence in it. And most importantly, Peggy, my wife and life partner. She has always believed in me, supported me and encouraged me to be more than I ever thought I could be.

HOYT A. BYRUM

The Chase is the product of Mario Busacca's belief that the message within, specifically the 3G Lifestyle framework for living the Christian life, needed to be told. Without Mario, there is no novel. Thank you,

Mario, for your encouragement and for your skillful creation of the storyline. I am indebted to John Advocate who shared with me the Gospel and helped usher me into a personal relationship with Jesus Christ. For those who saw potential in me that I never grasped, thank you for sticking with me and encouraging me. I am indebted to Kenneth E. Bailey, Th.D. for his insights to the Prodigal Son parable and to the Reverend Dr. E. Stanley Ott for teaching me how to share the Gospel using the PPPD method. My heartfelt gratitude goes out to Kathy Turner, who graciously extended to us her exceptional editorial counsel. My two precious children, Jennifer and Michael, have been in my corner cheering me on since I first started writing *The Chase*. Thank you. Most of all, thank you, Diane, my wife and my love, for standing by my side in this crazy adventure God has drawn us into.